MW01152637

Highlander's Bride

Moment in Time, Volume 1

Lexy Timms

Published by Dark Shadow Publishing, 2016.

This is a work of fiction. Similarities to real people, places, or events are entirely coincidental.

HIGHLANDER'S BRIDE

Also by Lexy Timms

Alpha Bad Boy Motorcycle Club Triology
Alpha Biker
Alpha Revenge
Alpha Outlaw

Conquering Warrior Series
Ruthless

Diamond in the Rough Anthology
Billionaire Rock
Billionaire Rock - part 2

Dominating PA Series
Her Personal Assistant - Part 1
Her Personal Assistant - Part 2
Her Personal Assistant - Part 3
Her Personal Assistant Box Set

Firehouse Romance Series
Caught in Flames
Burning With Desire
Craving the Heat
Firehouse Romance Complete Collection

Fortune Riders MC Series
Billionaire Biker
Billionaire Ransom
Billionaire Misery

Hades' Spawn Motorcycle Club

One You Can't Forget
One That Got Away
One That Came Back
One You Never Leave
Hades' Spawn MC Complete Series
One Christmas Night

Heart of Stone Series
The Protector
The Guardian
The Warrior

Heart of the Battle Series
Celtic Viking
Celtic Rune
Celtic Mann
Heart of the Battle Series Box Set

Justice Series
Seeking Justice
Finding Justice
Chasing Justice
Pursuing Justice
Justice - Complete Series

Love You Series
Love Life: Billionaire Dance School Hot Romance
Need Love
My Love

Managing the Bosses Series
The Boss
The Boss Too
Who's the Boss Now

Love the Boss
I Do the Boss
Wife to the Boss
Employed by the Boss
Brother to the Boss
Senior Advisor to the Boss
Forever the Boss
Gift for the Boss - Novella 3.5
Christmas With the Boss

Moment in Time
Highlander's Bride
Victorian Bride
Modern Day Bride
A Royal Bride
Forever the Bride

RIP Series
Track the Ripper

R&S Rich and Single Series
Alex Reid
Parker

Saving Forever
Saving Forever - Part 1
Saving Forever - Part 2
Saving Forever - Part 3
Saving Forever - Part 4
Saving Forever - Part 5
Saving Forever - Part 6
Saving Forever Boxset Books #1-3

Southern Romance Series

Little Love Affair
Siege of the Heart
Freedom Forever
Soldier's Fortune

Tattooist Series
Confession of a Tattooist
Surrender of a Tattooist
Heart of a Tattooist
Hopes & Dreams of a Tattooist

Tennessee Romance
Whisky Lullaby
Whisky Melody
Whisky Harmony

The Debt
The Debt: Part 1 - Damn Horse
The Debt: Complete Collection

The University of Gatica Series
The Recruiting Trip
Faster
Higher
Stronger
Dominate
No Rush

T.N.T. Series
Troubled Nate Thomas - Part 1
Troubled Nate Thomas - Part 2
Troubled Nate Thomas - Part 3

Undercover Series
Perfect For Me

Perfect For You
Perfect For Us

Unknown Identity Series
Unknown
Unexposed
Unsure
Unpublished

Standalone
Wash
Loving Charity
Summer Lovin'
Christmas Magic: A Romance Anthology
Love & College
Billionaire Heart
First Love
Frisky and Fun Romance Box Collection
Managing the Bosses Box Set #1-3

Highlander's Bride
Moment in Time: Book #1
By Lexy Timms

A MOMENT IN TIME SERIES

A Moment in Time Series

Find Lexy Timms:

Lexy Timms Newsletter:
http://eepurl.com/9i0vD
Lexy Timms Facebook Page:
https://www.facebook.com/SavingForever
Lexy Timms Website:
http://lexytimms.wix.com/savingforever

Description

One moment in time was all it took...

She shouldn't be here... She can't even recall how she got here.

Except for the dream. Mya Boyle remembers the dream. She knows it's somehow connected to her past, her present and the future.

Mya woke one morning in a field, a stag grazing close by as if it didn't even notice her. She lay bare, like a babe from the womb, except for a wool blanket wrapped around her tightly.

A grown woman with no memory, no family, no money, nothing. Kayden McGregor found her while hunting. He was after the stag and nearly shot her with his arrow instead. Unable to leave her to the wolves of his clan, he took her to his home.

He resents her. She can't bare to look at him. Or stop herself from staring when he doesn't notice. Trapped, and yet somehow destined to be together.

Remember enough of the past... You may be able to control your future.

Prologue

Mya ran.

Behind her ribs she could feel the beat of her heart, steady and strong. Her legs pumped, carrying her, swift and easy. The sensation of air flowing over her skin and filling her lungs made her light.

Her footing shifted.

She stumbled.

Overhead, thunder crashed, unrolling itself across the clouds with a deep, displeased rumble. Lightning forked down, burning the skeletons of trees across the backs of her eyelids in silhouette.

Rain fell, sharp as needles. It pricked against her skin and chilled her through to her bones. To her left, she could hear the sound of surf falling against shoreline, violent and ragged as the wind that drove it. She shivered, and pushed her stumbling legs forward.

Thunder boomed, and the ground went out from under her.

Mya fell.

There was nothing for her grasping hands to catch. Only emptiness beneath her, and pain. Pain that ripped through her chest and left her gasping in shock, struggling to breathe. Worse than anything she'd ever experienced. Enough pain to tear a heart.

She cried out, but no sound escaped her; all the air had gone from her lungs, her throat closed tight.

She woke.

Chapter 1

W hen her eyes opened, Mya saw the sky.

Night was coming, and the last vestiges of sunset spread pink and orange over the clouds, settling into the purple dim of dusk. A breeze moved over her skin, cool enough to set her shivering against the soft grass where she lay.

Beside her, a stag stood grazing on the long green stalks. For a long moment she stared at it, uncomprehending. What was it doing there? As she stared, she realized that the dun fur she had expected was in fact white, tinted faintly gold with the lingering light. A rack of heavy antlers crowned its head. The creature was breathtaking. It took no notice of her presence except the brief flick of one ear when she shifted, no alarm in its manner. Mya frowned at it.

A hiss whizzed by her ear.

Followed by a thud.

She startled back, and found an arrow embedded in the earth at her side.

For an instant, she stared stupidly at the thing, eyes moving over the black feathers held to its shaft with thread. Then the realization of what it was, and what it meant, shuddered through her. Someone was shooting arrows in her general direction.

She scrambled up, and it wasn't until she stood that she realized she was naked.

That probably should have given her more pause, especially considering that there was a man standing at the edge of the glade. But the man had a bow, and there was an arrow set to the string. The stag still grazed beside her, not even lifting his head.

Mya looked at the man, then back to the stag. She couldn't stand and watch him harmed. The thought of seeing the long legs fold and the noble, antlered head laid in the grass made her stomach turn. She could not explain it, but she could not let the stag die.

"No!" she shouted, darting forward toward the deer.

His head lifted, turning toward her, and his ears pricked.

"What are you waiting for?" she yelled at him. "Go! Get!"

"What in in the name of hades do you think you're doing, girl?"

Mya turned away from the stag, who still stood watching her with those big, liquid dark eyes. The man was staring at her, his bow lowered, his expression caught somewhere between question and anger.

"What does it look like I'm doing?" Mya snapped. She turned back to the deer. "Go! Get!"

There was a rustle of footsteps in the grass, and the stag at last bounded away, disappearing into the mist and the twilight.

"That was meant to be me dinner," the man said, his husky, rough voice loud in the evening quiet. "And several other meals besides."

"It is hardly sporting to shoot an animal that won't even run from the arrow." Mya knew as the words left her mouth that they were foolish, but she could not explain to him the urgent rush that had filled her when he raised his bow, the need to make certain the stag went on its way.

"Sport? Is it about sporting now?" The man laughed. "You'll pardon my coarseness, lady, if a lady you be at all, but I couldn't give much of a damn about sporting when starvation is the alternative."

A little late, Mya remembered she was naked and covered herself with her hands, her cheeks flushing hot.

"I've already seen everything you're trying to hide just now," the man said, white teeth flashing in the darkening night, eyes sliding over her body.

"Well then you can stop looking, can't you?"

He laughed, a low, rough chuckle that went straight to somewhere in the center of her, warming her up from the inside out. "Aye. I suppose I could at that. And while I'm about it, maybe you can explain to me why you went chasing my hunt off."

"I told you," Mya said, wrapping her right arm a little closer around her chest.

"And if that excuse is truly the one you wish you to use, you're more the fool than I pegged you to be already. What is it you're doing, running about the woods naked at the turn of the season, trying to freeze yourself to death?"

"My state of dress was not exactly a choice," Mya answered, glaring at him.

"No? Then what exactly might it have been?"

"I..." Mya's eyebrows drew together. "I cannot actually remember."

"You do not remember?" He echoed, disbelieving.

"I don't know how I got here."

"So you show up, with no idea of how you've arrived or why it is you're here, naked as the day you were born, and your first instinct is to chase off the stag that would have fed me and my clan for the next three days?"

Mya gave the thought a moment's consideration. "Yes."

"You are utterly mad, lass."

"I can hardly be blamed for losing my memory."

"No. Nor for the madness, I imagine," he said, and Mya glared at him.

"You're the one standing there, still staring at me," she pointed out. "If you think me so insane, what are you waiting around here for? Go find yourself another stag."

"In honesty? Making sure you don't wander off into a gully and die," he said. "A fine man I'd be if I left some naked woman out in the woods to die alone."

"Yes. You're such a great help," Mya snapped. "Doing absolutely nothing except drinking in the sight of my nakedness. Truly you are a gentleman."

"Losing your memory doesn't seem to have had any effect on the sharpness of your tongue, at least." He shook his head and muttered, "Seems more of an excuse if you ask me."

"And what excuse do you have for your attitude?" She'd heard him loud and clear. Oddly, she wondered why she wasn't panicking at the thought of not remembering why, or how, she got there. She should be frightened. Lost. But if she reached back, there was a sense of... She could not quite catch it. She felt as though something guarded her. As though she was meant to stand where she stood, looking into the dark eyes of the man still staring at her as though she were some strange novelty.

"You. Chasing off me dinner." He slid the arrow he was still holding back into the quiver and unstrung his bow, slinging it over his shoulder. "That would make any man a little less than polite."

"If the matter means so much to you, I'll cook you a dinner, for god's sake."

"With just what, pray tell?" He raised an eyebrow at her as he stepped in closer. "And can you even cook? You say you have no memory of why you showed up here in this field. What makes you think you would know your way around a fire?"

Mya thought about it, then lifted one shoulder in a shrug and let it fall again. "I could not say, honestly. And yet I'm certain that I do. Would I not have died well before now, if I did not?"

"Do you even know your own name?"

"Mya." She spoke slowly, tasting the word that had just come to her on her tongue. Yes. That was right. "My name is Mya."

"Well, *Mya*," the man said, as if tasting the name on his tongue as well. "I suggest you get moving. Being caught out here at night in naught but your skin isn't likely to end well for you. And not only because it grows cold with the winter coming on."

"I... Are there animals, then? I mean, more than just the deer?"

He scoffed. "Oh. Aye. Wolves. And they're always hungry."

Mya wrapped her arms a little closer around herself, shivering in the cold breeze at the thought of being caught alone and defenseless by animals that would readily have her for dinner. The man clearly didn't believe she didn't know why she was here. It must look to him as though she had been out in the wilds with another man, and he had run off with her clothes. She hoped to the heavens that wasn't what had happened. Images of starving wolves with amber eyes distracted her. She didn't want to be running from them. *Like my dream...*

"More than that," he said, interrupting the gory visions imposing themselves on her imagination. "Not every man in these hills will be as polite as I've been. Some of the men of my clan would ravage you worse than the wolves. So I suggest you be finding your way home before full dark falls."

With those words, he turned away. Mya watched his broad back move away in the dusk and wished she had a rock to throw at it. The least he could have done was tell her the way to the nearest shelter.

There was nothing. She didn't know where to go. So much for being a gentleman, he didn't even offer something to cover her body. Irritation boiled inside her. "When they find my body," she called after him. "I hope you feel responsible! I hope my spirit haunts your dreams!"

He sighed loudly, and stopped walking.

Chapter 2

"You know, lass," he said, stalking across the clearing toward her. "I think I will take you with me. If only because you must be the daughter of some rich laird to be so demanding, and the sum they give me for your rescue might even make up for the deer you chased off."

"Would you leave off the stag?" Mya snapped, exasperated, even as the chilly wind made her curl closer into herself, trying not to shiver in front of him.

"See? That is just what I mean. If you'd ever been hungry in your life, you might be a little more understanding of my frustrations."

"For all I know, I could've spent most of my life starving. Maybe losing my memory just made me forget how to hold my tongue."

"You'll excuse me for saying so, but you don't look like you've spent most of your life starving."

Heat flared in Mya's cheeks. "Would it terribly inconvenience you to keep your eyes to yourself?"

He grinned at her, his hand wrapping around her wrist to draw her forward, a shock of warmth against her chilled skin. "Likely not, but the view wouldn't be nearly so pleasant elsewhere."

If Mya's hand hadn't been busy shielding what little modesty she had left, she might have slapped him with it. As it was, she didn't have much choice but to follow him through the trees in the darkening night, his broad back outlined by the silver brush of moonlight.

"Lucky for you," he said as they approached a dim shape that lifted its head to watch them, snorting warm breath in a cloud of steam, "I've a horse and we won't have to walk back to the croft."

Mya, teeth clenched to keep them from chattering, just nodded. In truth, not walking sounded heavenly. Her legs were weak with shaking, and she wasn't sure how much farther she could have made it. His hand slipped from around her wrist, taking the only bit of warmth she had with it, and then he was pulling something off the horse's back, shaking it out and handing it over.

A blanket, she realized as her fingers closed around it. Mya wrapped it gratefully around herself, huddling into the rough wool, and almost asked him why on earth he hadn't offered it to her earlier. It would have been the least he could have done. But nagging at him now might mean risking the chance at a real shelter for the night, and she didn't want to be left out alone with the wolves, blanket or not. Under her bare feet, the grass was cold.

"Th-Thank you," she said, forcing it through a still-tight jaw, only aware that it probably sounded grudging as the words left her mouth.

"Aye," he said. "Come on. Up on the horse."

She didn't have a chance to try scrambling up herself. Big hands curled around her waist, fingers nearly meeting, and lifted her onto the warm back of the beast, build broad and sturdy as the human he served. She caught at the loose, coarse hair of his mane, clutching the blanket to herself with the other hand, and held on as the man swung up behind her, settling astride and taking the reins.

Like this, she was caught between his arms, feeling the roll of muscles in his biceps as he guided the horse into motion. He clicked his tongue, his breath hot against her ear, and she felt rather than heard the kindness he had toward the animal. Even through the blanket, she could feel the warmth of his chest against her back, and despite herself she leaned into it, her tired body sinking against the support. She felt him tense for only an instant, and then he clicked to the horse again and he seemed to forget her entirely.

Mya's eyelids fluttered, and lowered, despite her struggle to keep them open. Through half-lidded eyes, she watched the nighttime world glide by as the horse moved briskly out of the trees and onto open, rolling hillside. Overhead, the stars were a brilliant net on the black sky. Mya's limbs felt heavy, her body caught half in a dream.

Against her back, the chest of her rescuer—for that was what he was, despite the harsh words they'd exchanged—rose and fell. She could smell him, clean sweat and earth, closer than the warm, animal smell of the horse, and the sweet, chilly scent of the brush they passed through and the night that settled over them. There was another smell, something musky and sensual, making the hair on her skin rise. They rocked together with the motion of the horse, and distantly she thought her body remembered it, or something like it, a rhythm ancient as the hills they rode through. And her body woke, and wanted.

Heat sparked in the core of her, fanned from ember to flame by the strong arm that settled around her waist. She could feel the beat of his heart against her shoulder blade, steady as the beat of the horse's hooves. His breath stirred her hair. Mya pulled in a shuddering breath of her own and let it out again. Caught between sleep and waking, she wanted to know the way his hands would feel on her skin, warm and work-rough, big palms against her hips and the scratch of unshaven jaw against her thigh.

She couldn't explain why being close to him felt like home.

She didn't know him and he clearly didn't know her.

Their motion slowed, and stopped, and he shook her, more gently than she would have expected. Mya opened her eyes to the dark bulk of a small house against the sky and forced herself up, cold without the heat of him behind her as he slid from the horse. A low barn stood off to the right of the house, but other than that, she saw nothing more. Secluded and alone. It seemed that way apparently suited that roguishly handsome stranger.

"Down now, lass," he said, and she took the hand he offered, sliding awkwardly toward the ground. His palm against her side steadied her as her feet found earth once more, and then it remained there until she was inside, her steps on the grass and dirt uncertain on the uneven footing.

Inside, only the barest light brushed the sills of the little windows, and the corners of the house were black as pitch, full of shadows that shifted under her gaze, revealing nothing. The man knelt before the vague outline of a hearth, and there was a sound of metal against stone, reawakened coals glimmering in the ashes. They limned him in red and gold, and Mya curled her hands against her chest, resisting the urge to reach out and touch, trace the curve of muscle in the dim light.

He laid chunks of some material over the coals and leaned in, blowing on the embers. A moment later, the flames rushed upward, dancing hungrily over the fuel and lighting up the iron pot that hung over the fire, and the shadows were chased back to become faint, flickering things against the white-washed walls. The room filled with the scent of the fire, rich and dark and earthen.

There was a bed, she saw then, tucked against the back wall with a curtain pulled back to its edge, and at its foot a low chest with a basin sitting on it. On the other side of the single room sat a pair of chairs sharing a rough wooden table, and a cupboard for food storage, its top covered with stacked wooden bowls and cooking utensils. A fur rug was laid out in front of the fire, on the wall nearest the bed. It looked warm, and her bare feet wanted to sink into it, but the man was there, and so she stood on the cold earthen floor, wrapped in the horse blanket, and wondered what she was supposed to do next.

Would he expect some kind of payment for bringing her back here? Mya wet her lower lip nervously with the tip of her tongue and buried the idea, and the echoing thought that she wouldn't be entirely opposed to such an arrangement. Or opposed at all. The imagined image of him laying her out on the bed, his body settling over hers... She swallowed past her suddenly tight throat, and wrapped the blanket a little more tightly around herself.

"You know," he said suddenly, his voice making her startle, feeling absurdly guilty for a fantasy he couldn't possibly have known she was in the midst of. "There are folk that might consider endless staring a bit rude."

A bit— Surely that was a joke.

"As though you weren't doing exactly the same thing a short while ago," she answered, sharper than she'd meant it.

"There's no need to get yourself worked up about it, lass" he said, turning to look at her, his smile flashing again in the fire's glow. "I was only trying to help. You can hardly be expected to remember social niceties when you can't even remember where you've come from."

The desire to throw something at him was rapidly returning. Mya turned away, scanning the room for something that looked like it might contain clothes. It was a little much to hope for women's things, but he might at least have something she could feel a little less exposed in.

"I don't suppose," she said stiffly, "that you have something I can wear?"

"You're welcome to look, though I can't say there's much chance of anything that will be fitting you. But that chest over there will have a shirt or somewhat in it."

Mya sighed and went to dig through the chest, finding only a few garments folded on the top. She drew out a Jacobite shirt, the fabric cool and smooth under her fingers, and after a moment's hesitation pulled it over her head. It smelled faintly of him, and of the wood the chest was made from, subtle and strangely comforting. Mya breathed in the scent, smelling too the smoke from the fire and the damp stone of the walls.

"I'll take the rug," the man said, straightening up finally. "You can have the bed for the night, and in the morning we'll figure out what's to be done with you."

He turned, then, and Mya resisted the almost automatic urge to cover herself. On him, the shirt may have been perfectly decent, but on her it draped itself over curves, and the thin fabric did little to warm her. His eyes moved over her, lingering.

"You're making yourself rather familiar with my body for a man who hasn't even had the courtesy to tell me his name," Mya said, crossing her arms over her chest and staring him down.

"Kayden," he said roughly. He turned around again and poked at the fire, because he was determined to be as rude as he possibly could, apparently.

"A pleasure to meet you, *Kayden*," Mya said, in a tone that indicated it really wasn't.

When he didn't turn back around, she curled up in the bed, drawing the blankets over herself. They were chilly, and she shivered under them, waiting for her body heat to warm the space. It didn't seem to be doing much of that.

The sound of footsteps pulled her eyes open again, and Mya startled backward when she realized that Kayden was standing only a foot from the bed, one hand reaching out.

"What are you—?" The question died on her lips.

He was already stepping back, the blanket he'd let her borrow for the ride back in his grasp. "Just taking this, if you don't mind, seeing as you're using the rest," he said, amused.

Mya curled deeper into the coverlet, cheeks hot, and didn't say anything as he went back to the rug and laid himself out on it.

The room was slowly warming, but under the blankets on the borrowed bed, Mya still shivered, arms wrapped close around herself and legs tucked up to her belly. Her chilled body and frozen feet weren't giving the blanket much warmth to reflect back to her. Sleep called to her, teasing, just out of reach. It was too cold to sink beneath the comfort of it. She shuddered again and tried to drag the blankets in a little closer.

Was it warmer over by the fire? It must be. She listened to it crackle in the quiet and imagined the heat of it washing over her skin, taking away the shivers that kept running along her spine and over her flesh.

There was a rustle of motion, and then arms were wrapping around her, lifting her blankets and all from the bed. Mya caught at Kayden's shoulders as he carried her over to the rug and laid her down in front of the fire, settling down at her back. She thought maybe she should thank him, but wasn't sure how to say it, so she said nothing, lying still instead and watching the flames. With the fire in front of her and Kayden behind, the shivering settled. Wind whistled around the walls of the cottage, but inside it was warm, and she felt inexplicably safe, guarded by the man stretched out against her.

His breathing slowed, and fell into the pattern of sleep. Mya, strangely awake again after the half-dreaming ride from the forest, rolled carefully onto her other side. She propped up against her elbow and looked down at Kayden. Rest and firelight softened the hard edges of his face, making him look younger, his dark hair falling over his cheekbone. Mya reached out with a careful hand and tucked it back behind his ear. Her fingertips brushed against rough stubble on his jawline, and her breath caught with the memory of her earlier fantasies.

Her hand, like it had a will of its own, traced the curve of his neck down to the muscle of his shoulder, stroked against the slope of his collarbone, following the path as though it knew the way. He stirred, and she jerked it back to herself, hardly breathing. What if he woke?

But he only shifted, and sighed, and fell back into deeper sleep. She wondered what he dreamed about when his eyes moved behind the lids like that, his lips parting and his eyebrows drawing together above his eyes. Carefully, she reached out again and smoothed the frown away, turning her hand so that her palm curved against his cheek. Her heart was beating so loudly against the cage of her ribs that it was a wonder the sound didn't wake him.

When she moved to pull back, his hand caught her wrist.

Mya gasped, and his eyes opened, dark in the fire's glow, still hazy with sleep. He followed her wrist up to her shoulder, wrapping an arm around her to draw her in close, and then he was leaning over her, his mouth against hers.

Her lips parted, and his tongue traced the curve of the lower, slipping into her mouth to explore. She clutched at his bicep. A brief break, for breath, and another lingering, hungry kiss. Mya arched up into his body with a content sigh. It was slow, and languid, and she imagined it going on, drawing him down over her, letting him fill her. There were hardly clothes between them.

But the kiss broke then, and he drew back, and relaxed as he sank onto the rug again, the arm that had been tight around her going lax in sleep.

Nothing more than that kiss.

Mya let out a shuddering breath as she watched his face a moment. He'd kissed her like that and then slept? Had he even realized what he'd done? She rolled over again so her back was to him. She ached with wanting, and pressed her thighs tighter together to try and relieve it. Against her thigh she could feel the hard length of him through the blankets and the kilt he still wore. But he had hardly been awake when he had touched her. It had to have only been part of some dream, most likely one she had pushed herself into when she'd had her hands all over his face. She closed her eyes against the firelight, the heat of shame and desire in her cheeks. Tomorrow she would leave, and she could forget Kayden, along with his hands and his mouth, the way his body felt pressed warm against the stretch of her own.

Sleep came finally, and dragged her down into dreams.

Chapter 3

Morning woke her.

The fire had burned down to glowing embers, and Kayden knelt before it, stirring it back into waking.

"What is it you're burning?" she asked as he laid fuel over the coals and watched them light. She yawned and leaned onto her elbow to watch him.

"Peat," he said. "More abundant than wood in these parts."

The term felt familiar, but she couldn't recall where she'd heard it. Mya wrapped herself tighter in the blankets and watched as he poured water from a bucket into the pot over the fire.

"Breakfast will be ready in a bit if you're hungry. I have to go and milk the cows, but I'll be back in to get the porridge started, unless you know how to do it yourself?"

"Is it hard?" It seemed something she should know, and yet she was unsure if she did.

"You just pour oats from that bag over there into the water once it's boiling. Let it cook until it's not too thin. Make sure you stir it, though, or it'll get lumps." He gave her a look she couldn't quite interpret. "Use the wooden stick there. Right hand. And don't stir left."

Mya's eyebrows lifted. "What happens if I do? Stir left?"

He looked at her, expressionless. "The devil will take you."

"What? That's—"

But he was out the door before she could finish speaking, and Mya was left alone in the dark little hut with the smell of smoke. She sighed, and forced herself up from the reasonably warm nest of blankets, shuddering when the cool air hit her skin. The bedding she returned to the bed, but the wool cover she'd been given on the ride back from the forest the night before she wrapped around her shoulders as she settled into one of the chairs beside the fire, watching the water begin to steam.

He had kissed her. The memory made her whole body flush warm. He had kissed her, and he hadn't mentioned it at all. She wondered if he even remembered. He had hardly been awake when it happened. Had he thought it was all a dream?

The water was boiling, and Mya poured the oats into it, watching them sink to the bottom.

She could still feel his lips against her own. They'd been softer than she'd expected. Still lost in thought, Mya picked up the stirring stick that Kayden had pointed out and slid it into the pot, stirring to the right. Not because she actually thought the devil would take her—wherever she had come from, she was sure that they hadn't believed such things—but because Kayden had asked her to. And whether he really believed such a thing or not, she would indulge him in his own house.

The oats cooked down to a thick porridge by the time Kayden came back in, panting and stamping the dirt from his light boots at the edge of the doorway. He carried two heavy wooden buckets that, Mya realized, were full of milk. Setting them down carefully so that the liquid wouldn't slosh over the edges, he stalked across the room and glanced down into the pot.

"Looks about done. There are bowls on the cupboard top."

He wrapped a rag around his hand and pulled the pot from over the fire, setting it down on the stones of the hearth as Mya went to fetch the bowls and a ladle.

"So," he said. She turned to find him skimming the top of the milk for the thicker, richer part. A moment later he settled down in one of the chairs, pouring cream over the porridge she handed him. "You say you don't remember how you ended up in the meadow. Do you know where you're from?"

Mya, pouring cream into her own bowl, shook her head. "No. I don't remember that either."

"How old you are?"

She shook her head again.

"Is there anything you do remember?" he asked. "Anything at all?"

Mya gave the question some thought, trying to think back beyond waking in the meadow. There was the dream. Running through the woods. The pain. But that wasn't her past. Wasn't anything useful. She sighed. "I know my name. I know simple stuff, basic things like boiling water. But aside from that, I don't remember anything beyond waking in the clearing with you aiming the arrow at the stag." She took a bite of porridge. It was surprisingly good. "What about you? Where are you from? Here? Where is here, by the way?"

"Elsewhere," he said, his tone flat.

His tone told her not to push it. His information was none of her business.

She decided to push it anyways. "Here is elsewhere?"

"Excuse me?"

"I asked where here was?" She didn't want to upset him, but she had no idea where she was. She didn't even know *when* she was.

"The highlands, lass."

"When?"

He looked at her, his eyebrows pressed together.

"I just meant, is it spring?" She looked down, embarrassed she couldn't remember anything.

"It's autumn. Did you not see the colors of the leaves?" The words seemed harsh, almost accusing. She didn't know him and angering a large and unknown man in his own home hardly seemed like a smart thing to do.

"I did. I forgot. Distracted by... everything. And it was dark, last night." Mya bit her lip, and didn't ask him any more questions.

They ate in silence for several long minutes, the only sound the clack of spoon against bowl and the crackle of the fire.

"Well," he said finally. "There's no chance I'm sending you out into the world with no clothes and no memory of who you are or where you're from. Killing you with my own two hands would have about the same result. So you'll have to stay here until you've something to wear, and somewhere safe to be heading off to. A memory of some kind. Like as not, you're from the south. You haven't much of the Highlander about you."

She stopped with the spoon halfway to her lips. "What's that supposed to mean?"

Kayden raised an eyebrow at her. "Mean? Only that no Highland lass would chase off someone's dinner. We're not so accustomed to luxury around here that we can afford to be wasting food."

"Have you ever met a Highland girl with no memory? How do you know what she would do?"

"There are some things ingrained deeper than memory."

"I cooked the porridge just fine, didn't I?" Mya snapped, not sure why she was so annoyed with his claim that she had to be a southerner. What did she care if she wasn't one of his kind? But the line of reasoning had raised her hackles, and she found her fingers curling into a fist at her side. For a moment—the barest, flickering fraction of an instant—she thought she felt the hilt of a blade in her hand. Heard voices rise around them. But she blinked and the strange sensation was gone, leaving her alone beside the fire with a man who insisted on mocking her at every turn.

He laughed, like he couldn't tell how angry he'd made her. "Anyone with two hands and a set of eyes can cook porridge.

Hell, you could do it one-handed and blind, likely. That's not much proof of anything."

"So now I'm an idiot as well as soft?"

"Did I say such a thing?" Kayden looked at her like he thought she might be going mad.

"Tell me you aren't thinking it," Mya demanded.

"What I'm thinking is that you're a woman alone in hostile country and you'd do well to have a little courtesy," he said. His voice had gone low and rough in a way that made a shiver run up her spine, and not because she was afraid. "It would have been a great deal less trouble for me to leave you out there in the woods with the wolves to freeze to death."

"If it's such a burden, I am certain that I can find someone else to bother!" Mya regretted the words as soon as they had left her lips. The actual chances of finding someone who could help her were slim. Finding someone who would be as kind about it as Kayden, and not require anything in return, was going to be practically impossible. Not to mention that if she gave up his hospitality she'd have to give up the clothing and blanket he'd loaned her, and then she'd be out alone in the cold, as naked as she'd been back in that clearing.

And, if she was honest with herself, she didn't want to find someone else. She felt somehow drawn to Kayden, felt strangely safe sleeping beside him. As though she had known him once, in some long ago, forgotten time.

"As tempting as that is, I'd actually rather not deal with the consequences of kicking you out into the wilderness to die alone."

"You are too kind. Thank you." The words were sharp-edged.

Kayden got up from his seat and set the bowl down in the chair with a crack of wood against wood. "I have to go into the village to find you a dress. Or something to make one with. Whatever will get you out of my house faster."

"Believe me, I'll be as glad as you are."

But there was no answer. He'd already stalked out the door, slamming it behind him.

Mya stood, more slowly than Kayden had, and ran a hand through the fall of her copper-colored hair, sighing. There were knots in it, so she worked them carefully out with her fingers, braiding her hair and tying it off with a piece of leather thong she found on top of the cupboard. At least that would keep it out of the way while she scrubbed out the bowls.

When the door swung open, she was setting a clean pot over the fire for boiling water to clean the things they'd eaten with.

"Come back to apologize?" she mocked and glanced back around her. But it wasn't Kayden. From where she knelt by the hearth, Mya stared in shock at the trio of men standing in the doorway, gaping back at her. They were all as tall as Kayden, and even broader in the shoulders. One of them had hair as red as her own. The other two had the same dark coloring as her rescuer. She wondered if they were related. Were these the men he'd meant when he'd talked about his clan? Her stomach gave a nervous flip. Hadn't he warned her about them?

"What can I do for you?" she asked as she straightened up and got to her feet.

The shirt she was wearing didn't cover much, but she wasn't going to kneel on the ground and look up at them. She crossed her arms over her chest and lifted her chin. They were all three staring at her, their eyes roving over her body in a way that she didn't particularly care for.

"Are you Kayden's lass, then?" the red-haired man asked, eyebrows lifted.

Should she say that she was? Would they assume she had no right to be there if she didn't?

"I am staying here with him for the time being," she said finally.

The men exchanged glances.

"And where exactly did he find you?" the red-haired man pressed.

"I'm not sure I understand the need for the question." She wasn't going to explain to this man that she'd been found alone and naked in a clearing, with no idea of where she was from or what her past had been. There was something in his face that she didn't like.

He turned to look at the men with him. "Watch the door, would you, boys? The lass and I are going to have a conversation."

Mya took a small step back while his head was turned, not wanting to give him the satisfaction of seeing her sudden fear, but silently willing the other men not to leave. She was hardly so lucky. They turned and walked out, the door shutting behind them. Mya took a deep, shaky breath. "Just what kind of conversation is it that you want to have?" she demanded.

"Oh," he said, a slow smirk curling across his mouth, "I think you know."

Mya's stomach twisted.

That was exactly what she had been afraid he would say.

Chapter 4

"I'm not interested," she said, cutting him off before he could even begin.

"No?" He laughed. "You won't admit to being Kayden's woman, which means you're likely the kind of lass as doesn't have many scruples about bedding a man. Else what would you be doing, standing there in his nightshirt, hardly knowing him?"

"I've no interest in bedding you."

The laughter vanished from his expression. "If you think you'll be allowed to speak to me in that manner you've a lesson coming."

"Speak to you in what manner?" Mya met his glare with her own. "I've not insulted you. I've hardly been disrespectful. I simply told you I wasn't interested in going to bed with you. I don't see what reason you have to be so offended."

He took a breath, opening his mouth like he was about to speak, and then closed it again, and simply took a menacing step forward. In the firelight, his bulk almost seemed to fill the room, and Mya shrank back despite herself, though her jaw was still set and her eyes never left his face.

"You listen to me, lass. I—"

The sound of a scuffle outside cut him off, and he turned to look at the door just as it burst open to admit Kayden, breathing hard. He crossed the little space in a single stride and stepped between Mya and the man looming over her.

"Lachlan," he said, biting out the syllables. "To what do I owe the pleasure?"

"There's a clan meet about to take place," Lachlan said. He looked at Kayden with narrowed eyes. "We were passing this way, so we came by to inform you. You'll ride with us. We weren't expecting you to have company."

"Is there some rule against it?"

"Nay." Lachlan was still glaring at them. "Though you'd do well to teach that woman of yours a thing or two about how to behave herself here in the Highlands. Maybe men down south tolerated her tongue. We won't here."

Kayden stiffened. "I can't imagine Mya would be rude," he said, straight-faced, as though she hadn't just made him so angry he'd very nearly fled his own house.

"And while you're doing the teaching," Lachlan said, as though Kayden hadn't spoken at all. "You had better have her put on some clothes, before she gives someone the wrong ideas."

"And just what ideas are those?" Kayden asked, his voice coming out through his teeth in a growl that Mya felt all the way down her spine. "Inside my own house?"

The other man's glare tipped into a leer, his eyes sliding over Mya's body. "Just exactly the kind you'd think."

"Get out." Kayden was moving even as he spoke, wrapping a big hand around the other man's shoulder, against the base of his neck, and shoving him toward the door. As it opened, Mya caught a glimpse of the two men Lachlan had set to guard the door, both laid out on the ground. "Out!"

Kayden all but threw Lachlan out the door, slamming it behind him. When he turned to face Mya, her breath caught in her throat at the expression on his face.

"Are you hurt?" He was standing in front of her almost before the words had left his lips, so close that she had to tip her head back to meet his eyes. "He didn't touch you, did he?"

Mya shook her head. "No," she said. "No. I'm fine."

His hands caught her arms, the grip almost tight enough to bruise. When he looked down at her, she could feel the warmth of his breath against her face. "You're sure?"

She nodded mutely, not trusting her voice to speak with him so near. The hands around her biceps gentled, stroking down toward her elbows, and she shuddered a little, her whole body almost imperceptibly moving forward. Their breath mingled in the space between them, and for an instant she thought their mouths might meet. Her heart beat fast in her chest.

Someone banged on the door. Both of them jumped, startling apart. Where his hands had been, all Mya felt now was cold.

"Coming?"

Kayden called at the person on the other side, "I'll be right there."

Mya took a step back before he could turn around, putting further space between them.

"I can't leave you here," Kayden said when his gaze moved back to her. "You're not safe alone in the house."

"You can hardly take me with you, dressed like this."

Kayden spun on his heel and paced toward the other wall. "No," he said. "You're right. I can't take you with me. They're bad enough in my own house. If I let them get hold of you at the meet..."

"I'll be fine here." Mya met his gaze as he turned again. "Go. Do whatever it is you need to do. And I'll handle myself."

"No offense intended, but you've not done the best job of that."

She glared at him. "I will be. Just. Fine. Get."

"If you're staying, you'll stay with this." He moved as he spoke, toward the chest that she'd taken the shirt from the night before, and pulled a long knife from it. He handed it to her, and Mya curled her fingers around the sheath. "Keep that near to hand. I mean it. At the very least it will discourage anything that wants to get close."

There was another thunderous knock on the door, then, and Kayden swore under his breath and stalked toward it, flinging it open. "Yes?" he demanded.

Lachlan, standing on the other side, leaned half around Kayden like he was trying to get a glimpse into the house. Kayden moved to block his view. "We're waiting on you to head to the laird's house, and if we're late to the meet we'll all hear about it."

"Aye," Kayden said. "I'm coming."

He glanced over his shoulder once at Mya, his expression tight. She gave him a jaunty little wave, and got a scowl in return. His attention moved back to the men at the door.

"In the future," he said as he stepped through, pulling it shut behind him, the words muffled but still audible as they moved down the path, "I'll thank you to keep your eyes and your hands off my bride to be."

Mya didn't hear the response from the other men. She was too caught up in her own shock. Bride to be? What was he going to tell them when she left? That the engagement had been called off?

She shook her head. Whatever he was going to tell them didn't really concern her; she'd be well away by the time he needed an excuse, and she really didn't care whether his clansmen mocked him for losing the girl. Why would she? They had only just met. It was hardly her fault if he couldn't come up with a decent excuse for her presence. He was a handsome man—why wasn't he married already? With children running about the place?

The protests didn't even convince her. Mya sighed, and went to clean out the dishes they'd used at breakfast as the sound of the men and their horses disappeared into the distance.

When that was done, she gave her attention to the house. There wasn't much in it that she hadn't already taken note of. Bed. Cupboard. Chairs. Hearth. Chest. There was a butter churn she hadn't noticed the night before. Her gaze moved back to the chest sitting at the foot of the bed with the washbasin on top.

There was a part of her that told her she shouldn't be going through someone else's private things without their permission. Mya ignored it. Her host had been very close-mouthed about his history, and if she was going to be staying with him, she would need to at least know something about who he was. Anyway, he'd invited her to open it once; if he objected to her opening it again, he ought to have said so.

Setting the washbasin carefully aside, Mya opened the chest and set the clothes on the bed, still folded. Beneath was the wooden tray that held them separate from the rest of the chest's contents. Mya lifted it out and set it down next to her knee on the floor.

There wasn't much else in the chest, she was disappointed to discover. And certainly nothing that hinted at a past. There was, at least, a comb, which Mya gratefully borrowed, loosening her hair from the braid to work the knots her fingers hadn't caught from it. When that was done, she braided it again, and returned the comb to the chest. The only other items in it were a small sack of money in one corner, and two pins, one plain silver, and the other set with bronze and decorated with knot work. Mya lifted them out one by one to run her fingers over them, exploring the smooth metal. Then she set them back in their places and put the rest of the things in the chest where they belonged.

It was, she reflected as she closed the lid, going to be a long day alone in the little house.

Chapter 5

The afternoon passed slowly, and Kayden didn't return. Mya, restless and bored, eventually gave up on simply sitting in the house and wrapped herself in the blanket that had become hers, stepping out into the chilly day lit by a pale autumn sun.

Heather bent beneath her bare feet as she left the house behind.

It sat on a slope, and down below the land spread out, low and rolling. In the distance, dark hills closed the edges of the valley. Between her and them, water glittered in the sunlight, separating their hills from the village on the other side of the lake. At least she thought it a lake, though it stretched out to either side as far as she could see. She would ask Kayden, when he returned from the town, which must be the one she could see from her vantage point. It was large enough, houses huddled together around a market in the center. On the hill overlooking it stood the castle where, Kayden had informed her, more than one king of Scotland had spent time.

Lowing cattle pulled her attention from the view ahead, and she turned back toward the house and the stable that sat behind it. One of its doors opened on a pen, where a pair of shaggy red cows were grazing, chickens pecking around their feet. Mya wrapped her blanket closer around herself and picked her way up the hill to the pen. The cows watched her, unconcerned. One of them flicked an ear, and she was reminded suddenly of the deer, watching her just like that with his large dark eyes. She turned away from them and went back inside to sit beside the warmth of the fire.

As afternoon began to turn on toward evening, she got up again and went through the cupboard, finding flour and salt, meat, lard, cheese. A few other odds and ends. She wondered if Kayden expected her to cook some kind of supper. She had boasted that she knew her way around a hearth, after all. But it seemed that whatever kitchen she may have used in the past wasn't the kind of kitchen—if one could call it that—Kayden's simple home held.

Thankfully, further exploration revealed some kind of flat bread wrapped in a cloth and kept in a basket on top of the cupboard. That, she could at least work with. She set some of the meat to roast over the fire, and sliced cheese, then warmed the bread on a stone in the coals. All that finished, and the food keeping warm by the hearth, she went around the room and lit the candles she'd found scattered through it, filling the space with warm, golden light as night fell outside.

Hooves, at last, sounded in the yard, and Mya clutched the knife behind her back just to be safe. A few minutes later Kayden strode into the house, carrying a bag which he dropped on the floor next to the door as he took in the room. His eyebrows lifted. "Are you planning to run me completely out of candles along with everything else?"

"I made dinner," Mya said, ignoring the attitude as she dropped the knife on the table and grabbed the food. "If you're hungry."

"Little wonder there *is* anything for dinner. We'll soon be out, unless I can find a new deer."

"I'm sure you'll be able to find something." She wasn't going to rise to his bait. Clearly he'd had a bad day at the meeting. That wasn't her fault. And if he was going to take it out on her, she was going to ignore him until he could speak nicely.

Kayden sat down at the table, silent for a moment as he served himself bread and meat, slathering the bread and laying cheese on it. Mya followed his example. It was good, if a bit simple, and filling enough that her stomach at last stopped growling.

When they were finished, she stood and took his plate, preparing to clean up the remains of their meal. Kayden hadn't moved from his seat or said a word since their brief exchange at the beginning of the meal. Was he still angry, then?

"How was your day?" Mya ventured.

"My day?" He laughed, a bark of sound that didn't seem particularly pleased. "My day was about as you'd expect it to go after attacking another clan member over some strange woman that none of them knew was under my protection. Never mind that you were in my home, wearing my clothing. If that is not what 'under my protection' looks like, then I do not know what does."

"You were only defending me. Surely they could see that."

Kayden's dark eyes snapped to her face. "Could they now? No, they could not *surely* see it, because the man that I dragged out of the house like some common criminal is the cousin of the laird, and I'm hardly a member of the clan. It's little more than luck they didn't cast me out."

"You don't need to take it out on me," Mya said, her own frustration slipping into her voice.

"I'm not taking it out on you, lass," Kayden growled. "And if I were, well, it's your fault, isn't it? You're the one who had to show up in the middle of the woods wearing absolutely nothing, and you're the one who chased away the stag that could have fed me and half the clan. Which, as it happens, they were expecting from me, and are now also less than pleased about." He rose to his feet, slapping a hand down against the table. "And finally, might I add, you're the one who was running about my house in next to nothing, looking like some sort of—"

He had stepped half around the table, and they were standing close enough that she could feel the heat of his body against her own. Mya looked up at him.

"Like some sort of what?" she demanded.

"Like some sort of faerie creature," he hissed. "Here to lure me to my doom."

Her hand fisted in the shirt he wore. Her heart was pounding. She glanced down from his eyes to his lips, remembering the way they had felt on her own, then back, up. The look in his eyes was hot enough to set her aflame. Mya felt like she was burning. She wanted to be closer, wanted their clothes gone, wanted skin on skin contact.

She wanted *him*.

"And if I was?" The words were flippant, but they very nearly caught in her throat, her body almost trembling with his nearness and her desire.

He dragged in a ragged breath. "Then I would gladly go."

With the fistful of his shirt she yanked him forward, his body bowing toward hers, and their lips met. The kiss was rough and hungry, hardly leaving space for breath. Big hands curled around her hips and pulled her closer. His tongue ran across her bottom lip and he nipped at it slightly. She gasped and opened her mouth to him and his tongue slipped between her lips, filling her senses with the taste of him. The way his body felt against her own. The room around them could have ceased to exist in that moment; there was only him.

She ran the hand that wasn't gripping his shirt through his hair, fingers tangling in the dark locks and tightening just enough to pull as he turned them, pushing her back against the edge of the table. Mya broke the kiss, gasping.

"*Mya*," Kayden growled, voice wrecked with wanting. He pressed kisses against her jaw, her throat, refusing to let go. He tried to reconnect their lips but she turned away and he groaned, low in his throat.

"Kayden," Mya gasped. "Just—ah—wait a moment."

Their bowls were still sitting on the table, and she shoved them and the remaining food out of the way, clutching at his shoulders as he suddenly lifted her, setting her where they had been. Mya pulled him back down with a moan.

The kiss resumed, tongues stroking against each other, playing a game neither of them won. Or perhaps one they both could not help but win. He pressed his body down against hers, broad and warm, and she wrapped an arm around his neck and let him push her down, her spine arching and her legs falling open. He settled between them, one big hand moving to her thigh, stroking up its length. The other arm was wrapped around her waist, supporting her weight, holding her close.

Breathing became a necessity again. They broke apart once more, both of them panting. Kayden hardly paused. He dropped open-mouthed kisses along the curve of her throat, nipped at the skin there and made her cry out softly with the pleasure of it. There were no memories of this, any more than there were memories of anything else in her past, but her body knew it. This wild wanting. It moved instinctively, pressing up into every touch, needy and wanton. Teeth closed on her throat, just this side of pleasure. She jerked underneath him and whimpered. He licked a little spot in the juncture between her neck and shoulder and bit down again, hard enough to paint her skin with his mark.

"Kayden," she moaned, fingers curling tighter in his hair.

He pulled away with a growl and eyed his handiwork, lips curling into a smirk.

Mya tugged his hair again to get his attention.

"Mmm?" he hummed as he kissed her again.

"You're wearing far too much clothing," she said against his lips.

He pulled back just long enough to yank his shirt over his head, cursing when the piece of clothing defied his efforts. It came off in the next moment, and he threw it aside.

"Mine, now," she purred, leaning up to whisper the words against his ear.

He didn't bother struggling with her shirt. Just took it in both hands and ripped it roughly down the center, fabric giving way under the pressure. Mya's entire body shuddered, heat flooding her. Suddenly the need was desperate, her body aching for him. She wanted, in that moment, to drag him down to her and have him there on the table, hard and fast and hungry.

Her nipples peaked, the air in the room chill against her newly bare skin despite the fire. Kayden's eyes moved over her body like he couldn't bear to tear his gaze from her. Mya felt her cheeks heat, but she let him look, leaned back against her hands on the table so that her spine arched, her body bared to him. Her nipples tightened painfully at his scrutiny, demanding his attention. She tightened the hand in his hair and tugged, rocking her hips against his.

"Touch me," she breathed. If he didn't, she was going to have to do it herself.

His breath hissed through his teeth, and then he was on her, hands stroking up the curves of her ribcage until they rested just below her breasts, thumbs teasing along the sensitive curves of the undersides. Mya arched into the touch, reaching down with the hand that wasn't tangled in his hair to bring his hand up to her breast.

He gently squeezed, her peaked nipple pressing against his palm. Mya breathed in sharply. He stroked a thumb over her nipple, kneaded her breasts with his hands until she was almost dizzy with pleasure and need. She moaned Kayden's name and he thrust against her, letting her feel the length of him through his clothes, hard against her stomach. He nipped at her pulse point, and she whimpered.

Kayden moved in then, licking into her mouth again His moan was caught in the space between them, swallowed by the kiss. She rocked against him, and his hands tightened on her body, all but crushing her against him, as desperate for closeness as she was.

The kiss broke, and they panted for air. Kayden tilted his head so that the tip of his nose briefly brushed against her cheek. The barely there sensation sent a shiver along her spine. They were both breathing roughly, staring each other down, waiting for the next move.

"You are so lovely," he said, voice rough at its edges.

Then he leaned down and took one nipple in his mouth, swirling his tongue over the sensitive tip. Damn, *finally*. His free hand came up to tweak her other nipple. The sharp pleasure arrowed straight to her core and she arched her back, offering him more. He wasn't gentle. He increased the pressure until she cried out, body shuddering, but he gave her no rest. He merely switched sides, soothing the pain that was just the right side of pleasure with his tongue and causing more with his wicked fingers. She raked her nails over his shoulders and down his chest and his breath hitched.

He abandoned her breasts, then, despite her pleading moan, and kissed his way up her neck, pausing every so often to nip at the skin, leaving tiny bruises along the way. One hand lifted to cradle the back of her neck, his other still supporting her weight. Her pulse fluttered wildly. He bit down, sucking the bruised flesh into his mouth.

She sobbed at the pleasure, reaching for him—or for herself, she wasn't sure.

"No." Kayden caught her wrist and held it. "No touching."

"Please," Mya gasped, pulling at his grip.

"Hold tight," he ordered, and then he was moving.

Mya wrapped her legs around his hips and her arms around his neck as he lifted her from the table. It was effortless, as though she weighed nothing, and her stomach flipped at the ease of it as new heat coiled in her core. He crossed the room in a few long strides to lay her down on the bed.

He curled his fingers around her wrists, lifting them above her head and pressing them into the mattress. "Let me please you tonight, Mya. I want to watch you come undone for me. By my hands. My mouth." He smirked wickedly, his hand finally, finally moving down her body to stroke his fingers over her sex. "You are already so wet for me, lass."

This time, she growled. "Kayden. Dammit."

He chuckled at her choice of words. "Be patient, lass."

"What if I don't want to?" She breathed hard, clenching her thighs together. With a light smack against her inner thigh, Kayden spread her legs.

"Then you will wait until you have learned patience," he answered, the words a rush of hot breath against her ear.

"I will take the situation into my own hands if necessary," Mya informed him.

He chuckled. "No, you will not. Because I will not let you." His eyes were on her face, dark and wanting. "Can you play such games? Will you let me pleasure you?"

He slid his fingers over her again, cupping her and teasing at her entrance. Mya whimpered. Hunger filled his eyes and he leaned in for a bruising kiss.

Damn, he was wicked.

"You can't control me." Her breath came in hard pants.

"You'll be begging me to let you come," he purred. "I promise you."

She whimpered, and he paused, considering. Despite the want in his expression, his hands gentled on her body. "Tell me this is well with you? I do not wish to harm you."

"You'll do me no harm." She leaned up on her hands and grinned at him, wide and goading. He knew how to please a woman? Somehow she knew most men did not. "Come then. Make me beg."

"You'll not come without my word," he growled.

Mya shuddered.

He smiled at her, slow and utterly wicked, and sank the tip of his finger into her wetness. Then, he stopped.

Mya writhed, trying to get more of his finger into her, but he withdrew and slid his fingers a little higher, rubbing hard and fast at her clit. She moaned, head tipped back against the sheet, hips bucking up. Bloody hell, he was good. He captured her lips again, this time a little gentler, shaping her lips to fit his. He took her whimpers and groans into his mouth. Her muscles pulled tight, fingers curling in the sheets. The sparks were already running along her thighs, hinting at what was to explode, starting when—

She hissed in frustration, his hand suddenly gone. Her breathing heavy, she tried to rub her thighs together but he kept her legs spread, holding her effortlessly in place. He sat back, meeting her eyes, and smiled again. "Don't you wish to come? You are so wet. So wanting."

She shrugged, already coming down from the edge. "I can wait."

"Are you going beg me yet?"

She shook her head, baring her teeth in a grin. "Try harder."

He laughed. "You have asked for it, Mya. Remember that." He kissed her again, drawing her breath from her lungs. He stroked his hands up the inside of her thighs and down again, over the back of her knees.

He slid one finger into her, inch by inch, until he was fully seated inside of her. It wasn't enough. His other hand moved back to her breasts, teasing a nipple into a tighter bud, making her breath catch in her throat. His mouth attended the other, alternating with licking and biting.

She squirmed. "More."

"Impatient." He thrust another finger into her core, stretching her deliciously.

Her fingers tightened in the sheets, a moan caught in her throat. He swiped his thumb across her clit, pressing down harder each time until he was practically rubbing. He thrust harder. It built again, the pleasure coiling tight at the base of her spine, and it was right there for the taking. She could almost—

He kissed her, sliding his fingers into her hair and anchoring them at the back of her head. Her cheeks were flushed, her breath coming in harsh, ragged pants. Mya glared at him. Kayden simply looked smug, and she was beginning to regret giving him such free rein. It was obviously going to his head. Mya trailed her fingers down his chest and traced the waistband of his trousers before tugging them down. He let her, stripping out of them and tossing them to the side.

She smiled, then, and reached down, wrapping her fingers around the silky length of his cock. She swiped her thumb across the head, and Kayden groaned low but grabbed her wrist and raised it, shaking his head. "Not tonight."

"You are cruel," Mya snapped, but she drew her hand away, slowly, dragging her fingers against his skin.

A groan tore from Kayden's lips. He braced himself over her, his body hot against her own. Mya framed his jaw with her hands, tracing her fingers over his features. He was beautiful. She wanted him. Hands gentling, she ran her fingers through his hair, so dark against the white of her own skin. She looped her arms around his neck and tugged his head down, meeting him in a gentle kiss, almost tentative in contrast to the last.

He trailed his hand down her body, no preliminaries this time, and gently slid two fingers inside her. She groaned against his mouth, her hips rising to meet every thrust. She had already been denied twice, and it was only a moment's work before she was on the edge. Her body pulled tight, aching for release, and her breaths came in short, hard gasps. She was close. So fucking close. She dug her nails into his shoulders. He hissed and punished her with a sharp nip to the curve of her breast. "Do you want your release?"

Mya nodded, desperate. Her hand fluttered down to cover his, pressing him harder to her mound.

"It does not work like that, lovely one. Say it." He slowed his thrusts, teasing her.

Mya whined, bucking her hips, but he didn't speed up or touch her clit. She was growing desperate. The ecstasy she craved was there, just out of reach. Her center ached with wanting. She tugged his head down and pressed her forehead against his, their eyes meeting. "Please, Kayden. Bloody hell, please. Take me to the edge. Let me have it. Please."

His smile was scorching. "As you wish."

Another thrust. Another press of his thumb against her clit. Her eyes never left his as she reached the edge once more, pleasure sparking along every nerve. There was something profoundly intimate about that moment, their gazes locked together, both of them laid out before the other, all vulnerability and no secrets. It was that, as much as his hand on her that did it. She tipped over the edge, crying out his name and arching her body into his. His arm went automatically around her, his lips at her neck. Stars sparked behind her eyes as she rode the pleasure. A warm glow spread from her center to the rest of her body, painting the rest of the world in a hazy hue.

One arm was still looped around Kayden's neck, the other trailing patterns across her sweat-drenched skin. "Kayden." Her arm drew him closer. "I need you. Please. Inside me. I beg you."

He chuckled. "Are you saying my fingers were not pleasure enough? Have I deprived you, my lovely one?"

She laughed and shook her head, raising one leg to wrap around his hip and pull him straight across her. "They were nothing less than satisfactory. But I want more of you. All of you. Give it to me."

"But you just had your pleasure."

"I can have it again." She stole a kiss. "Let me care for you now. Let me feel you."

It was too much for him to take. He knelt between her legs, one hand on her thigh holding her open, and slowly slid himself into her, his eyes on her face. Mya's fingers curled against the back of his neck and her spine arched, her body unused to the stretch, but wanting it. Needing him. She moaned, and his own pleasured groan echoed the sound.

He pressed his forehead against her shoulder, face buried in the crook of her neck. And then he began to move, thrusting slowly, finding a rhythm. Their bodies met in a dance as old as mankind, the motion she had hazily remembered that first night when she had been wrapped in his arms. It was everything that she had wanted. Everything that she desired. He alternated between long and slow and hard and fast, his fingers finding her breast once more, lightly pinching and tweaking the tight bud of her nipple. She wrapped her legs tighter around him, dragging her nails down his back.

His hand tightened in her hair, low, choppy moans torn from his throat as he thrust. He reached one hand down to find her clit, rocking his thumb against her clit with the same rhythm his hips moved to. Mya bit back a cry, earning her a low, husky laugh. He pressed one last kiss to her neck and braced himself on his forearm, kissing her.

Pleasure coiled low in her belly again, wrapping her senses in its net. Her toes curled as she rode the wave higher, seeking the crash. She clung to Kayden, his cock rubbing perfectly against her inner walls, hitting the spot that made her entire body shudder with pleasure. Whimpers and gasps escaped her lips as Kayden held her head in place, his eyes never leaving hers. Damn it, she couldn't do this again. To see his desire so blatant and raw had pushed her over the edge the last time.

Mya cried out as the pleasure exploded outward, eyes falling shut. It was too much, too everything. He thrust hard one final time, groaning his pleasure, his head thrown back. She stroked his cheek, his shoulder, his back, and whispered words that she forgot even as they left her lips.

Chapter 6

When Mya woke, Kayden had already gone.

The bed was still warm where he'd been lying; her body still felt the press of his arm over her waist. She levered herself up onto an elbow, shivering in the rush of cold air as the blanket fell back.

There was a pot over the fire, and the sound of water bubbling reached her ears, mingling with the crackling of the flames. She would have to get up and start the porridge in a moment, but the thought of getting out of the warm bed and leaving nothing between her skin and the cold morning air felt daunting. The clothes they had scattered around the room the night before had been tidied away, and the only thing that remained was the folded skirt and top that Kayden had brought back from the village for her, sitting on one of the chairs in front of the fire.

Sighing, Mya pulled herself out of the bed and picked her way across the freezing floor to the chair. The skirt, when she pulled it on, slipped down her hips and nearly fell. She caught the waistband in one hand and pulled it back up, glancing around for something that might double as a belt.

There wasn't anything in immediate sight. She let the skirt drop, stepping out of it, and picked up the shirt still sitting on the chair. That, at least, wouldn't fall off. Hopefully.

It was a little big, but not so large that it was sliding off her shoulders, and at least it covered the important bits. There were shoes too. Mya pulled them on and laced them up her ankles, grateful for the warmth, despite the rough hide they were made from. They weren't perfect, but they were better than nothing.

She wrapped herself in the blanket and went to put the porridge in the water.

When Kayden came back inside, carrying eggs and a bucket of milk, he hardly looked at her. For the first time, he wasn't wearing the trousers that she'd first met him in. Instead, he was dressed in a plaid kilt like a skirt, draped to his knees and tucked into itself at the waist. He set the bucket down and moved to the washbasin without a word.

So it was going to be like that again.

Mya stirred the porridge to keep it from getting lumpy and didn't say anything.

"The skirt doesn't fit?" Kayden asked finally.

"It was falling off. I'll have to alter it."

"Can you actually sew?"

She glared at the porridge. "Honestly? I'm not sure. But it can't hurt to try."

"If nothing else, there's some rope in the barn. I can cut you a length."

"I would appreciate that."

She wondered if he noticed the same awkwardness, all the words that they weren't saying caught between them. The silence felt stretched. Brittle.

Mya spooned up the porridge and they took it to the table. Neither of them spoke. Spoonful after spoonful, they ate. The air between them so thick, it felt like a fog had rolled in from the meadow and into the house, settling directly between them. Finally, she couldn't take it any longer. She set her spoon down with a crack against the wood of the table. "So, we're not going to talk about this?"

"Talk about what?" Kayden said, as though the answer to the question was not entirely obvious.

"About what happened last night." Mya kept her tone tightly in check.

"Why does it need talking about? It was something that happened. There is no need to discuss it."

"I'm not asking to discuss it. I'm asking you to acknowledge that it happened at all."

Kayden didn't look at her. "I just did."

"Very well." Mya bit the word out, picking up her spoon again. "You acknowledged it."

"I don't know what more you want me to do, Mya," Kayden said, sharp. "Yes. It happened. You say that you aren't asking to discuss it, but that seems to be the path this is set to take."

"I am taking it nowhere. You acknowledged it. I agreed that you did. We can stop talking about it." Mya took a deliberately slow bite. "I'm done with the subject."

Kayden looked at her from across the table, his brows drawn down over his eyes, but he didn't try to push the conversation any further. He was likely just relieved that Mya had given up on it. She finished her porridge without another word.

When breakfast was eaten and cleared away, Kayden went out to the barn to cut some rope for her so that she had a way to tie up the skirt, at least for the time being. It was a relief to be wearing something more than a flimsy shirt, even if she did like the way that Kayden's eyes moved over her bare legs. Altering the skirt would be better, but Mya was too restless to attempt the project.

"Here," Kayden said, catching her attention.

Mya looked up, keeping her expression even. Her eyebrows lifted. "What is that?"

"It's called an arisaid." He took a step forward, holding the folded plaid out to her. "It will keep you a little warmer. Tuck it into your belt so you can wrap the top around yourself. There are other ways to wear it, but those are for less practical concerns."

Carefully, Mya reached out and took the fabric, unfolding it. It matched, she noted, the design of the garment he wore. She tucked it through the makeshift rope belt, letting the upper half fall over the lower so that she could have her arms free. "Thank you."

"It is of little consequence. I got it for you with the rest of the things." He moved toward the door again, pausing with his hand on it. "I'll be heading out to work in the garden. You can feel free to do whatever you like."

"And if I want to come out and work in the garden with you?"

Kayden stood for a moment, looking at her as though he was assessing her ability to handle manual labor of even the easiest sort. Then he nodded. "Very well, then. Come on out when you're ready."

He stepped through the door, pulling it closed at his back.

Mya took a deep breath and let it out again, running a hand over the fabric of the arisaid. It was soft under her fingers, fine wool woven tight. That Kayden had given it to her was somehow comforting, even when he was utterly infuriating, which was constantly.

She didn't understand why he was so distant. They had hardly done something wrong. Although she did have a feeling that... The details eluded her. Mya sighed, and headed out into the chilly autumn morning to help him in the garden.

"The oats are nearly ready for harvest," he said, not looking up from the weeds he was pulling.

Mya knelt a few feet from him and began working on her own patch, looking over the golden oats, planted just beyond the broad green leaves of the kale.

"So is that," Kayden said, following her gaze. "Once the first frost hits. Better for flavor. And the turnips too, a little after the kale. We'll be eating well in a few weeks if I can bring down a deer."

We.

He spoke as though he expected her to stay.

She'd thought he would want her out of his house as soon as she had something to wear, especially after their argument.

Maybe she had been wrong about his attitude after all, though that didn't make his obvious discomfort with their recent activities any less frustrating.

"You're quite stuck on that deer thing."

"I'm stuck on food for the winter. Especially if I'm going to be having a guest."

Mya paused halfway through pulling a weed up and turned to look at him. "A guest?"

"I know that I said you were out as soon as you had clothing, but you're still without your memory. I don't feel right sending you out into the world like that."

"A gentleman after all, then."

He laughed. "Maybe. Though I've never really thought of myself as such."

She pulled up the weed and tossed it on the pile with the rest. For a few moments they worked in silence, side by side, the space between them comfortable for once, instead of fraught with tension.

"Have you remembered anything more?" he asked.

Mya shook her head. "Not anything that I didn't know before. Except, well..." She paused, uncertain if she should go on.

"Except?"

She kept her eyes on the weeds she was pulling. "I have this feeling. That I was in love before."

"Before you lost your memory?"

"Yes," Mya answered. "I know it's maybe silly, to trust a feeling when you can't remember anything about yourself. But... love is stronger than that. Love is timeless."

Kayden didn't answer, and Mya wondered if she'd said too much. She wondered, too, why she didn't feel guilty about the night they'd just spent together when Kayden obviously did. He didn't have anyone he was betraying. At least no one that she knew. And though Mya couldn't be sure *who* was waiting for her, she couldn't shake the feeling that someone was. If love was indeed timeless, it shouldn't matter that she couldn't remember her past. But she didn't feel guilty.

With Kayden, she felt comfortable. She felt as though she belonged.

Chapter 7

Sometime in the early afternoon, their quiet labor was interrupted by the sound of hooves. Mya raised her head, looking up from the vegetable patch she was weeding, and saw Kayden straighten up beside her, turning his eyes toward the little track that ran down the slope toward the village. A moment later, a pair of horses topped the rise.

"Lachlan," Kayden said as the men riding the beasts came into view. His voice was tight. "Ealair."

"Kayden," the red-haired man said, lips curling into a smile that made Mya's skin crawl. "We've come to fetch you both so your lady may meet the laird."

Meet the laird? Mya turned to look at Kayden, her eyes wide, and caught sight of the guilty expression that flickered across his face before it vanished.

"You knew." Her voice was flat.

"Aye. They told me at the meet."

"Why in god's name did you not prepare me for it?" She hissed the words, quietly enough that the men on the horses wouldn't be able to hear them.

"I thought it would only make you nervous. It's not as though there's aught you could have done about it. And you hardly have visiting clothes to be changing into." He lifted one shoulder in a shrug and let it fall. "You would have only run about making yourself more harried."

"You have no idea what I might have done," Mya snapped. "Because you did not give me time to do it."

"Well, you've no time now. So I suggest you dust your hands off and get on the horse I'm fetching."

She could have happily murdered him, dirty hands from working in the garden and all. How could he have swanned about acting as though they had nothing better to do than tend to the kale when he knew very well that she was going to be summoned to meet the laird of his clan? Unbelievable man. Mya stepped into the house to make an attempt at cleaning herself up, knowing as she did that he had been right, at least, about her inability to do much more than dust the dirt from her clothing. There was nothing better to wear. Nothing to be done with her hair. She rearranged the arisaid to be a little more appealing, and hoped that would be enough.

When she stepped outside again, Kayden had the horse bridled and waiting. He gave her a hand up onto its broad back, swinging astride behind her, and then he was nudging the horse into a walk, guiding it to follow the other two down the hill.

A bridge waited at the bottom, crossing over the glittering water that separated Kayden's home from the village where most of the clan members resided. As they passed through the houses, Mya saw faces in the windows, watching them. Curious women and children, maybe, eager for a glimpse of the stranger in their midst.

Mya thought of lifting a hand in greeting, of giving them some sign that she was friendly, but she was not certain how they would react. She kept her hand lowered at her side, and contented herself with stealing glimpses here and there of those who were watching their little procession go by. She couldn't imagine that they often saw newcomers. It must have been a matter of at least a little excitement.

They rode into the yard of the manor house, built from the same rough stone as the hut that Kayden called home, and Kayden slid from the back of the horse to help her to the ground. Mya took the hand he offered, holding the too-large skirt out of the way so she didn't trip over it. He held her gently back as she moved to follow their escorts inside.

"Mya," he said, bending his head to whisper close against her ear. "Whatever you do, control your tongue for this one interview. If you displease the laird, we may both of us be forced from the clan's land."

She nodded, rather than answer in words, and saw Kayden's shoulders relax.

The men led them down a short hall and into a large room where the laird sat at the head of a great table.

He was a big man, bigger than Kayden, with hair as red as Lachlan's. She felt his eyes move over her with interest, but they didn't linger, at least. It seemed he either wasn't as interested in her as his cousin was, or he was capable of being more polite about it.

"Kayden," he said. "Welcome. And to your woman." His blue eyes narrowed. "Though I must say we're all very interested in how she came to be here, without a word from you before her arrival."

"Her... visit was something of a surprise, laird." Kayden's voice was steady.

"And how is it this visit came to pass?" The laird asked, turning his gaze to Mya.

That was the question she had been dreading; the one she had no answer to. How could she explain to him that she had woken up in a field, with no memory – nothing of her former life on her – and been rescued by Kayden? Even if she could have told the laird so, Kayden had already ruined that avenue for her by stating that she was his bride to be in an attempt at protecting her. And while the attempt was appreciated, it made things difficult.

"I came up from the south, laird." She tried on a smile as she said the words, hoping that he would accept them as they were.

"A southern bride, Kayden?" The laird sounded amused as he turned his eyes to her rescuer. "I would not have thought it of you."

"From the highland borders, laird."

"Ah." The laird sat back in his chair. "From the borders. Are you of one of the great clans there, then?"

Mya cast a quick glance at Kayden from the corner of her eye, then shook her head. "No, laird. I am from a small family. They live well to the west of here."

The man's eyes sharpened, and Mya's stomach twisted nervously. What if she had said something wrong? She could see Lachlan watching her from the seat at the laird's right hand. They had to tread carefully here. A mistake could mean Kayden's exile from the clan, though she did not think that would be the most likely punishment. But what did she know of the laird's justice?

"And how came you to meet Kayden?" Lachlan asked.

Mya swallowed. "Indeed, I had not yet met him when first I came. He made my father's acquaintance on the road, saving his life when he was attacked by lawless men, and as my father sought a man to be my husband, it seemed the encounter was fated."

That, at least, she seemed to have answered to their satisfaction. She saw several pairs of eyes move to Kayden, heard the quiet murmur of whispers rising at their backs.

"Your father sets high standards for the winning of his daughter's hand," the laird said. "So I must wonder why he sent you alone to our land, without introduction or escort. To live with a man when you are not yet wed."

"Ah." Mya bit her lip. "That is the tragedy, laird. I came on my own. My father was taken with illness some weeks back, and my mother and two sisters. My surviving brother had given himself over entirely to his work, and my home only brought back the memory of my grief each morning. So I left, to find the man to whom I am betrothed. It was, perhaps, foolish, but it seemed the right thing to do when the choice was made."

There was a moment of silence that Mya interpreted as stunned. She silently prayed that she had not just destroyed everything for them.

"We do strange things in the hold of grief," said a man who had not yet spoken.

He was older than the rest, Mya saw when her gaze flicked to him, his face craggy and lined with years. She hardly breathed, waiting for the laird's reaction.

"You speak the truth," the man finally mused. "Though I still wonder why Kayden did not bring you to us," he added. "When it would have been proper, nor ask among the clan that you be given proper housing while you awaited your wedding."

"She has only recently arrived," Kayden said. "And met with trouble upon the road that ended in the loss of what little she brought. I thought to give her some time to adjust to her new surroundings."

"It seems tragedy follows your bride wherever she goes," Lachlan said.

"I hope to turn that luck around," Kayden answered.

"See that you keep the rest of us informed of such events, in future," the laird said. "Your decisions affect the clan."

Kayden nodded. "I will do so, laird."

The room seemed to suddenly relax, then. It appeared that the laird had made up his mind, and Kayden's transgression wouldn't end badly for them. Some of the tension slipped out of Mya's shoulders. She followed Kayden's example as he bowed to the laird, dipping into a curtsey, and then followed him from the room.

"What are you going to tell them when I've left?" she asked when they were riding down the lane that cut through the village, her arms wrapped around his waist.

"That a member of your family came to claim you, most like," Kayden answered. His voice was tight, as though he wasn't sure he wished to say the words. "We'll find an answer for it when we need one."

Mya listened to the sound of the horse's hooves against the earth, and wondered if she wanted to have to come up with one at all.

Chapter 8

"I would like to teach you to use a weapon," Kayden said that night, as they were laying by the fire.

He hadn't touched her again. Even as they lay side by side, he was just close enough that she could feel the heat of his body, but he very carefully didn't let his chest press against her back. Mya tried to ignore the disappointment that crept along the edges of her thoughts. If he didn't want her, she wasn't going to lie around moping about it.

"A weapon?" she echoed, a little uncertain.

"If you are to be spending your days here alone, you need a way of defending yourself. I'll not leave you again with nothing and the likes of Lachlan McGill roaming about."

He wasn't wrong.

"I should be glad to learn how to use a weapon, then."

"Aye," Kayden said. "We'll start in the morning."

Silence fell between them, broken by the sound of the fire and the noise of the wind sighing around the house.

Mya bit her lip. "Thank you. For rescuing me from him. I did not say as much before, but I do appreciate it."

There was a rustle of fabric behind her, Kayden moving, and then silence.

"Thanks are not necessary," he said finally. "It was no more than any decent man would've done."

"And yet neither of the men who were with him did a thing," Mya pointed out. "So not every man is decent. I know that I was hardly kind about it before, but you've done more for me than anyone would have expected, gentleman or not. And I owe you a great deal."

"So finally you express a little gratitude." There was a smile in Kayden's voice that took the sting out of the words. "That is nice to see, I admit."

Mya resisted the urge to reach back and swat him for his teasing. She was trying to actually be serious about her feelings at the moment, and it would help if he'd listen. "I mean it," she said.

"I know you do," he answered, the laughter gone from his voice. "But what I did, I did because it was the right thing to do, not so that you would be indebted to me."

"Well, thank you. Either way."

"You are welcome, lass."

The words drifted into quiet once more, and this time neither of them spoke. Kayden's breathing slowed, and Mya let sleep rise up to claim her.

Morning came cold and gray once more, and Mya rose and made breakfast while Kayden milked the cows and collected eggs. When they had eaten, and cleared away the mess, Kayden took her out into the yard and handed her a sword.

Mya looked at it dubiously. "Do you think it safe to use a real sword from the start?"

"And what other sort of sword would you use?" Kayden laughed. "So long as you don't go chopping your own foot off or some such, you'll be just fine."

"I find very little comfort in that statement."

He grinned at her. "Relax. I won't be letting you maim yourself. Now," he said, and the smile was suddenly gone. "First, you'll need to learn how to hold it."

The blade was heavy in her hand, and the point wavered as she held it out. Kayden stepped in closer, warm against the morning chill, and wrapped one calloused hand over hers, guiding her fingers into place. He was so close that his chest almost pressed against her shoulder. Mya imagined the way his lips would feel against her neck if he dipped his head just a little, the way his fingers would feel curling around her hips the way they curled around the hilt of the sword.

But he did not touch her that way, only stepped back and gave further instructions in his low, smooth voice as Mya worked on learning the weapon he'd set in her hand.

"You're not going to be able to do much against an experienced fighter," he said as he helped her set her feet. "So you'll be going for the element of surprise. They're not going to expect you to be able to use a weapon at all. You must catch them unaware, do as much damage as you can before they realize what's happening, and then you run. You understand?"

"Why can't I learn to take them on? Afraid your teaching skills aren't up to the task?"

"You could, maybe, if we had a few years to work on it, but we don't, and it takes a special kind of skill to take on an opponent twice your size, even if you've a great deal of training otherwise." His hand caught hers again, lifting the wavering point of the sword, and for a moment his fingers lingered. Mya's breath caught in her throat. They slid away again. "Any of the men of the clan are going to have a far longer reach than you do, which means that they're going to be able to do you damage from a distance you won't be able to touch them at. And they're heavier. Weight can count for much in a fight."

Mya thought of the man who had cornered her in the house just days before, the way that he'd towered over her. She bit her lip. "I understand."

"In truth, there might be a teacher somewhere who could give you the right tools to win a fight like that." A smile slipped into his voice. "So I suppose my skills aren't up to the task after all.

But I've never had much cause to fight an opponent larger than I am."

No, Mya couldn't imagine that he had. She'd felt the muscles in his arms, the strength of his body over hers.

"So teach me what you can," she said.

"Oh," Kayden said, leaning in nearer and guiding her into the proper stance. "I absolutely intend to."

It was harder than she had expected.

If she had used a weapon before, in the life she could not remember, it had not been a sword. The weapon was clumsy in her hands, dragging her arms down with its weight. She followed Kayden as he led her through drill after drill, intended to make her body know the motions so well that she would move without thinking should the need ever arise, but they were a long way yet from that. Blisters rose on her hands where they had been wrapped around the hilt. Even in the chill of autumn, she felt hot with effort.

Later, when the sun had risen toward noon and Mya was panting with exertion, Kayden let her put down the sword.

"You've done well," he said, taking it from her hand. "Better than I might have expected, actually."

Mya gave him a sideways look. "I admit I am not certain whether to take that as a compliment or an insult."

"Take it how you like. Just don't forget to keep your point up."

She was hardly going to, when he'd spent the hours since breakfast lecturing her on the importance of it. Mya didn't point that out. She'd asked him to teach her; complaining about his methods was only going to sound childish.

"Tomorrow," he said as they stepped into the relative warmth of the low stone house, "I'll start you with the bow. It uses different muscles, so it should keep you from getting too sore. You won't be able to draw mine, but I've picked up one in town for you."

"You seem determined to make me into some kind of warrior maiden," Mya pointed out, laughing.

"Warrior maiden? No. I only want to be sure that you're capable of defending yourself should you have to. If you have any aspirations beyond that, you'll have to find someone else to aid you in reaching them."

Kayden moved to the hearth and began gathering together ingredients for what Mya realized was some kind of bread. She took a seat at the table and watched him, her chin propped up on one hand.

"Are you saying that you would not teach me if I wished to become a warrior maiden?"

"I am saying I am not the best teacher for such ambitions. For reasons we've already been over." Kayden looked up from the oats he was grinding into meal. "And in truth, I'm not sure that's the best occupation for you, though you certainly have the fire for it."

"That, I'll choose to take as a compliment."

He smiled. "You ought to. I meant it as one."

"Though I am curious," she said, "as to why it isn't the right occupation."

"In truth?"

"I would prefer it."

Kayden's hands stilled in their motions. "Then I'll admit that I don't like the idea of you in such danger."

The words made warmth bubble up behind Mya's ribs, filling her chest with a happy glow. She dropped her gaze to her hands, lifted it again to look up at him through her eyelashes. "I didn't know that you cared so deeply."

Kayden looked quickly away, hands once again busy, working butter into the coarse-ground flour. Mya swallowed the laughter that wanted to escape. All those rippling muscles and that fighter's courage, and he couldn't look her in the eye and admit that he might just have some feelings for her beyond obligation.

"You're my responsibility," he said. "I'm the one who brought you home. So I feel that I have a...duty to make certain you are safe."

"Just that?" Mya asked, voice deliberately soft. "Just duty?"

Kayden didn't lift his head. "You are worthwhile company."

Duty. Worthwhile company. Mya thought of the way his hands had moved over her skin as they tangled together in the bed, his mouth against hers, and wondered if he really believed that as much as he pretended to. She didn't ask him. Instead, she stood, and went to take eggs from the cupboard to accompany the bread for lunch.

Chapter 9

The blisters on her hands were becoming callouses, her wrists growing stronger. Mya was beginning to feel a little like the warrior maiden Kayden had told her he couldn't train her to be. She still struggled with the sword, but the bow came easier every day, and though he didn't often say it, she knew Kayden was pleased with her progress.

"I've things to be done today, so I'll have to leave you here," Kayden said as he carried the milk pails in and set them down on the floor.

Mya looked up from the porridge she was cooking. "Will you be gone for the entire day?"

He lifted one shoulder in a shrug and let it fall. "Likely I won't be back until close to sunset. You know enough to defend yourself, but the chances of something happening are small. You've been acknowledged by the laird. Even Lachlan will hesitate to cross that."

It wasn't Lachlan that had worried Mya. In truth, he hadn't crossed her mind until Kayden had mentioned him. Without Kayden, she would be alone in the house, with little to do. She supposed she could tidy things up, practice with the sword and the bow. See that dinner was cooked. There were things to keep her occupied.

"I was thinking that perhaps we might go down to the market," she said. "On a day when you don't have other duties."

Kayden turned to look at her. "Would that please you, Mya?"

"It would please me to be away from the house for a time," she said in answer. "I would like to see the village again."

"Then I will take you to the market one day soon," Kayden said, offering her a smile that made her feel warm all the way down to her toes.

"I will hold you to that."

They sat down together and ate, and then Kayden bid her farewell. Mya watched from the doorway as he rode down the slope, sighing a little as he vanished from sight beyond the ridge.

What had she done with her days, she wondered, before she had woken up in that field? Had she kept a home? Tended sheep? She laughed a little at the thought. Perhaps she had been a nobleman's daughter, lounging about and looking delicate. But her skill with the bow seemed to suggest otherwise.

She went about cleaning up the mess from breakfast, and was surprised at the sound of a knock on the door. Her thoughts went to Lachlan, and she wondered if Kayden had been right to believe he would not bother her. She picked up the knife he had left her the first day he went away, hoping she wouldn't need to use it. There was another quiet knock. It didn't sound like Lachlan. Not the kind of demanding anger she was sure would be in the sound of his fist against the door. Still, she paused before reaching for the latch.

Waiting for her on the other side of the door were two women. They smiled, and one of them proffered a basket she was carrying.

"I hope you do not mind us dropping by, dear," the older of the two said, already moving past Mya into the house as though she'd been invited. "It's just your man keeps you shut up so tightly here. We've hardly had a chance to meet you."

She still smiled as she said it, but Mya detected a note of disapproval in her voice.

"Kayden is very careful of me," Mya said, putting on a smile of her own and stepping back to allow them both into the room. She pulled the door shut behind them. "I'm certain he doesn't mean to isolate me from the clan."

"If he does not mean it, he ought not to do it," the younger woman said.

"Forgive us for not introducing ourselves," the older woman interjected before she could say anything more, shooting her a look that Mya interpreted as meaning she shouldn't have been so blunt. "I am Caoimhe, and this is Seonaid."

"It is a pleasure to meet you both," Mya said. "Please. Sit."

She waved them toward the seats at the table, but then wasn't quite sure what to do with herself. So she stood, hands folded in front of her, and waited for them to speak.

"We've brought you a gift," Caoimhe said, offering the basket she held.

Hesitantly, Mya reached out and took it, glancing beneath the cover that had been folded over the contents. Her eyes widened. It held honeycomb, rich and sticky, and she glanced up at the women.

"Are you certain?"

"We wish to welcome you to our clan," Seonaid said, smiling. "Please, accept the gift."

"I have nothing to give you in return."

"Gifts do not require return." Caoimhe's smile was as kind as Seonaid's. "That is why they are gifts."

"Thank you." Mya looked down at the honey again, thinking of the way it would taste in their morning porridge. "Both of you."

"Tell us something of yourself," Caoimhe said into the quiet space that followed as Mya set the basket on top of the cupboard and turned back to them.

The question made Mya's stomach twist a little with nerves. It had been trouble enough answering questions of her origin for the laird. The women were looking at her with attentive kindness, obviously expecting an answer of some detail.

"I am from the south," she said, because it was what she had told the laird. "Near the lowland border."

"Is it very different from here?" Seonaid was leaning forward a little in her seat, her wide green eyes full of interest.

"Not so different from here," Mya said. "Farmers, as here. Raising cows or sheep." She smiled. "Though I do not think the men are quite so rugged."

Seonaid laughed a startled, delighted sort of laugh. "To tell you true, more than one maid had her eye on Kayden. There are a few very disappointed young women in the clan, now that you've arrived."

"Are you one of them, then?" Mya asked, surprising herself a little with the question.

"Oh. No. I'm wed already, and quite happy with my husband." Seonaid shook her head as she spoke, curls bouncing on her shoulders. "And you needn't worry that Kayden's attention will stray. If he did not care for you, he would not be so protective."

"Speaking of protection," Mya said, the words slow and a little careful. "Might I be so bold as to ask you about one of the other men in the clan?"

"In what sense, lass?"

Mya turned to look at Caoimhe, hands twisting nervously together against her skirt. "There is a man called Lachlan..."

The faces of both women darkened.

"Lachlan is..." Seonaid shook her head, glancing across the table at Caoimhe.

"Lachlan is the kind of man that smart women walk wide of," Caoimhe said firmly. "And we keep an eye out for each other when he is about."

"Then I'm not the only woman who has had trouble with him." It wasn't really a question.

"No. You are far from the first. I doubt you will be the last. That he is the cousin of the laird makes him believe he can get away with much." Seonaid's tone was sharp.

"You seem to have had personal experience," Mya said, sinking down to sit on the low stool next to the hearth.

"I was the object of his interest for a short time. My husband stepped in before things could get too dangerous," Seonaid answered. "Though I do not doubt that if he had not taken up courting me Lachlan would not have left me alone easily."

"Then you think he will not challenge Kayden?"

"I could not say, in truth."

Caoimhe shook her head. "He is not a man of great courage, but that does not mean that he will let you go without a struggle if he believes there is any chance of his winning you over."

"There is no chance of that, believe me."

"It will take him some time to get that concept through his thick head," Seonaid said.

That was what Mya had been concerned about. Kayden seemed to have come to the conclusion that there wouldn't be any further trouble with the man, but she wasn't certain that he had put enough thought to it. That she had come seemingly out of nowhere to be named Kayden's bride likely made it more difficult. Lachlan had reason to be suspicious. And if Mya was honest with herself, she had to admit that his suspicions were not entirely unfounded.

"I will simply have to walk carefully, then, until he is dealt with," she sighed.

"Kayden will not let him anywhere near you," Caoimhe said. "He is a man that other men know better than to cross, if they are wise. And when he is not about, we will keep a watch out when we can. Women must help one another."

"If there is anything I can do for either of you," Mya said. "Ever. Please do let me know."

"That is what clan means," Caoimhe answered her. "It is family. And you are one of us now, whether you are wed yet to Kayden or not."

"Speaking of, there are gatherings in the evenings, particularly in winter. We sit around the fire, and listen to stories. Take up some useful occupation to make the nights pass more quickly. We would like to see you and Kayden there. He has kept too much to himself."

"I will speak to him about it," Mya answered. "I would certainly like to accept the invitation." She smiled. "Thank you both, very kindly."

"It is no trouble."

She had not offered them anything, she realized abruptly, and her face flushed a little with shame. "I ought to have asked you if you wished anything to eat," she said, rising from where she sat. "Perhaps some cheese?"

"I would not object to a bit of something," Seonaid said.

Mya fetched a plate and sliced some bread and cheese, then set it down on the table for all of them to share. A glance at the fall of the light through the window showed her that the afternoon was still early. Kayden would not be back for some time.

"Perhaps you would like to stay a while?" She offered. "Tell me a little something of the clan?"

The women exchanged glances.

"We have a little time," Caoimhe answered.

Mya smiled, and sat down to listen.

Chapter 10

Two weeks into Kayden training her with various weapons, Mya could almost always hit what she was aiming for with a bow. It was a thrill, to feel the bow drawn tight in her hands, straining to release, to watch the arrow sing from the string and thunk into the target. Her muscles, unused to the exertion, still ached when practice ended, but it was almost satisfying to feel it. She liked knowing she was learning a skill that she could use to defend herself. Liked knowing her arms were getting stronger, her hands were learning the feel of the string between her fingers. Kayden had her using a bow that had once belonged to one of the clansmen's sons, before he grew into the need for something bigger. With one of better quality, he'd told her, she would be able to hit her target more accurately. Mya had shrugged it off and taken more care in her aim.

The lessons with the sword were going a little more slowly. It wasn't that she was bad at it, precisely. Just that she hadn't taken to the blade quite as naturally as she seemed to have taken to the bow. Kayden mocked her for her clumsiness, but she had caught the fond smile on his lips when he thought she wasn't looking. Had caught, too, the way that his fingers lingered on her wrist or her shoulder, brushed against her hip as he moved her into place.

He wanted her, she was certain of it. She could feel it every time he got close, his body straining toward hers. But he hadn't touched her that way since the night he'd taken her to bed. Not in more than glancing strokes of his fingers that could be passed off as professional.

Mya wanted him. She wasn't ashamed to admit that to herself; anyone would want him. Those dark eyes. The strong arms. His kindness. Anyone would desire the man she shared a home with. Shared a home with, and yet could not touch.

But for all that, the lessons had brought them closer. He spoke to her now with more than brusque necessity. Smiled at her. Mya could be content with that, for now. Well, with that and the careful brush of his hands as he taught her how to stand, how to move.

"Soon," he said one morning as he watched her send an arrow into the target he had pointed out, "you'll be hunting deer of your own."

Mya laughed, lowering the bow. "Somehow I doubt that."

"You can pay me back for that one you scared away."

"Still stuck on that? You need to learn to let things go."

"I will let it go when you make up for having lost me half a winter's worth of food," Kayden said, but there was no real accusation in his voice.

"It's hardly my fault if you can't catch a different deer," Mya pointed out, archly. "Are you not supposed to be some great hunter? Go and kill something yourself, then."

"If I catch it myself, then you will not be making up for your crime."

When she turned to look at him, his expression was even, but laughter danced in his eyes. She smirked. "Maybe I have no intention of making up for it. What will you do then?"

"Let you get away with it entirely, most like." Kayden laughed, unable to keep up the stern façade any longer. "You're astonishingly persuasive, somehow, lass."

Mya grinned a little smugly and turned back to the target.

"I have something for you," Kayden said behind her.

She paused, fingers loosening on the string to allow it to slowly straighten, tension leaving it. "Something that cannot wait until I'm finished with the shot?"

"I think you'll want to see this first."

Letting the tip of the arrow sag toward the ground so that she wasn't pointing it at Kayden, Mya turned.

He was holding a bow. It was obviously brand new, made of some gleaming, golden wood that had been well-oiled recently. The string was taut and fresh, without any wear. In his other hand, he held a leather quiver full of arrows. She stared at him with wide eyes as he lifted his hands, obviously offering them to her.

"Where did you..." Mya un-nocked the arrow from the string and slid it back into the borrowed quiver on her back, holding the bow she'd been using in one hand. "Where did you get that?"

"The bow I made," Kayden said, as though it was hardly any effort, as though he had not spent who knew how long cutting it to shape and preparing it for use. The smooth sheen on the wood said that he'd finished it well. He had obviously taken great care in the making. "And the arrows and quiver I picked up in the market. I thought you ought to have your own. They needed to be matched to the draw of the bow anyway, and you can't have arrows without something to carry them about in."

Mya stepped sideways to lean the bow she had been using against the wall of the house, the quiver with it, and then reached out for the bow that Kayden held. He passed it across the small space between them, and Mya took it in her hands, running her fingers over the graceful curve. The wood was as smooth as it had looked.

"This is beautiful," she breathed. "Kayden. I don't know how to thank you."

He reached one hand up to rub at the back of his neck, a crooked smile on his face. "You needn't. It was just a practicality. Bows are simple enough to make, anyway."

"Not so simple that you don't deserve thanks for it," Mya said, stepping in closer to him and somewhat reluctantly dragging her eyes from the shine of her new bow to his face. "And you bought the arrows, and the quiver. I can't imagine that those were easy on your purse."

Kayden shrugged. "Not so bad. I traded milk for them. Not everyone in town is lucky enough to have a pair of cows as lovely as ours." He faltered a little as he realized what he'd said.

Mya hardly breathed, afraid that if she spoke wrongly he'd suddenly startle away, like the deer he so wanted to bring down. *Ours.* He'd spoken as though the house was not his, but theirs. As though they shared it. He'd spoken as though they were a couple, and despite the knowledge that it was hardly so, Mya's heart beat a little faster in her chest.

"No," she said finally, taking another step, now so near that she had to tip her head back to meet his gaze. "They aren't so lucky."

"Mya..." Kayden's voice caught rough in his throat. He looked as though he was reaching for the right words, trying to come up with an explanation for the brief slip of the tongue.

"What?" she breathed.

He looked away, out at the moors rolling upward beyond the house, and then back at her. "I ought to—"

"You ought to nothing," she said, though the words were gentle. "Until you've accepted my gratitude for the gift."

They were so close she could almost feel the warmth of his body against her own, a buffer against the chilly wind. She thought about taking that last step, pressing up against him with one hand on the breadth of his chest. The way his heart would feel beating under her palm. Was it racing as fast as her own? Did his breath catch with anticipation the way hers did?

"I'm glad you like it, but it was truly nothing."

"As nothing as taking me in when I had no one to turn to," Mya said. "You've been nothing but kind to me when others wouldn't take the time or the effort to do all you've done. You've spent your own money on me when I'm certain that you've very little. That is not nothing, Kayden."

Now he was looking distinctly uncomfortable. He shifted like he was going to take a step back, but wasn't certain where he wanted to go.

"I'm just trying to thank you," she said, softly.

His posture relaxed a little. "You're welcome," he answered, though he still looked as though the words were being dragged out of him.

Silence fell between them. Mya looked up into Kayden's dark eyes, and felt as though she could fall into them. Her body swayed, almost imperceptibly toward his. Did he feel the same pull?

One of his hands lifted, almost as though he would touch her. Mya could practically feel it against her skin already, every nerve tingling with readiness. She took a breath and didn't' let it out again.

His hand dropped back to his side. Disappointment rushed through her. But he hadn't yet pulled away, so there was that in her favor. She took a tiny step, hardly more than a shifting of her weight. His head tipped down toward hers, his eyes studying her face.

Her breath stuttered in her chest. She felt his wash warm across her skin. Her eyelids fluttered low, and her lips parted.

Abruptly, Kayden's head jerked up.

Mya startled back, surprised by the sudden motion. He was staring at the hill behind her, his whole body tense. She turned, slowly, to follow the direction of his gaze, her heart racing. Was it something dangerous?

But no. It was only a deer, silhouetted by the morning light at the top of the hill. She could see that the head was turned toward them, watching. As her eyes adjusted, she realized that the sun on its back had gilded its hide. It was not just a deer; it was the stag. The one she'd woken up beside.

"Kayden," she started to say, but he was already moving, snatching up his bow and heading for the stag.

It stood without motion as he approached. Mya's heart jumped into her throat. She had to stop him from shooting the animal. Her own bow still in her hand, she set the quiver down in the grass and jogged after him.

The deer watched them for another heartbeat, still as though it had been carved there, and then it turned and bounded away. Mya breathed again. Kayden, cursing, picked up his pace, but the stag was already long gone; he was not going to catch it. Mya turned and went back down to the range, setting an arrow to the string of her new bow and drawing back, aiming for the target.

She had emptied the quiver once already by the time Kayden returned, panting, his fingers curled tightly around his bow. Mya watched him stalk across the grass, his eyebrows drawn tight in a scowl, and resisted the urge to giggle.

"No luck?" she called, genuine rather than teasing.

Kayden shook his head. "Blasted thing took off into the hills. There was no chance of me catching it."

"I cannot understand your obsession with it, frankly," Mya said, aiming her shot.

She sighted down the arrow to the center of the target. These were straighter than the ones she'd been using: fresh, new wood not warped by weather or use. She breathed in. Breathed out again. Let go. The arrow zipped across the field and sank into the center of the target. Mya grinned so wide it almost made her face hurt, and turned around to look expectantly at Kayden, waiting for his answer.

"For one, it would feed us through the winter. As blithely unaware as you seem to be of the reality, if we don't have some kind of meat, we're going to go hungry. Or have to slaughter one of the cows. And for two, a white stag is a rare thing. The hide would fetch a pretty price in Inverness."

Mya thought of the sweet little Highland cows, with their fuzzy dark coats and wide eyes, and bit her lip. Maybe she was wrong to be so adamant about the stag. Wouldn't it be better to bring in wild game than to have to kill one of the milking stock? But there was something about that deer... She couldn't put her finger on it, but she felt it in her bones every time the creature was near. The thought of killing it felt like a crime.

When she looked up, Kayden was watching her. Heat flushed her cheeks.

"What's going on behind your eyes, there?" he asked, his voice surprisingly gentle after the brusque tone of only a moment ago.

"Just thinking," Mya answered.

"And the conclusion you've come to?"

"I don't know yet," she said honestly. "I... There's this feeling I can't explain. About that stag. I know it seems foolish to you, but I cannot stomach the idea of killing it. Him."

"You're right," Kayden said. "It is foolish, but I'll not hold it against you. You've a tender heart." He moved past, toward the door, brushing a hand against her shoulder as he did so. The warmth of it lingered even after he was gone.

For a moment, Mya stood, staring after him. A tender heart. She thought of the way he had leaned in toward her before the stag had taken his attention away. Thought of his hands on her as he taught her to draw a bow and hit her target. Sighing, she gathered up her things and followed him into the house.

It was dark inside, after the bright sun of a clear autumn afternoon, and Mya waited a moment for her vision to adjust, blinking against the shadows. When it cleared, she set the bows—new and old—in their places with the quivers. Her gaze lingered for a moment on the graceful curve of the one Kayden had made her, and she felt a swell of warmth in her chest. He had created it with his own hands. A part of him that could belong to her, even if the rest of him did not. Mya smiled, and turned away from the weapons.

Kayden sat at the table and waited for her to join him. He had set a few bits of food out for them. The bread, which he had called bannock, and leftover porridge.

Mya watched his face in the afternoon light spilling through the small windows and thought about the white stag and why he wanted it. Though about the way she had frightened it off. "Tell me something," she said.

Kayden met her eyes, his expression questioning.

"That first night, when you said you were going to leave me out there... Would you have? Truly?"

His eyebrows lifted. "Are you sure that's a question you want to ask, Mya?" There was something in his voice that said the answer might not be one she liked.

She suddenly wasn't sure if she did want to know or not, but the words had already left her lips. "Yes."

Kayden sighed. "No," he said. "I wouldn't have. Had I left you there, you'd have died. And I would not have allowed that. Not even for a woman as utterly infuriating as you are."

Mya smiled.

She woke that night abruptly.

For a moment she lay still in the firelight, listening to the sounds of the little house, uncertain what had woken her. Then Kayden moved again, thrashing under the blanket they shared, and she jerked upright.

His breathing came out fast, making cut-off sounds that sounded like distress. Mya reached out for him and hesitated, uncertain if he would appreciate her waking him. When he groaned like he was in pain, she decided it didn't matter. He could be embarrassed in the morning that she knew he had a nightmare. It made him no less of a man in her opinion. He might feel different, but that didn't matter right now.

Especially as he cried out again and shuddered, his feet twitching as if he were running.

She reached down and curled a hand around his shoulder, shaking him gently. "Kayden," she said, leaning over him. "Kayden, you dream."

His head tossed against the pillow, then he rolled over and pulled her on top of him.

"Kayden. Wake up. It is only a nightmare."

He startled awake. For an instant, his body was tense under hers, every muscle straining. Then he relaxed, a shuddering breath escaping him as he slumped against the fur under him.

He inhaled a long, shaky breath. "I am sorry I woke you."

"There is no need for that." Mya resisted the urge to reach out and brush a hand over his forehead, stroke the tousled hair back from his eyes. She glanced down, remembering she lay on top of his hard, tense body. She rolled off and sat beside him. "Everyone has dreams."

Kayden didn't answer. He lay back against the pillow, staring up at the ceiling, only just visible in the dim light.

"Do you wish to speak of it?"

"No." The word was sharp, bitten off.

Mya's hand still rested on his shoulder. She wondered if she should take it back, if he didn't want her to touch him anymore, but he hadn't said anything about it. She left her hand where it was. "If you desire to—not now, but later... If you wish to, I will be here." She wanted to tell him that she had scary dreams sometimes too. Flashes of light, uncertainty, fear, racing hearts, a horrible feeling of loss. Waking up scared and alone. Flickers of her dreams pressed against her memory, trying to break forth. She held back, unsure of how to explain her wild dreams and terrified of them at the same time.

Kayden's eyes moved to her. "Thank you, Mya."

She opened her mouth to answer, and suddenly his hand was wrapped around the back of her neck, drawing her into a kiss. It was only a moment, just a brush of lips against lips, and then his fingers were sliding from her skin and Mya was pulling in a surprised breath.

She gave in to the urge, then, to brush the hair back from his face. Kayden caught her wrist gently in his hand and lifted it to his lips, kissing the backs of her knuckles.

"You are unlike anyone I have ever known," he said, voice soft, still rough with sleep.

Mya's breath caught in her throat. "I hope that's a good thing."

"It is."

Then why, she almost asked, *don't you touch me?* Why had he withdrawn every time they had become intimate with each other? But asking would ruin this moment, and she was going to take what she could get.

Slowly, she sank back down to join him under the blankets, her head against his shoulder. After a moment of startled immobility, he wrapped an arm around her and drew her close.

"It's strange," he said. "Sleeping beside someone else. I haven't done so in a long time."

"I can't remember it," Mya said. "I have this feeling that I have. That I shared a bed with someone once, but the memory of it, that's gone."

His embrace tightened. For a moment, Mya thought he was going to speak, but he said nothing, only held her. Gradually, his breathing slowed, and he slept again, Mya sinking into dreams beside him.

Chapter 11

The first frost came a few days later and the workload increased. In the mornings, Mya's feet made the frozen heather crackle underfoot. They harvested the kale, and then then turnips. Though she had mentioned to him the gatherings held by the clan, they had not yet gone, but he had promised her that they would attend at least one. Mya was beginning to wonder if she would have to drag him to it. But other things were more satisfactory. At night, they slept side by side on the fur in front of the fire, and while Kayden hadn't kissed her again, he no longer pulled away when she curled close against his side. He'd hold her when the room grew chill.

Then one afternoon, he came home with a pair of rabbits.

Mya looked up from the skirt she was altering at the sound of the door opening. Her heart beat a little faster at the sight of him.

It had taken some time and more than a little trial and error to get the sizing of the skirt right. Mya was certain that she had picked out more stitches than she had put in. She'd found a method that worked in the end, though, and the new skirt under her hands was shaping up nicely. It would be good to have a second, for when the first needed washing. Though there was a part of her that wondered if walking around the house in nothing but Kayden's shirt might lead to a repeat of that first night. She hoped, but she doubted it would happen. The man seemed determined not to give in to his desire for her.

"They're not a deer," Kayden said, slapping the rabbits down on the table. "But they're meat."

Mya looked dubiously at the limp creatures lying on the table.

"What do you want me to do with them?" She swallowed, trying to erase the sudden dryness in her mouth.

"Cook them," Kayden said simply. "I would do it myself, but I have to go out again today. There's another clan meeting that I need to attend."

"No worries about leaving me on my own this time?" Mya teased.

"Should I have any?"

She sobered. "I will be fine. I know how to protect myself now, and there was no trouble when you left me last."

She still held in mind the other women's warnings about Lachlan, but she was not so worried about him now she knew how to defend herself. And he had caused no trouble for them yet. Perhaps he had decided that fighting with Kayden was more than he wished to involve himself in.

"You do have a decent grasp of how to use a sword and a bow. I think you can handle yourself for a few hours."

"I'm glad you have such confidence in me."

Kayden finished slicing the meat, throwing her a grin. "I'm not sure how well-placed it is just yet, but I suppose we'll see."

"You're too kind, sir."

"Behave yourself. I have to leave." His eyebrows pressed together in frustration.

"I'm not a child," Mya said mildly. "I think I'm more than capable of being alone for a few hours."

"The last thing I would mistake you for is a child."

There was something in Kayden's voice that made her feel warm, made her wonder if... But he was turning away before she could look for the answer in his face, wrapping the upper part of his kilt around himself against the cold afternoon as he opened the door.

"I'll be back by the time the sun sets. We'll eat then."

"Be safe," Mya said.

The door closed behind him. Sighing, Mya turned to the rabbits, and tried to decide what on earth she was going to do with them.

In the end, she cut them up and threw the meat in water to boil. That done, she washed her hands and sat down at the table a moment, wondering what she was going to serve the rabbit with. Turnips seemed likely. Or kale. Perhaps both.

Her thoughts turned away from food.

She had been trying not to think about the fact that she was at the house alone for the rest of the day, about what had happened the last time Kayden had attended a clan meeting. But she couldn't shake the thoughts. Her hands curled in her lap, and she glanced over at the sword that sat near the door, keeping her bow and quiver of arrows company.

Swordplay still was not her particular talent, but she could use it well enough to at least defend herself against an intruder. Though that would only hold out so long. If Kayden was not already close...

The bow, though, that would stop a man from a distance, and she knew she could hit her target with it. She rose from the chair and checked the rabbit. It did not look as though it would be done soon. And it could hardly burn in a pot of water. Mya took up her bow and quiver, and went outside.

Overhead, the clouds hung low, but there was no rain yet. A chill breeze wound its way down from the higher hills. Mya tucked her arisaid into her belt, out of the way, and took up position in front of the target. She braced the lower part of the bow against her foot to string it.

She set an arrow to the string.

The steady motion of the bow—draw back and release, draw back and release—calmed her nerves. If trouble did come, she would be ready for it. She wasn't some helpless damsel needing to be rescued.

Lachlan had caught her by surprise the first time, but he'd find her better prepared now.

Mya ran through a few more shots, then went to fetch the arrows from the target, sliding them back into the quiver and heading inside to check on the meat.

It was boiling happily away. She stood over it for a moment, considering what she was going to add to it. There was still kale out in the garden, and it might make a good contrast to the meat and the turnips. Decided, she picked up a bowl from the cupboard, and headed back out.

A breeze curled around her as she walked from the house to the little garden plot at the side, catching her skirt and tugging at the hem. Mya took a deep breath of the fresh air and felt a smile settling on her face. She had grown surprisingly domestic, lately, and she found that she rather liked it.

Kneeling in the soft earth of the garden, she began picking the ruffled green leaves and laying them in the bowl. She was humming softly to herself, pleased with the preparations she was making for dinner, when she felt something watching.

Her heart skipped a beat.

She had, she realized, left the sword inside, where it would be of absolutely no use to her. Kayden had told her to carry it, but she'd been sure she would be safe in their own garden, hadn't even thought of it as she'd walked out of the house.

Slowly, heart pounding in her chest, she looked up. Her breath left her in a rush of relief. It was only the stag, white hide gleaming dully in the muddy light of the cloudy afternoon. He was standing at the edge of the garden, head up and ears pricked forward, staring at her.

Mya laughed. "You know, I'm not sure who taught you not to be afraid of humans, but it's a bit of a bad habit, do you not think so?"

The stag huffed a breath through his nostrils and shook his head like he was trying to get a fly out of his ear.

"No?" Mya picked up the bowl of kale and got to her feet. "Because the way I see it, not all humans are as nice as I am. Most of them will be glad enough to put you on a plate."

He watched her as she moved closer, sides heaving with his breath. Mya held out a kale leaf, and he looked at it as though it might be a trap for a long moment, then reached delicately out and took it between his teeth, pulling it from her hand and crunching it down.

"Now go," Mya said, flapping a hand at him. "Shoo. Before Kayden gets back and decides to take another shot."

The stag stood there a moment longer, and then he turned and was gone, vanishing over the hill.

Mya felt strangely bereft as he disappeared.

Back in the house, she pulled the rabbit from the water and set it aside to heat on the griddle so she could start the turnips boiling. That done, she turned her attention to the rest of the room, looking for something to occupy her time while she waited on dinner and Kayden's return. Her eyes fell on the basin sitting on the chest at the foot of the bed.

A wash might actually be just the thing she needed, and while stripping down and soaping herself up in front of Kayden would likely get his attention, doing it while he was out of the house was maybe a better choice.

She set the kettle at the edge of the fire to heat and began unbuttoning her blouse, sliding it off her shoulders and dropping it to the bed. Her arms broke out in goose bumps at the chill in the air of the room, and she shimmied quickly out of her skirt so she could take the basin over by the fire. The fur rug was warm and soft under her feet.

She thought of Kayden. Wished he was standing behind her in the firelight, his hands on her hips and his lips against the back of her neck. An entirely different kind of warmth coiled in her belly.

When the kettle began to hum, she pulled it from the fire and poured the steaming water into the basin, adding a dipper of cool from the bucket to make the temperature a little more comfortable. Then she dipped a rag into it, twisting out the excess water, and began washing herself.

There was soap. A little cake of it that smelled faintly of some spicy herb. Mya lathered up, breathing it in, and sighed happily. It felt good to be truly clean, the sweat and dust of the day washed away. She rinsed the cloth in one of the buckets before dipping it in the warm water again, rinsing the lather from her skin.

When it was done, she felt scrubbed and fresh, still pleasantly warmed by the flames in the hearth. She almost considered lingering there, lying on the rug and feeling the soft fur against her bare skin. That would be a sight for Kayden to come home to. She imagined him stopping dead in the doorway, his eyes moving over her body.

But there was dinner still to be made; the turnips were nearly ready to mash, and the kale still needed to be cooked, so Mya reluctantly clothed herself again, and went to throw the dirty water out into the grass. The floor was cold away from the fire, and she shivered a little with it, grateful when she could close the door behind her and move back to the warmth of the hearth to start mashing the turnips and throw the rabbit on the griddle in preparation for Kayden's return.

"That smells promising."

Kayden stepped inside, shaking drops of water from his plaid as he shut the door on the lazy drizzle falling outside.

"Considering the amount of time I spent on it," Mya said, not looking up from the turnips she was stirring on the hearth, "it ought to."

"For a woman with no memory, you're a surprisingly accomplished cook."

Mya smiled down at the food, the expression hidden behind her loose hair. It maybe wasn't much of a compliment, but she knew Kayden well enough after their weeks together to know that, coming from him, it was high praise indeed, and she couldn't quite help the fluttery feeling it woke in her stomach. "It's not exactly difficult to put turnips over a fire. Food. Heat. Success."

"I've eaten food that was not a success."

"Then I'm glad I can provide a satisfactory experience."

"More than satisfactory," Kayden said, and again there were the warm flutters in her stomach, a smile that she hid behind her hair.

"It's almost ready," she answered. She shifted to the other side of the hearth instead of stepping in close to Kayden the way she wanted to and pressing her body to his, feeling the warmth of his skin against her own.

The turnips were steaming when she scooped them from the pot and onto the plate, heavy with butter and cream. She served out the rabbit on top, and they took their food to the table.

Kayden took a bite, and his eyes widened.

"This may be the best thing I have ever eaten." There was a moan in the words.

This time, Mya didn't hide her smile. She looked up at him from under the fan of her lashes, a satisfied grin on her face, feeling maybe just a little smug. "That good?"

Kayden just nodded, his mouth completely full. There were no words from him, in fact, for the rest of the meal. He seemed content to eat without speaking, too busy dishing up seconds to bother with conversation. Mya took it as the compliment it was, too busy enjoying her own dinner to be particularly bothered by the lack of conversation. Kayden hadn't been wrong when he said it was good; she was pleasantly surprised with the results. When he'd brought in the rabbits, she hadn't been entirely sure that she would be able to make anything with them.

When both their plates were clean, Kayden got up from the table and cleaned the dishes while Mya watched, more than a little shocked.

"That's not a sight I ever expected to see," she said, leaning comfortably back in her chair with one leg crossed over the other.

"I did wash my own dishes before you came along, you know," Kayden pointed out. "I am capable of it."

Mya smiled. "You should do them more often."

"I'm not so sure of that. You might be spoiled by such treatment."

She didn't dignify that with a verbal answer, only gave him a look that set him laughing.

"Very well, then. I'll do the dishes more often," he said when the laughter had faded to chuckles. "You do make most of the food."

"It seems only fair," Mya agreed.

The dishes were done, and Kayden dried his hands. For a moment, he did not move from his place, and Mya wondered what kept him there, his head bowed over the bowls he had just finished cleaning in the basin.

"Kayden?" She pitched her voice soft.

He turned at the sound of his name, and looked at her with dark eyes.

Mya felt the flutters return, this time paired with a coil of heat that wound its way to her center, slow and lazy. She knew that expression written across his face.

"Mya..." He did not finish whatever he had been about to say.

Instead, he moved across the small space between them to lay a hand against her cheek, cradling her face in his palm. And then, slowly, he leaned down. Mya's heart beat fast in her chest. The moment seemed to take forever, his progress obviously meant to give her time to back out of the touch before his lips met hers if she wished to, but she had no desire whatsoever to avoid the kiss. His mouth found hers, and she moaned softly into the space shared between them.

Kayden pulled back for breath. For an instant, it looked as though he would speak, but she dragged him down into another kiss before the words could leave him. She didn't want to hear his excuses for why they shouldn't be doing exactly what they were doing, because there was no reason. What they were doing was exactly what they both wanted, and she wasn't going to dance around it any longer. Her body refused to be denied again.

Another brief break, both of them pulling in air before their lips met once more. Then Kayden's hands were on her shoulders, drawing her up out of her chair. He walked her backwards, and she went with the push of it until she found her back against a wall, cool even through the fabric of her clothing. Kayden was warm against her chest.

"Tell me you desire me," he said, the third time that they broke for air.

"I desire you," Mya answered before she'd even had time to consciously consider the words. There was no need for it. She knew what she wanted, and what she wanted was him. "I have wanted you since the moment we met."

This time, his mouth was rough against hers, taking and hungry. Mya curled her fingers around his shoulders, tightening until she could feel the fabric begin to give under her nails and arched into his body and his kiss.

"Tell me," she said between kisses, "why you've waited so long for this when I can see you watching me. When I know how much you want me."

Kayden went still in her arms.

Mya wondered for a moment if she'd asked the wrong question. Would it break the moment between them? She didn't want to go back to pretending that they had never kissed, never touched.

"I waited," he said, "because I had to be sure." He brushed a kiss against the curve of her jaw. "I had to be certain this truly was what you wanted. That I was not just imagining things because I wished so strongly for you to be mine. I would rather have only what little of you I can if you do not want me, than lose you altogether."

Mya kissed him, long and slow, stepping forward to guide them back toward the bed, giving Kayden no choice but to move with her.

"Does this answer your worry?" she broke off long enough to ask.

Kayden didn't have the chance to answer before she kissed him again. They sank down to the bed together, her body over his, and parted for breath.

"Tell me true, Kayden," she murmured, bending forward so that her nose was just barely brushing his, hair falling along one side of her face. "Do you desire me?"

"Yes," he groaned, hands sliding down her arms as she began to slide down his body. "More than I have ever desired anything."

His eyes were on her hands as she knelt between his legs, reaching out to unbuckle his belt that held his plaid in place around his hips. He propped himself up on his elbows to watch, and she took a moment to slide the broach at his chest free as well, letting the fabric that hid his body fall away. It was a surprisingly pleasing sight, all that bare skin against the backdrop of his open kilt, but Mya let him pull it out from under himself and toss it to the foot of the bed.

He was hard already, his length arched up against his belly. Mya didn't wait any longer. She curled her hands around his hips for leverage, and lowered her mouth. Sucking in just the head of his cock, she laved her tongue against the underside, intentionally teasing him in a way that was sure to drive him to distraction. His hips jerked up against her, one of his hands fisting in the blanket.

"Oh fucking hell," he groaned, meeting her eyes when she flicked them back up, his own dark with shock and arousal. Arching one eyebrow, she held his gaze as she lowered her mouth further over his cock and then hummed as she pulled back up, sliding off of him with a pop. He let out a rough grunt, biting hard into his bottom lip as he nearly shook with the effort of staying still and not rocking up in search of her mouth.

"You were saying?"

"Heavens above, woman." He was panting heavily, his cock erect between them. "If I had known you were going to do that, I would never have waited so long."

"That is what you get," Mya said, tucking her hair behind her ear and smiling up at him. "If you had only spoken to me, you would have been perfectly aware of my thoughts on the matter."

Kayden muttered another curse, pushing himself up onto both elbows. "C'mere, lass," he muttered roughly, reaching down to tug her forward so that he could capture her mouth in a searing, desperate kiss. "Are you sure you're not some sort of succubus, sent to tempt me?"

"Kayden," she said on a low laugh, "I think if that were the case, I'd have had you in bed long before now."

Brushing their noses together, she leaned in for another heated kiss.

"And yet you are like no lass I've ever met," he said, hissing as her hand found his erection and gave him a few teasing pumps. "You are utterly bewitching."

She stroked her hand along his length again, and Kayden groaned against her mouth, parting her lips so that his tongue could slip between them, sending sparks dancing through her whole body.

Mya pulled back, sliding forward to straddle him. As she settled into place, she felt Kayden's mouth press a wet, sucking kiss at the top of her breast, just above the neck of her shirt. A soft sound of surprise escaped her, and one of his hands curled up along her ribs, holding her in position above him. Pulling the top three buttons loose with a fervor she was quite sure had removed them from the shirt entirely, he gently sucked her nipple into his mouth, scraping his teeth against it just enough to have her trembling above him.

All too soon, he leaned back, leaving her shirt to gape open. "Don't take it off," he murmured, ghosting his lips up over her cheek as she tried to meet his mouth with her own. "Not yet."

Mya laughed breathlessly, panting a little rapidly for such brief contact. "I admit I don't quite understand the appeal of me being fully clothed."

"But you aren't quite," he replied blithely, smiling when she laughed again. "Are you?" His hips rolled up against hers to prove his point. He hadn't exactly picked up undergarments for her in his search for clothes, and his length rubbed against her bare thigh.

"Does that do something for you, then?" she deadpanned.

"Seeing you rumpled and half-clothed?" Kayden laughed. "Aye. It does."

A mischievous grin split her face, and she reached up slowly to undo one and then two more buttons. The shirt fell farther open, leaving her breasts completely bare.

Kayden's hand tightened around her waist, and he pulled in a breath before speaking, his voice low enough that it sent shivers down her spine. "I want your mouth on me."

"I think you already experienced that particular treat, did you not?"

Kayden looked up at her, expression heavy with want. "Aye. And I want more of it," he said, a growl at the edges of the demand. "Please."

Mya bit her lip to hold back a moan. His begging only furthered her need for him. "Only if you thoroughly satisfy me after," she teased in response, clambering back down so that she was leaning over his erect cock.

"It's a deal," he groaned just as she took him in hand and gave him one firm lick along the underside of his shaft. "Oh *yes*," he groaned, breath catching when she swirled her tongue over the head. "Bloody hell, *Mya*."

Her favorite thing about this, she decided, was the way Kayden tried so intently not to show how much her ministrations affected him. But she could see it in the way he followed her every move, in the way his fingers curled so tightly in the blanket that his knuckles went white; she could feel it in the constant stuttering of his hips, in the tensing of his muscles as he wound up tight beneath her.

He groaned her name again, and it tipped her over the edge, igniting her need to slake her own desire. So, sucking firmly on his cock one last time, she pulled away.

She met his gaze as she straddled his hips, noting the tension in the clench of his jaw with a flush of heat in her core. Instead of lowering herself immediately, though, she reached under her skirt to press his rigid shaft against her clit, her eyelids fluttering at even that brief relief.

Kayden swore, hands coming to grasp hard onto her upper thighs, sliding the skirt up them to bare her skin as she rubbed his cock against herself and whimpered. "Come on, Mya," he rasped out, hips twitching at her unintentional teasing. "Dammit, lass. Stop teasing or you'll drive me utterly mad."

Blinking her eyes open to meet his, she lined them up with her hand and then sunk sharply down onto him, stifling a cry of pleasure at the movement. Kayden let out a low grunt, bucking up into her as she ground down against him.

"Oh, yes," she breathed, dropping her head back and turning her face to the dimly lit ceiling overhead. "Oh *yes*, Kayden!"

"Come here," he muttered, tugging on her hand so that she was bent over him, hands pressed to the blanket beneath. "Gorgeous," he said, just before capturing her lips with his own, both of them moaning as she rose and sunk onto him again.

Moving her hips in firm, deep thrusts, Mya reveled in the fullness of Kayden inside her, of that perfect stretch that sent arousal singing through her at every stroke. It was a new source of pleasure, being pressed so close together. The intimacy of moving as one being, with one thought and one purpose, made her breath catch. She could not remember the other men she had lain with, but she thought that none of them must compare to Kayden.

Their noses brushed together as she undulated against him, her mouth curving into a smile. When he caught her eyes, he gave her a reflexive smile in return, one hand reaching up to bring their lips together for messy, open-mouth kisses. She couldn't hold that position for long though, her muscles beginning to protest, and she pushed up so she was sitting over him. Her next thrust had gravity working in her favor, stroking his cock against something deep inside her that made her gasp in pleasure. Reaching out, Mya tangled one hand with his and propped her other against his chest, moaning low under her breath as the added support helped her hit that same delicious angle at each and every rock of her hips.

Kayden bit out a low curse, and before she knew what was happening he'd bundled her against his chest, flipped them over on the blanket, and begun taking her in earnest. The noise of protest she made as he moved them become one of pleasure as his cock stroked against that place inside, and she bit down on his shoulder to muffle the sound. Mya just reached down to curl the fingers of both hands around the curves of his buttocks, his muscles flexing as he thrust into her. Her skirt fanned around them as she spread her legs further apart and rocked back up to match his rhythm. Kayden's hands slid it further up her thighs, baring her completely to him.

A breathless giggle escaped her throat, slipping into another whimper of pleasure.

"Did you just laugh?" Much to her disappointment, Kayden slowed enough that he could peer down at her, confusion written across his brow.

"No," she tried to assure him, but another traitorous laugh bubbled out of her almost immediately. "I'm sorry," she giggled, wrapping one arm up so she could smooth her hand along his neck. "But I'm just so—" She cut herself off on a shuddery moan, back arching as his next thrust pressed directly against her clit. "Fuck," she gasped, determined to explain herself, "I'm just so very happy. I know it's maybe the wrong time to laugh, but I can't help it. It's just... It's filling me up."

Kayden laughed, then, though for an entirely different reason than she had, and Mya swatted at his shoulder.

"That joke was not intended," she snapped, but the words came out full of laughter, and she couldn't keep the straight face that she had been trying for.

"No, but it was funny all the same," Kayden answered. His voice was rough with need.

The thrusts picked up their pace, making her cry out, and for a moment he faltered.

"Don't stop." She nipped at his earlobe and rocked up against him again. "I like when you lose control."

With his face hidden in her neck, she could see the firelight dancing across the ceiling, gold and red. Her eyes wandered back to Kayden, and she reached up to thread her hand through his dark hair, feeling the soft strands sliding over her fingers.

Just as she was about to attempt to goad him back into that delicious, nearly punishing pace, Kayden groaned, and then pulled off of her, sinking back onto his knees.

"What...?"

"Here," he said, breathing heavily as he reached out to pull her up after him. "I don't want to hurt you. I want you on top again."

Mya didn't answer immediately, her attention fixed on the way he looked with the light dancing over his skin, painting shadows along the arches of his cheekbones and the rippled muscles of his abdomen. It picked out biceps and hips, his cock standing at rigid attention between them. Kayden stared at her with unabashed desire. His hands reached out for her and he was breathing heavily, those dark eyes made even more striking as they reflected the hearth's glow.

The thought that he was everything she'd ever wanted, though she could not remember what she had wanted before the time she met him so perhaps her perspective was a little off, flitted through her head.

Then she blinked, her senses returning in a rush.

"You wouldn't hurt me," she said, but even as she spoke she grabbed for his hand, allowing him to help position her as she straddled his lap. The second they were lined up, Mya tilted her hips to take him in as far as she could in this position, both of them sighing shakily as they were joined once more. It took them a few seconds to sync up their movements, but at last they found just the right rhythm, with him thrusting up as she rocked down. It was perfect. It was what she had longed for all those nights lying beside him in the dim dark, hearts pounding to the same beat. Each stroke sent scattered threads of heat through Mya's whole body, and she moaned low in her throat, back arching.

One of Kayden's hands curled around her backside through her clothes, helping her increase the strength and speed of their thrusts, and his other hand came up to cup her chin, trying to steady her enough that he could slide their lips together. She pressed her hands to his jaw, only barely managing to do more than simply pant against him, forcing her eyes to stay open and fixed on his.

She wanted, she thought, watching the firelight on his face, to make love to him outdoors someday. To see the sunlight shining down on them both, lighting them with more than the dim glow in the house. Wanted to be able to pick out every detail of his expression. But that was later. For now, she had this. Had him in the flickering light of the fire, and that was enough.

She could not break her gaze from his. A breathless smile broke across her face and she pressed their foreheads together, curling her fingers around the back of his neck to hold him close.

Shifting beneath her, he adjusted the angle so he could buck upwards faster, and that change, small as it was, sent Mya rushing toward the edge. Toward orgasm. Surprise pushed his name from her lips in a soft gasp, only just audible above the crackling of the hearth and the wind singing along the walls. Pleasure shivered through her veins, arcing out from where he moved inside her. Her vision blurred, and all she could think to do was keep moving, keep holding on. She reached for the ecstasy that waited, lingering on the edge of the fall. And then, suddenly, it was there. Heat washed from her head to the tips of her toes, her thighs squeezing hard around his hips, and a hoarse cry of his name escaped her lips.

Kayden groaned, buried his face in her neck, and bucked frantically up into her, holding on to her a little too hard as he rushed toward his own orgasm. His cock sliding roughly against her already sensitized nerves sent more waves of pleasure coursing through her, and she whimpered, digging her fingernails into his shoulder. With a last, sharp stutter up into her, Kayden came undone, muffling a shout against her neck. She melted forward against him, and his arms closed around her, holding her close.

A satisfied hum rumbled from Kayden's chest to hers, and he lifted his head. He looked relaxed in a way that she had only seem him look after the first time they had fallen into bed together, in those moments after orgasm had left them both boneless and satisfied. But there was more in his expression. Affection, warm and soft. His feelings bared at last. Giving her a half-smile, he swept loose hair out of her eyes and tucked it behind her ear, adjusting his hold around her so that she didn't slip away before she was ready.

"I think I'm in love with you," Mya whispered, keeping her eyes trained on his. An uncertain smile flickered on her lips. It was maybe an awkward time for her to confess something so momentous, with him still inside her and both of them sweaty and exhausted. But she couldn't stop the words from escaping, couldn't go on letting him think that this was anything but what it was.

He had been there for her from the moment she woke up, alone and lost in what felt like an alien world. Despite the way they fought, he had brought her home with him, given her somewhere safe, given her clothes and food. And yet, all along, the thing that had given her the most happiness was him. Just him, close to her. Holding her. The realization had maybe been a long time coming, but now waiting didn't feel like an option at all.

Instead of holding out for a reply, Mya tucked her head against his neck and let out a little sigh of contentment. The words had been sudden, she knew, and the she wasn't sure he would answer them in return. Wasn't sure that she hadn't rushed everything along too quickly. But in that moment, she had his arms around her, the warmth of his body against her own, and that was enough.

"Mya," he said, voice soft.

She slowly looked up and met Kayden's dark eyes, her heart stuttering in her chest at the expression on his face.

"I think," he said, "I'm in love with you too."

Chapter 12

When Mya woke in the morning, Kayden lay beside her. He stirred when she shifted, and drew her closer with an arm wrapped around her waist, sleepily pressing a kiss to her temple. Mya curled nearer to hide her smile against his shoulder.

"Morning," Kayden rumbled, still heavy with sleep.

"Good morning," Mya answered.

The smile must have been audible in her voice, because he leaned up on one elbow to look at her, stroking his fingers over her cheek. "You seem content this morning."

"I am." Mya turned the smile up at him. "I had a good night last night." Her hand stroked over his chest. "And I can't think of a better way to wake up than this."

"No?"

Kayden leaned in and kissed her then, slow and sweet, his hand on her cheek. When they broke the kiss, they were both smiling.

"I admit, I've tried to think of a better waking, and I think you're right." He kissed her again.

A short while later, they finally dragged themselves from bed and out into the chill of the room for breakfast. Mya hummed softly to herself as she made the porridge. Realizing suddenly that she was being watched, she turned to find Kayden in the doorway with the milk buckets, leaning against the frame and watching her.

Her cheeks flushed hot. "What're you staring at?"

"You," he said, completely unapologetic as he pushed off the door frame and crossed the room. "You're the most beautiful thing in the room."

"And you're a flatterer."

"Is it flattery if it is true?"

Mya laughed and served the porridge. "How was the clan meet yesterday?" she asked as they took their seats at the table.

"Exactly like every other clan meeting I've ever been to," Kayden answered. "Men arguing with each other. Arguing some more."

"Did they ever come to a conclusion?" Mya took a bite of porridge.

"Not this time. There's some talk about a boundary disagreement with another clan, but I don't know that they're going to go through with it. The other clan has better resources, which won't necessarily stop them, but there are some people in the group who realize that jumping into a losing fight right before winter could end badly."

"Them. You talk as though you do not consider yourself part of the clan."

Something crossed Kayden's face that Mya couldn't interpret, and the expression was gone almost as soon as it appeared. She tipped her head a little to the side, as though that could help her discern what it meant, but there was no flash of sudden insight, and in the next moment Kayden was speaking.

"I'm not, quite," he said. "I'm still a bit of a newcomer, and most of them don't hesitate to remind me of that."

Mya reached across the table and laid a hand over his. "I'm sorry. I didn't realize that was the case."

He turned his hand so that he could slide their fingers together, shaking his head. "Don't be. It is no great tragedy, just a simple fact of life. They'll accept me sooner or later, just as they'll accept you."

"Will they?" Mya's porridge was growing cold, and she took a bite, swallowing before she spoke again. "I haven't really even met them. The only ones I did have the... luck of being introduced to were not exactly the kind of people I'd be interested in spending a great deal of my time around.'

"Lachlan and his men are not the entire clan. There are better men in it."

"I would hope so," Mya said. She wondered about the other women in the clan. Being with Kayden felt like enough most days, but she sometimes felt isolated. Though she had met them briefly, it had been only once, and they had hardly had time to truly speak before Kayden returned. She wasn't sure she yearned for the company of other women, but she was curious about them. How did they act? Who were they married to? Did they carry a fire and independence that she felt she had? Part of her didn't want to know. Didn't want to see anyone for the fear that someone would recognize her and send her to a life she had no idea even existed anymore.

The conversation died between them, and for a moment they were both looking at each other across the table, unsure of what to say.

Mya turned her attention to her breakfast, and Kayden followed suit.

"Keep your guard up!" Kayden swung at her, and Mya scrambled to get her own sword in position, blocking him with a ring of metal on metal.

It was cold out, rainy autumn giving way to the first signs of winter. Soon the land would be gray and empty, though Kayden had said there would also be snow. Mya shivered; even under the warmth of layers of fabric she could feel the cold.

"Keep your eyes on your opponent."

He came in from the side as he spoke. Mya spun on her heel and met the next blow, taking a step back as he advanced.

"Good," Kayden said.

There was a certain exhilaration to the activity, Mya had to admit. She was quickly warming up, and her heart beat fast in her chest, her breath coming in quick bursts that left plumes of white vapor in the air. Another swing, another block. The grin on Kayden's face was enough to make her smile back at him. He looked pleased with himself and he looked pleased with her.

"So," she said conversationally as she stepped into his space, pressing the brief advantage. "Am I warrior woman material yet?"

He laughed, dancing back from her attack, and came at her again. "Not quite. Though I would say that you're certainly getting there. You're shockingly good at this."

"Shockingly?" Mya gave him a mock hurt look and attacked. "I wouldn't think it should be that surprising. I'm a very fast learner."

"You are that."

He was the one advancing again, and Mya backed up, giving ground. In truth, she didn't think she was anywhere near warrior woman level. For all that he'd claimed she was shockingly good with it, the sword still didn't come as easy as the bow. It left her wrists and arms aching after a bout, the callouses on her palms and fingers rubbed rough.

She took another swing, and Kayden blocked it, moving in closer and forcing her sword back against her body until she was arching away from him, trying to hold her ground against his strength and failing. It was proof that he'd been right about bigger opponents with longer reaches, that if she truly wanted to be good with the sword she would have to find a teacher who could train her in how to turn those strengths into weaknesses. But she wasn't genuinely looking to be a master with the weapon. Only good enough that Kayden wouldn't be worried about leaving her home alone.

Kayden, who was currently giving her a look that was entirely too smug for her liking. She let herself bend a little farther back, and the shift put him off balance as he leaned in to counter it. Mya pushed suddenly, hard, and he stumbled back. In the next second, his footing went out from under him on some hidden stone, and he fell flat on his backside, the sword sliding across the grass.

For an instant, Mya was worried that she'd hurt him. Her mind ran through all the ways that could have gone very wrong. But it hadn't, and he didn't seem damaged. She let herself laugh.

"Having some trouble there?" she asked.

"You're entirely too amused," Kayden said, scowling up at her.

"I just watched a great brawny Highlander fall on his arse." She grinned. "Of course I'm amused."

He opened his mouth like he was going to say something else, but Mya didn't give him the chance, dropping lightly into his lap and pressing her lips to his, a salve for wounded pride. Kayden moaned, one of his hands closing around her hip and the other pressing against her back between her shoulder blades to pull her in closer. Mya looped her arms around his neck and wondered if he was remembering the night before the same way she was, their bodies moving together in the firelight.

"Pick up the swords," he said when the kiss broke, a little breathless in a way that was entirely gratifying.

Mya picked them up, and then he was rising, lifting her as effortlessly as though she weighed nothing, and striding across the grass toward the little house.

"Sword lesson over?" Mya asked, looking up at him with wide eyes and a too-innocent expression.

He laughed, low and already a little rough at the edges, making heat curl under her skin. "Sword lesson is over."

They stepped inside and the door closed behind them, Kayden setting her carefully on her feet and putting the swords in their proper place. He stoked the fire until it was crackling, sparks jumping in the hearth.

"I was thinking perhaps tonight we might attend one of the clan's gatherings," he said as he tended the flame. "I know where they are held."

The words were not quite what Mya had expected, after the heat rising between them as the lesson ended, but she tucked the desire away to rise later. He had not offered before to take her, and she intended to take advantage of it. "I would like that."

He turned and smiled at her over his shoulder. "Then we shall do so when we have eaten."

They sat and ate largely in silence, though when Mya looked up she found Kayden's eyes on her, his expression soft. She smiled back at him, dipping her head again and looking up at him from under her lashes.

When dinner was done, they rose, and Mya cleaned the dishes while Kayden went out and saddled the horse. She was more than a little excited. More than a little nervous. It was the first time she would really be interacting with a large number of clan members, and though she had met Caoimhe and Seonaid, and seen a few of the men during her introduction to the laird, there were likely to be many of them she had not met.

Kayden would be with her, at least. So whatever came, she would have someone who knew her. Who cared for her. She smiled at the thought, and set the clean dishes away.

The ride was so very different from their first one together, through the chill night, the hills around her blending into something like a dream as they moved past. But there was something about it that put her in mind of that, all the same.

Perhaps it was the twilight around them, Kayden's arms wrapped around her waist. She was not tired, but she let her head tip back so she could look up at the stars that gleamed in gaps between the clouds. Watched them wheel overhead.

When they arrived in the village, Kayden helped her down from the horse outside the little house that belonged to Caoimhe and her husband.

"I admit," Mya said. "That I am a little bit uncertain about this."

Kayden looked down at her. "If you are afraid, you need not be. They will treat you with nothing but kindness."

"I am not afraid. Only a bit nervous, perhaps." She leaned closer into the arm that wrapped around her shoulders. "I am sure all will be well."

When the door opened, warm firelight and the sound of laughter spilled out into the darkness. Kayden ushered her inside, and Mya found herself greeted with smiles by both Caoimhe and Seonaid. Others looked up as well, and Mya saw a few heads bend toward each other, whispers no doubt exchanged between them. A few children scrambled around the adults' feet, and an elderly man sat by the fire, half dozing.

"Please," Caoimhe said. "Come in. Take a seat."

Kayden was there, then, his chest warm against her back, his voice murmuring in her ear. "I will only be a moment," he said. "I must speak with someone, but then I will come and sit with you."

"I am sure that I will be fine here."

There was a small huddle of women in one corner, all of them with knitting needles busily clacking away. Mya noticed them watching her as Kayden moved away, disapproval on their faces. When she turned, Seonaid was standing beside her.

"You needn't mind them," she said, her eyes on the same set of women.

"What is the trouble with them?" Mya asked quietly. "I don't believe I've met them, and yet I think they dislike me."

"They think badly of you because you live with Kayden and have not yet wed him," Seonaid answered after a moment's silence, obviously uncertain whether she ought to tell Mya so.

That had not occurred to Mya. She was not certain why it had not. Perhaps because in the loss of her memory she had forgotten some of the customs of society. But she was hardly going to move out now, and it would do little to redeem her reputation in the eyes of the women.

"I suppose I ought to have expected that."

"In truth, we were all a little surprised when we found out, but we heard from the men who were there when you met the laird that your family had died, and we could hardly blame you for wishing to live with someone you knew, when you'd lost everyone else."

A little surprised, Mya turned to look at the other woman. "That is kind of you. To understand. Thank you."

Seonaid smiled. "I am not one to judge. I find that there is always something for which you can be judged, when you are judging others."

"That is more than a little true." Mya looked up as Kayden approached, and gave Seonaid one last smile. "I will keep that in my thoughts."

"Do you wish to find a seat?" Kayden asked as he reached her.

Mya laid her hand on the arm he offered, leaning into his side with a glance at the disapproving women. If her expression was a little smug, well, she thought she had reason to be pleased with herself. She had Kayden, after all. Their opinions hardly mattered.

Kayden led her to a seat at the edge of the circle. Next to them, Mya saw a young woman winding yarn on a drop spindle. The motion of it was a little hypnotic, and she realized she was staring after a moment, lifting her head to find the young woman looking back at her. She smiled a little uncertainly, hoping the other wouldn't see her watching as rude. Glancing quickly away, she found her eyes suddenly meeting Lachlan's. Her stomach dropped.

He was staring at her, his eyes narrowed and his expression hard. When he realized that she had seen, he smiled, slow and cold. Mya looked away from him. Wondered if she ought to say something to Kayden.

"Would you like to learn," a soft voice said beside her.

Mya looked up to find that the young woman had gotten up from her chair and approached them. "Learn?"

"I noticed that you were taking some interest in the spindle," she said. "And I thought perhaps you might like to learn how to use it. It's a good skill to be having, and useful on long nights beside the fire."

"I'm certain I could obtain you some wool," Kayden said, flashing a smile at the girl that Mya noticed had her flushing a rather fetching pink. "If you wished to practice such things."

"I would very much like to learn," Mya answered. It was only partly to take the girl's attention from Kayden. She honestly did have some interest in spinning, and if they were going to be attending more of the meets, it would be pleasant to have some means of occupying her hands.

"Then I should be glad to teach you." The young woman smiled at Mya, pulling her stool in closer to theirs so that she could lean over and speak softly.

Up near the fire, there was some stirring, and then the voice of the elderly man rose over the quickly quieting room as he began to tell a story. The girl's hands guided Mya's on the spindle, and Kayden's body was warm at her side.

It was, Mya thought, an altogether delightful way to spend an evening.

Chapter 13

The days passed, and the world outside grew colder, but inside the little house there was warmth, and light, and Kayden. There were no more awkward mornings. They made love by the fire and fell asleep wrapped in each other's arms, woke in the morning to kisses and wandering hands. In truth, Mya couldn't keep her hands off him, and it seemed the feeling was mutual. More than once in the fortnight that had passed since they had fallen into bed together for the second time, they had left the breakfast dishes and the day's duties until well into the afternoon. It was hardly sustainable, but Mya was going to take it while she could get it.

They attended more of the gatherings. Mya had found that she liked them. Liked the chance to talk with the others, and listen to the old stories of the clan and the lands around them. Perhaps she felt especially connected to them because she could not remember her own past. Hearing the history of others gave her something to hold onto. She had made a better job of avoiding Lachlan since the first, and though a few of the women still spoke to her only when necessary, Mya was sure they would not go on that way forever.

She was making dinner one winter afternoon when Kayden came in out of the rain, shaking the water from the plaid he'd pulled over his head. The animals were tucked away safely in the barn, warm and protected from the winter wind. In years past, Kayden had told her once, they used to be brought in with the family for the winter, kept in a pen against one wall. Mya was more than a little glad that wasn't the case any longer; she wasn't sure that she could have done what they did the night before while a cow stared at her from across the room.

The night before had been... She flushed thinking of it, and looked down at the turnips she was cooking over the fire to hide a smile. For such a strong man, Kayden was so very gentle. The memory of his hands on her skin was enough to wake a new wanting heat in her core, and she looked speculatively at him as he sharpened the swords near the hearth. Maybe they could make dinner quick.

She was turning away when a motion from the corner of her eye stopped her. Mya paused, and turned back to look at Kayden again, wondering what it was that had caught her attention. There. His hands were unusually clumsy with the whetstone, and her eyebrows drew into a frown as she watched him work.

"Kayden?" she asked softly.

He turned toward her, and in the firelight Mya could make out the flush in his cheeks.

"Are you well?"

For a moment he seemed to consider that, and then he shook his head. "No," he said, rising from the chair and almost swaying on his feet. Mya darted over to catch him before he could stumble. "I don't think I'm feeling well."

His skin felt too warm against hers, and Mya carefully guided him to the bed, tipping him into it despite his protests.

"No," she said when he tried to rise. "You're ill. Lie back and rest."

Kayden subsided with a huff, and Mya went to get him a glass of water. When she returned, he sat up and drank it slowly, his dark eyes fever-bright.

Mya's stomach flipped nervously. What if he got sicker than she could take care of? Was there a doctor in town? Someone who could help?

As he settled back against the mattress and she tucked the blankets around his shoulders, she could feel the heat coming off him. Though she had likely touched every inch of his skin in recent days, it still felt surprisingly intimate to smooth her palm over his forehead.

"You have a fever."

He blinked up at her. "I'm sure it's nothing a little bed rest and some good food can't cure," he said, reaching out to tuck a stray lock of hair behind her ear.

"If it doesn't— If you start getting worse, where do I go for a doctor?"

For a moment, it looked as though he wasn't going to answer the question, but then he sighed. "Inverness. The town across the firth. Ask for a doctor at the church. I don't want you going into the taverns looking for someone to aid you. But it won't be necessary. I'll be just fine by morning."

Mya wasn't sure, as she turned to serve up dinner, that those words were true. How could he know if he would be fine or not?

He insisted on feeding himself, despite her offers, giving her such a look when she attempted it that she had to turn away to stifle a giggle behind her hand. For a sick man, he could look very fierce, but he did not frighten her.

When he was done, he let his head fall back against the pillow with a sigh. Before Mya had even eaten her own dinner, he was asleep, his breathing ragged with illness. Mya sat in the chair next to the bed and watched him, the familiar lines of his face in the firelight. It seemed so long ago that they had met in that clearing. Almost another lifetime. Sitting there, she could not imagine a world without him in it. Could not imagine herself without him by her side.

In the end, she got up from the chair and went to curl up on the rug in front of the fire, not wishing to disturb what sleep he was getting. She slept lightly, concern for Kayden keeping her from the deepest levels of dreams. He slept soundly for a few hours, but when she woke before dawn, he was moaning and shifting restlessly, burning hotter than before.

"Kayden." She laid a hand on his shoulder and shook him gently. "Kayden, darling, wake up. Please?"

His eyelids fluttered open, and he looked up at her, his expression dazed.

"Your fever's worse. Can you still speak to me? Do you understand what I'm saying?"

"My head hurts," he said. "There is some—" He broke off to cough once, sharply. "There is agrimony leaf in the cupboard. Tea with that. And honey."

Mya nodded and went to start the water boiling on the hearth. As she turned to go back to his side, she paused, some half-recalled idea trying to slip through. She glanced at the bucket of cool water she'd dipped his cup from before, and then she went to the chest and pulled out one of the scraps of cloth from altering the skirt, wetting it in the water before she returned to Kayden's side.

"Water," she said, picking up a cup from the side of the bed where she'd left it. "Drink."

He blinked up at her as though she was speaking a foreign language he couldn't translate, so she lifted the glass to his lips. He swallowed once automatically, then gripped the wood and drank the rest down in quick gulps she hoped would not upset his stomach.

"Easy, easy," she said, but at least the cup was empty. She set it on the floor again and pressed the wet cloth to his forehead. He moaned and leaned into her touch.

"Does that feel good?"

"Yes," he said, voice rough.

The cloth warmed quickly, so she flipped it over before pressing it to his cheeks and the back of his neck. When there were no longer any cool spots left, she went to the bucket and filled a bowl with water. At his bedside, she rinsed the cloth in the bowl and continued to sponge off his feverish skin.

Over on the hearth, the kettle whistled. Mya got up and pulled it from the fire, then went to the cupboard to search for the appropriate leaf, steeping that in the boiling water and sweetening the tea with honey before she took it to him. That, he drank in slow sips, careful of the heat, while Mya helped him hold it. When time passed and his stomach seemed okay with that and the water, she refilled his glass and helped him drink more. He settled in then, and slept. It was not a deep sleep, but at least it was not so restless as it had been. Despite the little sleep she'd gotten, she was too worried to be tired, and continued her ministrations while he dozed.

His skin felt a little cooler as dawn came and spilled into the room. Mya set the bowl and the cloth aside and smoothed the hair back from his forehead. He stirred slightly before falling back into sleep with a sigh. She was, she realized as the light brightened in the room, going to have to do his usual morning chores.

Collecting the eggs would be easy enough. The hens had never seemed particularly inclined to peck her to death for them, for which she was grateful. Milking, though, was a whole other matter.

Kayden had taught her how to milk the fuzzy brown Highland cows one morning, but most of that lesson had involved him failing to hold back laughter at her expense when she failed in some aspect. She was not particularly looking forward to trying again. But Kayden could hardly do it; had he attempted to she would have stopped him. So she put on her shoes and went out to the barn, huddled in her arisaid against the chill of the wind.

It was warmer inside the rough little building, her steps cushioned by hay instead of sinking in soft mud. The two cows and the horse looked at her with large, liquid dark eyes. Mya reached out to stroke the horse's silky nose, and he butted his head into her hand, coaxing a tired smile from her lips. She couldn't stay with the horse forever, though, so she moved to the cows, biting her lip as she looked them over. The roosting chickens fluttered their wings with little rustling noises. The whole place smelled rather comfortingly of animal.

The first cow looked at her warily when Mya stepped into her stall, but she stood obediently still as Mya set up the milking stool and the bucket. It would be fine, she told herself. As long as she didn't hurt the cow, all would be well.

Her hands were hesitant as she reached out, and the cow startled a little when they made contact, but only stamped one hoof against the hay-covered floor. Mya sighed a little in relief. It took her a few tries, but soon milk was squirting into the bucket, foaming and warm. She let herself lean forward enough to rest her head against the cow's warm flank.

Kayden would be pleased with her, she thought. When he woke. He would be proud of her for doing the chores he could not. And it was proof, wasn't it, that she was capable of making it in the Highlands. She was not the weak woman he'd supposed her to be when they first met in that clearing.

The first milking finished, Mya moved on to the second, which went easier than the last, her nervous fear gone. When she was done, she stroked a hand along the thick fur of the cow's back, scratching at her shoulder. The cow leaned into the touch with a snort, and Mya almost found herself laughing. Maybe milking cows wasn't so bad after all. Buckets of milk in hand, Mya returned to the house and set them in the corner, then returned to the barn for the eggs. When she came back in, the wind blustering through the door behind her, Kayden was awake and blinking at her groggily.

"You milked the cows," he said.

"Yes," Mya agreed as she unwrapped her arisaid and let it fall back to its place over her skirt. "Someone had to."

He smiled. It was tired, but there, and warm. "I would not have guessed it when I found you."

Mya laughed. "No. I was just thinking that. I suppose I'm not what either of us expected."

Kayden held out a hand for her, and she crossed the room to sink down at the edge of the bed, looking into his dark eyes.

"You," he said, smiling tiredly, "are exactly perfect."

The words warmed her like sunlight.

Chapter 14

Kayden was ill for another two days. Though by the third he was sitting up in bed and moving around the house, Mya forbade him going out in the cold, not wanting to set off the sickness again before it had completely run its course. Kayden complied, grudgingly.

"There are ways to pass the time," he said, watching her make bannock at the hearth.

Mya looked over at him, eyebrows lifted. "And what might those be?"

He grinned back. "What do you think, my lady?"

As tempting as the prospect was, Mya had other things she needed to finish, including churning the butter from recent milkings, and in truth she had no interest in contracting whatever illness had laid him out in bed for three days. "I think I will have to pass, for the moment."

Kayden slumped against the pillows stacked behind him and drank more of his tea. Mya stifled a laugh and went back to her work.

The acceptance of her momentary rejection, however, was short-lived. As the day went on, Kayden seemed determined to drive her to distraction. He got up from the bed and moved around the house in nothing despite the faint chill the fire couldn't dispel, washing himself at the basin. Mya tried not to watch the way the firelight moved over his skin, highlighting curves of muscle sheened with water. It was entirely unfair to use that against her, and she told him so. He only laughed and went back to bed.

"Are you certain," he said as she made dinner, "that you wish to go on waiting?"

"I'm cooking," Mya said, her voice coming out more breathless than she would have liked.

"I can think of something I would much rather eat than turnips."

Heat spilled over her cheeks. "You shall have it. When you are well."

"You are utterly cruel," he retorted.

"I'm practical," Mya answered. She turned and carried his plate over to the bed. "One of us ill is enough. I hardly want to join you in the sickbed."

That seemed to get through to him. He gave her a little smile and took the plate that she offered, eating his food without any more teasing offers. Still, Mya felt guilty for shutting him down as she'd done, and resolved that when he was well again a surprise might be in order.

Evening had settled over the house, and Kayden was out seeing that the animals were situated for the night. Mya took the linen nightshirt she had worn in their first days together out of the chest. In all her mending, she had not remembered to fix it; it was still ripped directly down the center. She stripped out of her skirt and blouse, and pulled it on instead over her shoulders. It hung from them, threatening to slide off her arms, and after a moment's thought she reached for Kayden's extra belt, winding it around her waist to keep the shirt from coming off entirely. Above, the rip made it fall open, baring a stretch of white skin and the curves of her breasts. She smoothed the fabric over her thighs, and sat down in the shadowed corner at the back of the table to wait for Kayden's return.

He came back in whistling, and stamped the dirt from his boots. His eyes had not yet found her, half concealed in the dim room. Mya waited until he was sitting on the edge of the bed, untying his shoes, then rose, and stepped out into the light.

Kayden froze. For a moment he didn't say anything at all. Mya took another step forward, hips swaying.

"God in heaven, woman. Are you trying to kill me?"

Mya laughed. "You wouldn't be much use at all to me dead." Her eyes roamed down his body, settling considerably farther south than his face. Even through the kilt, she could see that he was already hard. Her lips curled into a smirk.

"You're doing this on purpose," he accused when he saw how smug she was, and she feigned innocence with a smile, looking at him wide-eyed as she walked forward.

"Doing what?" she asked, blinking down at him.

"Driving me to the edge of madness," he remarked, dryly, kicking his boots aside and reaching out to grasp her around the waist, pulling her to him as she giggled.

"Who knew a simple shirt could do all that?" she asked teasingly, letting him bring her onto his lap as he kissed her temple, breathing in the scent of her hair.

It was, of course, entirely a lie. She knew *exactly* what she was doing to him. Had, in fact, been planning it for an entire day.

"You did," he muttered, adjusting her slightly so she was more comfortable, and Mya smiled once more, allowing him to jostle her before she pulled away slightly and kissed his forehead.

"Mmmm, but it makes *such* a great good evening, doesn't it?" Mya asked as she brushed kisses along his jaw while her hands dipped down to his hips.

She tipped her head up and pressed her lips to his. The tentative motion was matched easily, and he leaned into her, explicit permission for her to kiss him more deeply. The low groan he made in the back of his throat got louder when Mya rubbed his thighs, pushing the kilt up to get at bare skin, nipping at his upper lip and taking it into her mouth. Carefully, he pushed the torn shirt off of her shoulders so that it hung low on her arms, bringing one hand to the autumn red fall of her hair and the other between her shoulder blades, pressing her toward him.

Mya smiled against his mouth just before she pulled away from him, kissing over his cheek and across his jaw once more, drawing a sigh from him. As she reached his throat, he tipped his head back, and she left an open-mouthed kiss over his Adam's apple, feeling him swallow as one of his hands trailed downward, cupping her backside as he ground against her, letting her feel his arousal.

Slowly, Mya's lips made their way to his ear, licking at the shell before she nuzzled him, swiveling her hips so she was rubbing against his erection, making him gasp. Her fingers crept up his side, tracing the arc of his ribs before she curved her palm over his shoulder and to the back of his neck, grasping his hair. Gently, she kissed his ear, grinding down against him once more as she whispered, "You're already so hard, Kayden," and pulled on his dark locks just hard enough to punctuate the point.

He sucked in another harsh breath, opening his eyes to look at her as she pulled away and she smiled at him, the hand on his hip rubbing soothing circles into the warm skin under his shirt. Her lips curled into a wider smile, and she leaned forward to kiss his nose, making his own mouth twitch upward.

"It's hardly something I can help," he told her, and she lifted a brow as she played with his hair, seated in his lap and feeling the hard line of his length against her thigh.

"Oh? Are you so easily controlled?" she asked, the playful grin on her face getting even more mischievous. His eyes narrowed slightly and Mya giggled. "No? It's not that?"

"I'm not entirely certain after all that you aren't some kind of fae creature," he replied, cupping the back of her neck and kissing beneath her jaw. Mya hummed, letting her head fall back. "Come here to claim me."

"I suppose you'll just have to take it on faith that I'm not."

"Mmmm," he replied, finding her pulse point and tenderly kissing it. "I'm not entirely convinced, but I'm not a smart enough man to back out now."

"Better to die happy?" she asked, the teasing tone evident, and Kayden only sucked at her neck, sure to produce a darkened mark.

Mya let a small, breathy sound of pleasure escape, and felt his lips curve into a smirk against her skin. He only pulled away when she started grinding wantonly down on his lap, and he nipped at her playfully.

"When I am done with you," he informed her, almost casually, though she could practically feel the shiver of pleasure that hummed through him, "you'll not be teasing. Or saying much of anything at all."

Mya bit her lip as Kayden pressed burning, open-mouthed kisses down to her collarbones, kissing across them and nipping delicately.

"Is that—mmmm—is that a threat?"

Kayden's lips had finally trailed to her sternum, right atop her heart, and he gently pressed his lips to the spot, the overwhelming tenderness of his touch making her breath catch in her throat. His eyelashes tickled over her skin as he pressed his cheek atop her left breast, his touch approaching worshipful as his hands trailed over her back, stroking her spine and massaging her skin through the thin linen of the shirt.

She could practically feel his smile against her flesh. "It's not a threat. It's simply what will be, Mya."

He couldn't see her grin with his face against her chest, but she thought he could feel it, feel the happiness warm and bright under her skin.

"Someone is rather cocky," Mya said, squirming atop him, bringing herself backwards slightly, letting his hardness press to her belly. When she looked down, taking in his erection, her grin deepened. "Literally."

Kayden snorted, splaying his palm between her shoulder blades and pushing her forward once more so he could kiss over the other side of her neck, leaving her to tangle her fingers in his hair as he left a wicked burning sensation everywhere his lips touched her skin.

"You are terrible," he muttered, biting her earlobe and tugging gently at the flesh between his teeth. Mya giggled, though it was broken up by the wanting, breathy noises that kept slipping from her throat.

"I'm sure you are somehow to blame," she informed him, relaxing backward in his hold and bringing her legs around him, running her hands through his hair and circling where the nape of his neck met his skull as he located every spot on her throat and shoulders that made her shiver and gasp.

Mya swallowed hard when he brought his hands to her hips, grinding against her and connecting their mouths, his tongue sliding over the cushion of her lower lip. Mya parted her lips for him, tilting her head and deepening the kiss, even as he wrapped an arm around her, settling his large palm over her ribcage, his other hand massaging her hip, gently running over her backside. She felt too warm, gasping when he pressed his fingers over a spot that had her jolting, jumping in his lap and rubbing over his erection.

The groan he gave off was intoxicating, and she could feel his desire slicking her skin, making the slide of her belly against his length easier. His tongue came to twine with her own, his hands exploring her body with lazy thoroughness, and she sighed against his mouth, one of her hands coming between them, intent on touching him, making him feel as good as he was making her feel.

But he pulled away as her fingers gently brushed over his flexing stomach, the hand that had been roving over her side grasping her wrist, instead, and she caught his strained, particularly dark smirk before he maneuvered them, laying her flat on her back with no warning at all.

Mya gasped, her free arm flying around his neck as the world went dizzy for a moment. On her back, her head tipped off the edge of the mattress, exposing her neck even more, and, this time, Kayden settled one knee between her legs, grinding against her slightly, inspiring a warm moan as he licked her throat.

"None of that, Mya," he said, and the way he uttered her name made her feel electric, his teeth coming to scrape over her sensitive skin even as he palmed at her breasts, cupping them, letting the weight settle in his large, capable hands. Mya arched up to his touch as he kissed behind her ear, a whimper coming from deep in her throat. "This is about you."

As he tenderly caressed her, he brought the fingers of one hand down her flexing stomach, his index finger extended as he barely touched her, drawing a line down her torso. Mya breathed in harshly, swallowing hard as his left hand continued lightly stroking her breast, rising and falling with her breath.

Slowly, teasing her, he moved his knee away so he could press two fingers between her thighs, smirking when he took note of how wet she was. She strained, flexing her hips to try to get more friction as he traced the underside of her breast, making her quiver beneath him. His eyes found the marks he had no doubt left behind. They would be stark against her pale skin, an obvious sign of their connection. Of his desire.

She thought of how she must look to him as his gaze explored her body. Her head was tipped back, her face flushed, partially from the position, but mostly from his ministrations, her lips swollen and well-bitten. As she fluttered her eyes open, she knew her pupils must be blown as wide and dark as his own. Her chest rose and fell with her breath, his free hand moving up her body to play with her nipples, already hard and aching with want. The touch made her whimper once more. His gaze continued trailing down, taking in her flexing stomach, the flush over her thighs.

"You are so lovely like this, Mya," he informed her.

She only fluttered her eyes shut, breathing hard as she tried to rut against his hand. He leaned over her once more, biting down on her earlobe. Mya gasped, her hips bucking up off the bed as she shuddered with the perfect ache of it. He moved his head down, kissing her nipple with a rush of warm breath. She shuddered.

"Mya," he said, taking his hand from between her thighs and away, and she whined, eyes snapping open.

"Kayden," she pleaded. "I want you. I need you. Please do not tease me." Her hand lifted to his jaw and caressed the line of it, feeling the roughness of stubble.

His grin was wicked as he leaned into her touch, all the while bringing his fingers to his mouth. In the scant light of evening, she could see how they were glistening, and she swallowed hard when, he licked them and tasted her.

Her fingertips dug into his cheek, slightly, as he licked his fingers. His grin widened, and Mya arched up, yearning for his touch, pushing her breast further into his hand so he could massage her skin, feeling her writhing body, her hips twisting and her chest heaving. Her nipples were hard and flushed, and Mya moaned softly as he bowed his head and blew on her skin, catching the wet spots he'd previously left and making her shiver. The different sensations were making her desperate, making her whole body spark with pleasure.

Mya's fingers tangled in his hair as she gently whispered his name, and he growled low in his throat, nuzzling against her neck and biting down softly. Mya's hold on his dark hair tightened as he molded his hard body over hers, pushing their hips together so he could hold her down with his weight. Slowly, as he sucked on her neck, he trailed his touch on her breasts inward, spiraling toward her sensitive nipple.

She arched toward him, her entire body shaking as he tapped his fingertip against it, a tease of a touch. Her chant of his name faltered, and he continued suckling at the bite he'd left on her neck, rocking his hips against hers.

"Kayden!"

He grinned, biting down on her skin once more and shifting his weight to offer a new angle, rocking his body against her own. Mya could not remember words. Her ability to speak had fled her, her body speaking for her instead. Lightly, he traced her areola, allowing his fingernail to barely brush over her flesh, and she strained against him harder, her eyes closed tightly as her breathing came faster, panting and needy, carrying scraps of his name. He continued tracing around her nipple, the motions maddeningly slow, and Mya ground her hips against him, aligning herself against his erection and only succeeding in teasing them both with the slide.

Immediately, he arched away, moving his hands off of her. Mya let loose a high whine, boxing his head in with her arms and holding him close to her, whimpering.

"Mya—"

"Don't stop," she begged, her voice harsh and pleading, high and breathy. "You make me feel so good. Please, don't stop."

He nuzzled against her jaw, complying with her demands. His hand stroked over her ribs.

"Keep—keep going—" she cut herself off with a moan, arching almost painfully off the bed, her legs spread wide, her fingers looping his hair and tugging him toward her.

"Tell me how it feels, Mya," he whispered, kissing her jaw before he maneuvered atop her, relinquishing one hand to hold her head up, looking into her eye as he cupped her other breast. She fluttered her eyes open, her entire face warm and pink, bringing her lip between her teeth.

"Kayden..."

"Tell me," he commanded once more, gently kissing over her cheeks, missing her lips on purpose and sucking at her jaw.

"So good," she panted out, maintaining eye contact with him as his fingers kneaded at her flesh. "It feels s-so good. Warm. Pleasure sparking under my skin."

He kissed her as a reward, swallowing her soft moan as he thumbed her nipple, and Mya bucked harshly, unable to help it. The pleasure filled her up, her body electric and her thighs trembling.

Kayden's hands were strong as he shifted his hold so he could roll her nipple between his fingers, pinching and twisting almost immediately. She broke away from his mouth with another soft, pleased sound, throwing her head back as he latched onto her pulse, licking and sucking at the skin of her neck, adding one more mark to the many she already had courtesy of him.

She arched up higher, her legs splayed open, and he gently trailed his lips downward, listening to her panting, feeling her shiver. Slowly, ever so slowly, he released his hold on the back of her head, letting it fall back once more, and Mya moaned as he breathed hot air between her breasts, over her ribcage, her belly, and to her thighs. She spread her legs even wider for him, so wanting for his touch, and felt him smile against her skin.

He kissed over her inner thighs, slowly, his gaze lifted to her body, drinking in the sight. With one hand still caressing her breast and the other resting atop her hip, he finally reached to where she wanted him. His calloused fingers crept over her hipbone before he extended a finger and brought it between her lips, watching her buck.

"You're practically dripping, Mya," he breathed out, and she whimpered.

"I want you, Kayden. Please. I want you."

"Do you?" he asked, though she was certain he knew full well she did, looking up at her and playfully running his hand down her leg. He must know just how wanting she was. He could see the way she writhed helplessly against the mattress, could feel how wet and ready she was. But he didn't touch her.

"Yes!" she gasped finally, knowing he wanted her to say it.

"Do you want me to fuck you, Mya?"

Her breath hitched at the question, a soft groan accompanying the nod she gave. "Yes," she said, her voice tipping higher." Yes, please?"

He hummed as though still unsure. "How badly do you want me to, lovely one?"

She practically sobbed, his finger stroking her maddeningly slow. "I w-want you so badly. Please? Oh, Kayden, please?"

"*How* badly, Mya? Tell me exactly how badly you want it."

He was grinning, and she wanted to reach down and drag him up to her, taste the smile on his lips. She had shown him that she was not weak. That she could hold her own even in the harsh north. But that did not mean that she wanted to always be strong. And here with him, his finger caressing her clit with the ghost of a touch and his hand on her breasts, she could unwind so completely, tell him exactly how desperate she was to shatter.

His finger kept stroking. The glide between her lips was effortless, and, if anything, she only grew more slick as he looked up at her, sucking on her inner thigh, leaving marks everywhere his lips touched her. She levered herself up on her elbows, her body trembling, and looked down at him and the smug expression on his handsome face.

"Kayden. I will die if you do not let me find release."

"That bad, hmm?" he teased.

"Yes. Dammit. That bad."

"Well," he said, contemplatively, the motion of his stroking getting slightly faster, much to her delight. "If that's the case..."

The ache he had ignited between her legs must be as unbearable for him as it was for her. She had felt how hard he was. How wanting. And how was it that her surprise, meant to tease him, had been turned around on her so thoroughly? Slowly, all too slowly, the finger that was between her lips came to her entrance, and she gasped, falling back against the mattress as he slid it into her.

"Is this what you want, Mya?" he asked her, biting down gently on her hipbones and the skin of her belly, not yet leaning forward to taste her, though she wanted him to. Was sure that he wanted to.

"Yes. Yes, yes, yes," she chanted, her hands fisting the sheets, her body meeting every motion.

"Do you wish for more?"

The moan that tumbled out of her was rough at its edges, her body arching and the muscles of her stomach fluttering as she tensed. "Yes. Oh. Yes. Please?"

He slicked up a second finger and slid that one into her as well. Mya hitched her legs up higher, laying them over his shoulders. He brushed kisses against the insides of her thighs, and then the backs, nipping gently. Then he breathed warm air between them, making her shiver in anticipation as his fingers kept up their motion, sliding in and out of her.

"Kayden," she gasped.

"This," he said, voice low and rough with arousal, "is my favorite part, Mya. Watching you take me. Watching you want it. Damn lass, you're lovely." He curled his fingers, pressing deeper inside her, catching the spot there that made her gasp.

Mya was a shaking, shuddering mess. She was doing little more than panting, begging him to put his mouth on her. The syllables of his name were fragments breaking against her teeth as he pushed her higher into pleasure, drove her to the brink of ecstasy.

He rested his head against her thigh, seemingly content to just touch her like that. Content to make her completely mad with desire. Mya groaned and clutched at the blankets. She couldn't speak any longer. Not even the scattered attempts at his name.

There were only shuddering, cut off noises of pleasure and need, and when his fingers didn't let up, thrusting swiftly into her and curling in the perfect way, she bucked upward, crying out.

He leaned in, then, and pressed his lips against her folds, giving long, slow, deliberate licks over her entrance, taking his fingers out for short, swift moments as his tongue laved over the opening. Then he thrust them back in, leaving her gasping and moaning. His nose nuzzled her, his lips caressing her clit, sucking softly and consistently, interspersed with circling his tongue around her. Mya's hands found his hair as she shuddered, her body brought right to the edge, tingling with pleasure that was almost too much.

Her moans came shorter, rising in pitch, catching on her breath. She was so close. Right on the edge of orgasm. Another touch. She wanted to beg him, to tell him how much she needed it, but the words would not come, and she could only writhe. He must know how much she wanted it. How much she needed him.

He pressed a third finger inside her, fast and hard, and brought his mouth down over her clit. Pleasure exploded through her, colors bursting on the insides of her eyelids. Mya sobbed with the intensity of it. And all the while Kayden was there, holding her close, speaking in a low murmur. She couldn't make out the words, knew only the sound of his voice wrapping around her like a caress as the pleasure came in wave after wave, filling her utterly.

She was whimpering by the time he had slowly kissed back up her cheek, and the hand that had been caressing her breast came around her, sliding beneath her back and the mattress, adjusting her so that her head wasn't tipped over the edge of the bed anymore. Mya threw her arms around him, though she felt mostly boneless, nothing but contented pleasure, shuddering in his grasp as he held her. Only when the aftershocks had eased to gentle flutters did he take his fingers out of her, kissing over her nose and cheeks and brushing over her mouth as she breathed out his name.

Slowly, her heart stopped racing, and Mya let herself be held, utterly relaxed. She caught her breath with a deeply satisfied sigh, her smile content and lazy, basking in his affections. She bumped their noses together, kissing his mouth as he grinned down at her.

"Is it still being cocky if I was correct, Mya?" he asked her, then, the expression on his face entirely too pleased with himself.

She only hummed, still smiling, curling in close to him.

Pressed that close, though, she felt the hard line of him against her belly once more and remembered that he had not yet had his pleasure. Her brows furrowed and she looked down, taking in the hard length of him.

"Still cocky," she said, leaning in to brush a kiss against his shoulder. "You've had nothing."

He kissed beneath her ear, softly stroking her side, their legs tangled together. "I have had a great deal of pleasure," he said.

"That is not enough. I wish to make you feel this good," she said, cupping the back of his neck, her thumb coming to stroke over his jaw. "I want to make you feel as good as you made me feel."

"You do," he assured, curling up to her, but Mya rolled her eyes.

"Do, as in general. Not did, as in just now."

Kayden nuzzled at her, apparently fully prepared to go without when she had planned the entire thing for him. It was sweet, and completely ridiculous. "You don't have to, Mya."

"But I want to," she replied, curling her fingers over his shoulders and pushing him back slightly. She leaned in and kissed the bridge of his nose. "Can I?"

The smirk that curled over his face was lazy and endearing. "You can do whatever you'd like with me, Mya."

"Mmmm, you might regret that." She gave him a wicked smile. "I could tease you as you teased me. I think you will find it is not quite so much fun on the other side."

He laughed, looping a lock of her red hair around his finger. "Have I rubbed off on you, then?"

"In more ways than one."

That earned her a chuckle, and Mya smiled sweetly at him, kissing his jaw and pressing him down onto his back. He looked at her, eyebrows lifted, and she grinned down at him.

"Let me do something for you," she said, watching him swallow.

His lips curled into a smile to match her own. "Go on, then. Do as you wish."

Chapter 15

She gave him one more soft, gentle smile before she kissed his throat, intent on leaving him with as many marks as he'd left her. He didn't moan for her, didn't fall apart under her touch. Not yet. But she knew how to play him, after all their nights together. She knew how to judge his reactions from the flex of his hips and the way he swallowed, hard, how he brought his hand to the top of her head to encourage her.

She unfastened the belt that held his kilt in place, and he arched from the mattress as she slid it out from under him and tossed it down onto the chest at the foot of the bed. Then she kissed her way down his chest, focusing on the line of his sternum. She might have teased, if she wanted, but she wanted to watch him writhe for her. Wanted to see the pleasure wreck his expression. She was focused on making her way down to where he most wanted her, returning the favor that he'd given her moments ago. She wanted to give him what *he* wanted. She wanted to see him break open, gasping her name. So when she got to his hips and the perfect cut of muscle there, she only stroked her fingers over his side before she glanced up at him, smiling, kissing his belly, watching the way his eyes darkened.

"Are you glad I coaxed you into this?" she asked.

He hummed an agreement, bringing a hand to the top of her head and brushing her hair back from her face. Her heart skipped a beat in her chest as he looked at her, tenderly looping the strands behind her ears, bringing her hair to one shoulder so it wasn't in her way. Kayden showed affection mostly in small ways: in careful, swift caresses, in absentminded comforts, and this was no different. Mya smiled warmly, the affection she felt toward him almost overwhelming, as though it was swelling in her chest until her body could hardly contain it.

"I love you," she told him, resting her cheek against his hipbone for a moment.

"Mya..." he said, low and soft. "I love you, too."

He cupped her cheek, and she brought one of her hands off of his hips, resting it over his and turning her head slightly to kiss his palm, her fingers settling into the spaces his fingers left.

She gave one more kiss to his palm before she moved back, just enough to lower herself down, and she let go of her hold on his hand so she could curl her fingers around his length. Mya heard him groan, his hand falling from her cheek and down to her shoulder, stroking over her in encouragement.

Her tongue slipped out to wet her lips. He was so big. She thought of the way he felt inside her, stretching her so perfectly, and had to swallow a moan. Her thighs rubbed together, trying to provide some stimulation; she wanted him inside her again.

Slowly, she kissed the underside of his cock, holding him at the base as she maintained eye contact with him, and he groaned breathily while she breathed hot air on his sensitive skin. She parted her lips to wrap around him, then. His fingers carded through her hair and she relaxed slightly, letting her eyes slide closed and slowly taking him in, inch by inch.

She didn't rush. She felt him tense under her, trying not to thrust up, his body shivering with the effort of control. It was incredibly hot. Mya slowly stroked his thigh with one hand, the other squeezing him gently at the base. Kayden's choked cry when she sucked on the head was intoxicating, and she could feel herself growing wet again, wanting him.

Mya took another inch, and he groaned, sliding a hand through her hair again. She wanted, she thought as she slid back up slowly, teasingly, to give him more. Wanted to do something they hadn't yet done. She gave it some thought as she lifted up entirely, hearing him choke off a moan. She smiled and kissed at the base of him, her nose gently bumping against his skin.

"I want to try something new," she said, running a hand up his side.

"Do as you wish," he answered, his expression a little dazed, and she grinned, crawling over him, placing both hands onto his chest and pressing him into the mattress. She felt his hand slide down from her shoulder, curling over her spine until he cupped her backside, grinding against her, hungry and wanting. Mya smiled at him, setting a kiss atop where his heart was beneath his sternum, feeling his thumbs rub soothing circles against her skin, making her arch into the touch.

"I am going to turn," she told him, and she looked into his eyes, dark and wide with want.

"Mmm," he answered, seemingly beyond words, and she nuzzled beneath his jaw, tenderly kissing his pulse point before she pulled away.

It didn't take much maneuvering at all, really. In only a moment, she had her legs on either side of him, her back to him. She arched, throwing her hair back over her shoulder as she bent over him, shifting so that her spine was arched, her body on display to him. The knowledge of just what he was seeing made her flush, but if his groan was any kind of answer, he was pleased with the view. She gently tapped the inside of his thigh so he wouldn't jolt when she brought her lips to his hips, kissing and nipping at the thin skin there, making him moan.

Looking at him, again, she bit her lip as she took in how hard he was. His cock bobbed in front of her, big and heavy, and she wanted him like she had never wanted anything or anyone.

She grasped him once more, her hand wrapping around his cock, before she bowed her head and shimmied backward to get more comfortable, her tongue coming out to lick at the ridge. She heard him gasp and she kissed his tip, leaving a line of kisses down the length and then opening her mouth and circling the head with her tongue.

She felt him shift beneath her, moaning, and she finally opened her mouth for the head of his cock, sinking slowly down him.

Mya almost jumped when she felt his hands on her back, massaging her skin, and she moaned lowly at how the pads of his fingers dug in against the muscle. Kayden had calloused, well used hands, and he knew just where to touch her to make her boneless with pleasure. She felt her body sink down, relaxing a little further against his. The quick, shallow intakes of air through her nose morphed into slow, deep breathing, and she found that she had far less trouble taking more of him into her. She bobbed her head back and forth, taking him deeper every time, feeling him shudder. She cupped his balls with the gentlest touch, feeling herself warm even further as he groaned.

She answered the sound with a moan, and the vibration against his length broke his control. His hips bucked up, just enough to almost be too much. She pulled back, but his hands were on her, and there was nowhere to go. But there was something about the restraint, being held by him, that made her want him all the more, her body aching to have him inside. She moaned again. This time he was prepared, and did not move, but the groan that escaped him was hungry, almost a growl. Mya was certain that Kayden had an explicit view of just how much doing this for him had turned her on, and she felt his fingers soothe down her spine, managing to force out a strangled apology for the abrupt motion before as he trailed his hands down to the curves of her buttocks, cupping both cheeks.

She didn't mean to squirm, spreading her legs farther as she slowly slid upward, but her body had a will of its own, and the pleasure was too much. Mya stroked her hand over what she couldn't take in her mouth, and Kayden arched off the bed, squeezing her backside and kneading the flesh, his moans growing deeper as she began to pump him before she licked back up to the tip and sucked it into her mouth once more. He growled her name, and she bucked against nothing, aching for some kind of touch.

With both of her hands on his body, she couldn't even reach down between her legs and relieve the near painful arousal she had been brought to. Kayden hummed deep in his throat, still stroking her buttocks, and she arched into the touch, trying to beg him without words to give her something. Anything.

Kayden found words somewhere, hands tightening as he breathed out, "Fuck, Mya. You're so wet."

She moaned, taking him deeper into her throat, pleasure sparking down her spine. Heat coiled in her belly.

"I want to have you again," he growled. "Want to hear you scream for me."

Bloody hell. The words were almost too much. It was cruel to do that to her, and as the words went on, Kayden telling her how much he wanted to taste her once more, she thought it was a little unfair that she was the one on top and he still had her quivering and breathless with need. She couldn't help but remember the way his mouth had felt on her. That she had found her pleasure like that.

When she felt one of his hands leave her ass, trailing downward, she couldn't help but make a painfully eager noise, making him groan with the vibration.

She felt him trail a finger between her lips, starting at her entrance before slowly moving up to her clit. It felt so good that she strained to lean into his touch, rutting against his hand, silently begging for mercy and release. He slid a finger inside her the same way he had just a little earlier, and she moaned, muffled and desperate. He was too lost in his own pleasure to tease, sliding a second finger into her, thrusting them roughly and mercilessly stroking over all the places that drove her wild with pleasure. She felt his thumb come over her clit, rubbing harsh, swift circles against it, and her hips bucked.

Kayden's other hand was still curled around her buttock, and she had taken him in so far that there was no room for her hand to pump him anymore. Instead, her lips met her hand and she could only work it around at the base of him, her other hand palming his balls, bringing the pad of her thumb to the sensitive skin there and rubbing. He had given up any semblance of control, and she barely even had to move. Instead, he was rocking into her mouth, his speech sliding into syllables she couldn't make out. Only her name was recognizable.

She couldn't help but grind against his hand, rocking her body down against the touch, but it wasn't enough and he knew it, and when he said her name again, the *"Mya"* so low and ragged that she barely had it in her to stay upright, she felt his hand leave her backside to grab her hair. It was all the warning she got before he pulled his fingers out of her. Mya cried out in frustration. She wanted to tell him to keep going, but her mouth was still full with him, even as his hand in her hair pulled her gently but inexorably upward.

"Stop. Mya, stop," he managed to growl, and Mya lifted her head with a gasp, breathing hard through her nose.

"Kayden?" she asked, her voice hoarse before she felt him move her, wrapping an arm around her waist and lifting her as he sat up.

His mouth came to her shoulder immediately, kissing across until he got to her neck, biting down as he brought his other hand back to her sex and stroked her once more, making her buck into the touch with a cry.

"I want to take you," he muttered, repeating the phrases over and over as he left a trail of kisses up to her jaw, and she moaned and caught at his arm for leverage, her other hand reaching down and under her to grasp his cock.

Mya whimpered, tossing her head back and over his shoulder, her hair spilling over her shoulders and his. "Yes. Yes, please. Dammit, please," she gasped, shifting from her spot on top of him as her eyes closed once more and she settled more comfortably on her knees, lifting herself and pressing him against her, waiting until he hummed out an affirmation before she lowered herself down. They came together in one easy slide, and he kissed over her jaw, his lips brushing over her chin before they found her mouth.

He curled one hand around her hip and the other found her clit, stroking it as he moved her in his lap. Mya went boneless in his grasp, letting him thrust and grind into her as she reached up to curl her fingers in his hair. Her body arched as he moved the hand from her hip so he could cup one breast and then the other, rolling her nipples between his fingers.

She pulled away from their kiss with a harsh cry, throwing her head back once more and burying her face against the crook of his neck and shoulder. She left soft but fevered kisses all over his neck and the underside of his jaw, dropping them between scrambled words and pleading noises.

He lifted her off of him without warning, and she all but sobbed in frustration before he laid her out on the mattress, only taking the barest of moments to settle between her legs and slide back into her. Mya cried out at the new position, wrapping her legs around him and wrapping her hands around his shoulders, her moan pitching up when he resumed the pace he had taken before, grinding and rolling his hips.

This time, facing her, his cock stroked over that perfect place inside her, and her thighs spasmed around him as she lifted her knees higher, opening her to him. Her head tossed against the pillow, hair spilling around her. He brought one hand back down to rub her clit as the other cupped her cheek, directing her gaze back to him.

"Eyes—eyes on me, Mya," he choked out, and Mya's eyes locked onto him as he desperately moved in her and she met his thrusts with equal fervor.

"I love you so much," Mya gasped, her lips parted and her eyes half-lidded even as they met his own. One of Mya's hands curled tighter around his shoulder, her nails digging in before she dragged them down his back, every muscle in her body wound tight with pleasure. She was close again. So close. "Harder," she pleaded.

Her teeth nipped at his lip, and he lengthened his thrusts, giving her what she wanted. Mya threw her head back, gasping, before she managed to open her eyes and connect their gazes once more, and she held him tight to her.

"Kayden. Kayden. I—" The words faltered and fell away, her body shuddering.

He rocked deeper into her, curling his body over hers. Skin pressed to skin, every inch of them so intimately close. His rhythm faltered. He thrust in again, hard, and pressed his thumb down on her clit.

She very nearly screamed his name, her body jolting with pleasure as orgasm rushed through her. It sang along her veins, lighting up her nerves, and she gasped and arched under him. He rocked into her again and then he was following her, calling her name. He turned his head, trying to find her mouth, bumping their noses before he kissed her, hard. His hand cupped the back of her head, holding her close as they both worked through their orgasms.

His arms were like steel, clutching her to him so tightly it was like he was trying to mold their bodies to each other, and she held on to him just as tightly. Just as desperately.

Mya was still gasping when he let his head drop to her shoulder, breathing out a long sigh and pressing a kiss to the skin. He brushed another to her collarbone, her throat, easing her through the last of her release. When she was completely limp, relaxed entirely, he moved to pull out of her, only to be stopped by her hand on his hip.

"Not yet," she said, stroking over his shoulders and sinking into the comfort of the mattress and his hands. He smiled and kissed her cheek, catching his breath. Mya grinned back up at him. "Worth the wait?"

He laughed. "More than."

"Good."

There were dishes still on the table, but Mya didn't care about them. They could wait. She wasn't getting out of bed for anything until dawn. Everything that she needed, everything she could possibly want in the world, was right there with her, holding her close in the quiet night.

"Kayden," she said, voice soft.

"Yes, lovely one?"

She smiled at the endearment, wrapping herself closer around him.

"I love you," she said. The words caught a little in her throat, not said in the heat of passion or the golden moments just after, but spoken with a clear head. Genuine and vulnerable.

His hand found her cheek, and her eyes met his. The dark pools of them seemed to reflect the light of the fire, making them endless. She could drown in them.

"I love you too," he said.

Her heart felt full to bursting. Whatever had come before, whatever the future held, in that moment the world was perfect.

Chapter 16

"Mya," Kayden said when they had both been up to wash despite her initial refusal to leave the warmth of his arms. Bathing, he had stripped her out of the torn shirt and his belt, dropping kisses against the newly bared skin of her shoulders and arms. "There is something I wish to... Something I wish to talk about. With you."

"Hmm?" Mya tipped her head back to look up at him, a question in her expression that she knew he could see even in the dim light.

"I want you to stay with me." He said the words quickly, like he wasn't sure that he would have the courage. "Not just for the winter, but forever. If you want to."

Mya's sleepy contentment splintered into fragments, and she levered herself up on an elbow, suddenly completely awake. "You what?"

"I want you to stay with me," he said again, this time more slowly. His eyes met hers. "I'm in love with you, Mya. I don't want you to go."

For a long moment, Mya was silent, trying to wrap her mind around the request he had just made. He wanted her to stay. He wanted—

"Truly?" She tried to keep the wavering uncertainty from her voice, part of her afraid somehow that he couldn't mean it. That it must be some kind of trick.

"Truly," he said, his voice catching on the word, as though he too was afraid.

"I-I don't know what to say."

"Say that you'll stay with me."

She looked up at his face, the want and the love written clearly in his expression, and thought of the past that she couldn't remember. Before, she had told him once, she was sure that she had been in love. But she could not remember his face. Could not remember who he had been. No one had come for her. What could her unremembered past offer that she did not have here, with Kayden?

"What if there are people out there looking for me?"

He reached down and stroked a hand against her cheek. "If you want to look for your family, Mya, I'll take you to look for them. I will do everything I can to find them for you." His expression faltered, twisting with pain. "Whether you wish to stay with me or not."

Could a man that she didn't remember, who hadn't looked for her, be as good as the man in bed beside her now? Would she find anything better than the love looking back at her from those dark eyes?

I love you, she had told him. And she had meant it. Mya smiled.

"Yes," she said, and the word spilled over with the joy suddenly bubbling up inside her. "Yes, Kayden. I will stay with you."

His arms wrapped around her, crushingly tight, and he was kissing her, hard. She held him close and gave herself over to the rush of want and brilliant happiness. Before, she had thought the world was perfect. Now she knew that was not perfection. This, sharing in his absolute joy, knowing that she would spend the rest of her life with the man holding her close, that was perfection. It was everything.

Finally, Kayden pulled back. They were both breathing hard, smiling wide, dazed smiles at each other. He slipped suddenly out of the bed.

"I know it's hardly the proper time," he said, sinking to one knee beside it while Mya stared at him with wide, startled eyes. "And I imagine I could be wearing something more romantic than my birthday suit, but I can't wait another moment, Mya. So, while it may be a bit redundant, seeing as I've already asked you to stay, there's something else I want to ask you."

Mya's breath caught in her throat.

"Mya," he said, "you've no last name I can use in this proposal, but that doesn't matter. I'm offering you my own. You are the light of my life. The best thing that has ever happened to me, and will ever happen." The smile broke out across his face again. "Mya. Will you marry me?"

This time, the answer came without hesitation, Mya scrambling down from the mattress to throw herself into his arms.

"Yes," she said. "Yes! Of course I will, you ridiculous man."

He kissed her again, rough for a moment, but gentling into slow. Tender. Mya sank into it with a sigh that caught between them. She didn't feel the cold floor under her knees. Didn't feel anything but Kayden, wrapped around her and holding her close, filling her every sense with his presence. It didn't matter that she couldn't remember her family and he wouldn't speak of his. They had each other. That was enough. That, Mya thought as the kiss broke and they pulled apart to look into each other's eyes once more, would always be enough.

"I love you," she said, and he laughed.

"And I you, Mya. My lovely one. Always and utterly."

Another kiss, and they might have been well on their way to a third round of lovemaking, had Mya thought either of them could take another release as intense as the ones they'd had. But the floor had started to hurt a little, and when Mya shifted uncomfortably Kayden pulled back. He gathered her up into his arms and lifted her onto the mattress, wrapping himself close around her and pulling the blanket over them both. Mya curled into the support of his chest.

"You," Kayden said, pressing a kiss to the nape of her neck, "are the thing I love most in this whole world."

"And you are mine," Mya answered.

"I'll get you a ring," he said then.

Mya hadn't even considered a ring. In the moment, all she had cared about was Kayden. "We don't need one, if you don't have one."

"We do," he answered, stubborn. "I'll not have you walking around without one. Every man in the Highlands needs to know that you're off limits. That yer mine."

That brought laughter bubbling up from behind Mya's ribs. "A little possessive, don't you think?"

"With a lass as fine as you? It's simply a necessary precaution." His tone was teasing, and he kissed her again, on her shoulder, pulling her in closer against his chest. "And besides, I rather like the idea of you walking around wearing my ring. It's a little more appropriate for mixed company than you wearing my shirt."

"That is true," Mya agreed, laughing again. "I'll wear your ring then. And gladly."

His arms tightened around her. Mya felt safe wrapped in them, as though the rest of the world could not touch her. Could not touch either of them, safe in the warmth of their little house on the hill. She smiled.

There were details to discuss, of course. When would they have the wedding. And where. Who would they invite? Undoubtedly Kayden's clan would be in attendance. But all of that was for a later time. She would not worry about it now. Now, she was lying beside the man she loved most, content in the knowledge that she was loved, and all the world was right.

She curled into the warm embrace, and slept.

Chapter 17

Mya had grown used to waking with Kayden at her side. But when she woke that morning, he was gone, the bed already cold where he had been. She sat up, frowning, and checked the room to see if she could find any sign of him, but there was nothing. The milk pails had already been brought in, and the eggs were sitting in the basket on the table. His shoes were gone from their place. She bit her lip as she looked around the empty room. Where had he gone?

Rising from the bed, she dressed and made her way over to the table. There was a note, sitting under the edge of the basket that held the eggs.

Gone to town. Returning soon. I love you.

Mya smiled down at the little slip of paper. He might have woken her and told her in person that he was leaving, but he had likely thought it was better to let her sleep in after the night they'd had—and what a night it had been—and she had to admit that the extra sleep had done her some good.

The cows were cared for, and the chickens, so there was little to do there. She made herself breakfast, wondering if Kayden had anything to eat before he left. She hoped he had. If not, she was going to have to talk to him, she decided. No making trips on an empty stomach, especially when he had been so recently ill. She finished up her breakfast and cleaned up after herself, then stepped out into the early morning fog to see what the day promised.

It was a surprisingly nice day for a Highland winter, warmer than she would have expected, and after a moment's thought she went back in to retrieve her coat and shoes. A walk might do her some good. They'd been cooped up in the house for days, and she had hardly left it before that. Breathing the fresh air would be nice.

She started out along the hill, looking down across the firth at Inverness. She could see it just starting to wake, tiny figures moving along the streets at the water's edge, and she smiled.

The land around her was gray, and dim with winter, but the hills rolling up toward the sky were still beautiful, the rocks that jutted up from them commanding the view. She took a deep breath of damp air and wondered why they hadn't gone on more walks together. That was something she would have to change.

Behind her, the house was receding into the gray landscape, even as the sun rose high enough to begin burning off the fog. Mya glanced back at it once, fixing its location in her mind. It wouldn't do to get lost. While she was sure that Kayden would find her if she did, she didn't really want to explain to him that she'd gone out for a walk and forgotten her way home when he inevitably appeared. His mockery she could take. Frightening him, though, was something she didn't wish to do.

He had asked her to marry him. The thought sent a frisson of joy up her spine. Kayden had asked her to stay, and to be his wife. She could not think of anything in the world that would make her any happier.

They would have a summer wedding. Or maybe one in the late spring. A time for beginnings. Perhaps, by then, she might have made some friends in town. It would be nice to have a few. Kayden was a wonderful man, but he could not provide the particular company that she was sure, despite her lack of memories, that other women would.

The sun was rising high enough now to burn off the fog, opening up the view. Mya hummed softly to herself as she made her way down the rolling slope of a hill, skirting the valley below, still filled with drifting moisture in the air. Ahead, trees rose against the rocks, dripping and deep green against the dim landscape.

Abruptly, she became aware of the sound of hooves behind her.

They were not loud, muffled by the damp earth and the soaked heather, but she could hear them, coming up quickly. She had not checked to see if Kayden had taken the horse. Perhaps he had, and had realized that she had gone out for a walk. She hadn't expected him back quite so soon, but she was hardly complaining. She turned with a smile on her lips.

But it was not Kayden who rode up behind her.

It took her only an instant to place the red-haired man on the horse. Her heartbeat picked up its pace, and her stomach flipped. Lachlan.

"Well, well. If it isn't Miss Mya. What're you doing out alone on such a dreary morning?"

"Taking a walk," Mya answered, grateful that her voice was steady.

"And where is Kayden?"

"My betrothed," Mya answered, keeping the words even, "is in town. Though I'm certain he'll be home shortly."

"A lass as lovely as yourself shouldn't be out wandering alone," he spoke with a leer that belied any attempt at concern.

"It's a kind offer, but I need no company. Thank you." Her hand curled into a fist against her side, and Mya silently prayed that he would take the words as she meant them and go. Surely he wouldn't dare to lay hands on another man's wife-to-be.

"You know, I've never liked a woman who thought she was too good for me." Lachlan's voice dropped lower, rough and angry, and Mya's shoulders hunched against the sound as much as against the cold. His presence made her skin crawl. "And you've a very disrespectful attitude."

"I think," Mya answered, ignoring the words because she didn't know how to answer them without angering him further, putting herself in more danger. "That I should be turning for home."

She turned as she spoke, stepping to the side to avoid his horse. A hand closed around her wrist.

"I think not," he said. "I'm still talking to you."

"Take your hands off me!" Mya bit the words out, yanking against his grip. It didn't loosen. "I'm a betrothed woman!"

Please let him listen to that, if he would not listen to anything else she said. If he wouldn't leave her alone for her own sake, maybe he would at least respect another man's claim.

"You say that," Lachlan said. "But I don't know that I actually believe it." His horse pranced nervously in place, and Mya tried again to pull away, avoiding the hooves. "You see, girl, you're not wearing a ring on your finger. I've heard nothing about wedding plans. No bakers hired. No seamstress making a dress. And Kayden kept you shut away in his hut nearly since you arrived. You've hardly seen the clan. Yet you wish me to believe you betrothed to the man?"

"I am," Mya said, forcing the words out past the tight constriction in her throat. "Ask him, if you don't believe me. He's kept me in the house to protect me. To be near me. Take me home, and we'll talk to him when he arrives."

Lachlan laughed. "No," he said. "I don't think so."

Before she had a chance to protest, he was leaning down, one brawny arm catching her around the waist and pulling her up onto the horse. Mya struggled, but caught as she was with her belly against the horse's shoulders, his arm holding her down, she couldn't get enough leverage. Tears prickled threateningly behind her eyes, but she was not going to cry. Not for him.

Would Kayden even know that she had been taken? She had no way of knowing when he would be returning from town, and when he did, where would he think she had gone? She hadn't left a note. What if he thought she'd changed her mind about marrying him, run away because she decided she wasn't ready?

The thoughts spun around each other, driving her closer to panic.

The jostling of the horse's motion, shoulders knocking against the space between her ribs, forced the air from her lungs, making it impossible to catch her breath. Worse than that was the humiliation of being thrown broadside over the back of a horse like a sack of flour. Like an object. Her cheeks burned with it.

Lachlan's arm moved down, his hand sliding over the curve of her hip. Mya kicked out, but there was nothing to hit. Over her head, he started to laugh. The sound made her stomach threaten to rebel.

Her body ached where the horse's motion jostled it. Mya tried to watch the land around them, to have some idea of where they were going, but the rush of it made her dizzy, and with a jolt of empty despair she realized it was likely Kayden wouldn't know where to find her. She was being taken farther and farther from the man she loved, and he had no idea she was even gone.

Chapter 18

The horse slowed, and then stopped. Lachlan finally loosened his tight hold on her and Mya was able to lift her head. Before them, there was a house sitting at the top of the hill, much larger than Kayden's. A barn stood behind it, cows milling around in the pen out front.

He'd taken her to his home.

Lachlan slid off the horse, dragging her with him. His big hand was curled around her upper arm tight enough to bruise. Mya went with the yank, stumbling on almost numb legs as he dragged her toward the house.

Surprise, Kayden had said when he was teaching her how to use a sword. She wouldn't be able to fight a larger, more skilled opponent if he knew it was coming. But Lachlan didn't expect her to be able to use a weapon.

She stumbled again, this time planned, and as he turned toward her she yanked the sword on its belt from his sheath, bringing it down on his arm.

He dropped her with a curse. Mya caught her skirt in one hand and ran for the track they'd come down, the sword clutched in her fist. Behind her, she heard Lachlan yell. She didn't turn to look.

She should have taken the horse, she realized too late. He could jump on the animal's back and come after her. But if she'd stopped to swing herself into the saddle, he might have caught her before she ever left. So she forgot about the horse, and ran.

There were trees up ahead, and she made for them. If she was lucky, the undergrowth would be too thick for the horse to follow.

Her breath came fast. Her heart pounded in her chest. Mya ignored the ache in her side and ran on.

Horse's hooves followed behind her. She heard Lachlan swearing, screaming her name. He was getting closer.

Absurdly, Mya suddenly remembered the dream she'd had the night Kayden found her. Running through the trees, sure and fleet-footed, faster than she could ever be in the waking world. But she was not so fast now. Her feet wanted to falter under her.

Ahead, through the trees, Mya thought she caught a glimpse of white. For an instant, the shadows seemed to be the shape of a stag. He lifted his horned head, unperturbed by the scene before him. And then he was gone. Her heart cried out for Kayden.

Mya gained the trees, stumbling in the bracken and last year's fallen branches.

"Bitch!" Lachlan roared behind her. "Get back here or you'll regret it!"

"Lachlan!"

Kayden's voice.

Kayden was here.

Mya nearly sobbed with relief. She stopped running.

That proved to be a mistake.

Mya had thought she would be safe in the forest, but she had only made the fringe of the trees, and the horse had caught up with her. Lachlan grabbed her by her hair, yanking her back.

Despite the pain in her scalp, Mya swung around and stabbed upward, blade cutting through his forearm, scraping sickeningly against bone. He made a sound caught somewhere between a growl and a scream, but the hand in her hair only tightened.

"Mya!" Kayden called from the tree line.

She looked up as he swung down from his horse, racing across the space that still separated them.

"You take your hands off her, Lachlan!"

Lachlan laughed. "And if I don't? What are you going to do about it, Kayden no-name? You're hardly a member of the clan. Who do you think the laird is going to listen to?"

"The laird," Kayden said, "has already given his blessing to my marriage. And you know as well as I do that the laws of the clan forbid stealing another man's bride."

"Both of you claim marriage, but I've yet to see any proof of this happening."

"I'm not obligated to give you proof, Lachlan," Kayden growled, "But if you insist on it, I've the ring on my person. Now let her go."

Lachlan didn't. Mya pulled against his hold, but when she swung the sword again, he caught her by her wrist and held her still struggling.

Kayden reached them.

He grabbed Lachlan around the arm she'd wounded and *twisted*. Lachlan howled. The hand that had been fisted in her hair let go. The other, however, still held her wrist, and he glared down at Kayden.

"For my own safety, I'm not releasing her until she lets go of my weapon," he hissed.

"Mya," Kayden said, hand on his own sword, ready to defend her.

She dropped the one she was holding, and Lachlan dropped her wrist. Quickly, she took a step back, and then another. Then Kayden's arm was around her, warm and solid, and she was shaking in his embrace.

"Kayden," she gasped, the word catching on a sob.

"I'm here, lovely one," he said, pushing her back behind him and moving away from Lachlan's horse without ever taking his eyes from the man who rode it. "I'm here."

Lachlan spat at the ground in their direction and climbed down from the horse to collect his sword, arm still bleeding in two places where she had connected with the weapon. Kayden pulled her away, not lingering to watch, and Mya went willingly with him.

But Lachlan wasn't done.

He was there, suddenly, swinging his sword, and Kayden dodged out of its path, pulling his own blade from its sheath. When Lachlan swung again, Kayden blocked the attack with a ring of metal on metal.

"Lachlan! What are you doing?"

The red-haired man growled. "I've put up with you long enough. Forcing yourself into our clan. Claiming things you've no right to. Drawing the attention of the laird while better men than you, who have been part of the clan for longer, are passed over."

He attacked again, and again Kayden blocked. They circled around each other, feinting and slashing, stabbing. Mya watched with her hand pressed to her mouth. Kayden could be hurt. He could be killed. She sucked in a breath through her teeth and bit back a shout as he stumbled.

Kayden caught himself, and pressed forward. Metal clanged. There was a flurry of motion, swords flashing in the morning light, and then one of them was falling. For an instant, Mya didn't breathe. But the sword was Lachlan's. In the same moment, Kayden stepped into the bigger man's space and hooked an ankle around his leg. Lachlan stumbled and fell, and before he could lift his head Kayden had a sword at his throat.

"You are done," he growled. "You'll not come near Mya. You'll not touch her. Swear it to me."

Lachlan glared up at him. Kayden pressed the sword harder against his neck, digging into his skin.

"Swear it!" he growled.

"Fine!" Lachlan hissed. "Fine. I'll not touch her. Are you satisfied?"

"Not quite. But I'll let it slide. If I ever see you touching her again, I will kill you. I'll do the same if you so much as look at her."

Kayden withdrew the sword and took a step back. When Lachlan didn't rise, he slid the weapon back into its sheath, and turned to hurry back to Mya's side.

"What happened?" he asked as he lifted her onto the horse, glancing over his shoulder to be sure that Lachlan wasn't following.

"I was out for a walk," Mya said, partially wondering why Kayden hadn't simply killed the man. It was wrong, but she still wished him dead for trying to take her. "I—" The word caught in her throat.

Kayden swung up behind her on the horse and nudged him into a canter. With Kayden's chest pressed warm and sturdy against her back, Mya glanced over their shoulders in the direction of Lachlan, who was getting on his horse, turning its head toward the house on the hill and kicking it viciously into motion.

"You went on a walk," Kayden encouraged as they rode away from the house, his arms wrapped around her, supporting her.

"I went on a walk and he was there," Mya said, trying to keep her voice from trembling as she spoke. "He grabbed me, and pulled me onto his horse, and brought me here."

"And the wounds on his arms?"

Mya bit her lip. "I did that," she admitted. "He pulled me off the horse and I acted like I was going to fall, then grabbed his sword from the sheath and attacked him with it."

She wasn't sure what his reaction would be, if he would be angry with her for taking such a risk. To her surprise, he laughed.

"You," he said, "are the best kind of surprise."

"I was only doing what you told me," Mya pointed out.

"You managed to injure a man more than twice your size. Not once, but twice. That is more than many fighters I know would be able to say." Kayden brushed a kiss against the top of her head. "You saw an opening, and you were brave enough to take it. I'm proud of you, my lovely one."

Mya felt her cheeks flush with heat, and her chest fill with pleased warmth. She leaned back into the support of Kayden's chest and felt safe, and loved. Lachlan, and the terror she had felt in his grasp, was already little more than a memory.

As though reading her thoughts, Kayden said, "I'll not let him touch you again." The words were a growl. "Not if I have to kill him to keep his hands off you."

Mya shivered a little at the power in his voice, want pooling in her center despite the recent circumstances. Kayden must have felt it, because he pulled her nearer, the hand that was not on the horse's reins sliding down to her hip.

"Was your trip into town successful?" Mya asked, trying to distract herself from the desire, an almost inaudible hitch in the words.

"For that, you'll just have to wait and see," Kayden said, but there was a smile in his words that gave away the answer.

Riding in front of him once more, the motion of the horse a steady rocking beneath them, Mya remembered the first night. She had been half in a dream, his body warm against the chill of her skin. She remembered the way the desire had risen in her then, lazy curling warmth.

She had always wanted him, she realized. From the moment she first saw him, standing at the edge of that clearing. And now, she had him. The thought made her smile.

"Did you truly seek the blessing of the laird for our marriage?" she asked, suddenly remembering what Kayden had said to Lachlan. That he had asked the laird already.

"I met him in town," Kayden said. "And spoke with him. It is tradition to seek the blessing of the clan's chief before undertaking such a venture as marriage. It's well I thought to do it, or we might have had a harder time with Lachlan."

"Can he truly just do that? Take a woman like an object?"

"No," Kayden bit out. "The laird will not be pleased to hear what he has done. That he knew you are my bride and attempted to lay claim to you anyway, that is not something the laird will allow to pass, cousin or no."

Mya almost asked what the laird would have done for a woman who was not engaged to a member of his clan, but she wasn't sure she wanted to know the answer. She let her head tip back against Kayden's shoulder, and said nothing. In silence, she watched the scenery flow by, growing slowly more familiar as they neared the house overlooking Inverness on the far bank of the firth. She could not remember what home had been before, but as they crested the final rise and came into view of it, she was certain that no home could look quite as inviting as that low stone house with smoke drifting from its chimney on the chill winter air.

They dismounted, Kayden sliding down first and offering a hand to help Mya. She took it, stepping carefully onto solid ground once more. Kayden's hands pulled her close.

The kiss was hard and hungry, verging on desperate. It carried in it all the worry that Kayden hadn't given voice to, the fear for her safety and the joy at her safe return. Mya sank into it with equal fervor, tangling her fingers into his dark hair.

When he withdrew at last, they were both gasping a little.

"Thank you," Mya said. "For coming for me."

Kayden caught her hands in his own, drawing her close. His dark eyes met hers, and she felt her heart beat faster.

"I," he said, voice low and earnest, with the air of a vow, "will always come for you, Mya."

"Always?" she echoed.

One hand moved up, palm cupping her cheek. "*Always*," he said again. "Love finds a way."

She leaned up on her toes, dragging him down to her with a hand on the back of his neck, and kissed him until both of them were more than a little weak in the knees. He was everything she hadn't known she needed. Like a man from a dream too good to be true, and for a moment she was afraid that he couldn't be real, that nothing as perfect as what they shared between them could exist.

But he was there in front of her, real and solid, and he was hers. And whatever had gone before, whatever she had lost, she felt, somehow, that she had woken in that clearing for a reason. It was fate that Kayden had found her there, or destiny. Because they belonged together. The truth of that resonated through her bones, filled her with bubbling joy at the touch of his hand. She had him, and he had her.

What more could she possibly want?

Chapter 19

She could, Mya decided after a moment's thought, want another kiss. Kayden drew back, and she chased his mouth, coaxing him into it, long and slow. He curled a hand around her hipbone and dragged her closer, holding her against him. Her arms slid around his neck and her fingers intercrossed. There was hardly space for air between their bodies.

Mya could have gone on kissing him forever. The world faded away around them, until nothing but Kayden existed. Nothing, that was, except him and the horse, who abruptly reminded them of that fact by sticking his head between them. They broke apart.

"I have to put the horse away," Kayden said, warm laughter in his voice as he tried to disentangle himself from her.

The horse butted his head against her shoulder, and Mya reached up to stroke the silky-soft fur of his nose. He pressed into the touch, but only for a moment, before he started nosing at her, searching for treats.

"Your horse is just a bit greedy, I think," she pointed out.

He grinned at her. "Not at all. He's just friendly."

"A little too friendly." Mya giggled when the horse's nose nearly went down her blouse. "Go take care of him before he expires from lack of proper spoiling."

Laughing, Kayden leaned in and stole another brief kiss, then turned and headed for the stable, leading the horse, who trotted happily after him. Mya shook her head, a smile on her lips, and leaned against the frame of the door to wait for him, looking out over the hills.

If Kayden had been just a few minutes later to her rescue, what would she have done?

It was true she'd had the sword and Lachlan hadn't, but she'd only trained a few weeks with it. He was a warrior of the clan, and far bigger than she was. The memory of him looming over her made her stomach twist. She wished suddenly that she had gone to the barn with Kayden. Standing alone on the gray landscape was too much like that moment, and she found herself subconsciously listening for hoof beats. Would Lachlan try again? Her breath came shallow and too fast. Kayden had rescued her, this time, but what if there was a next time? What if next time he couldn't?

"Mya."

There were big hands on her shoulders and Mya startled back against the closed door before she realized that they were Kayden's hands, that Kayden was looking down at her with his eyebrows furrowed, concern in his expression.

"Mya? Are you well?"

"Yes," she said, throwing her arms around him and burying her face against his shoulder. "Yes. I'm sorry. I'm fine."

His hand slid gently through her hair. "You do not seem fine, lass."

"I was just..." Mya leaned into the touch. "I was just thinking what might have happened, if you hadn't arrived when you did."

"That doesn't matter," Kayden said. "What might have happened? It did not. And it's never going to. Don't think on it, lovely one. Don't give him any more of yourself. He's not worth it."

Her arms tightened around him, and for a moment they just stood there, wrapped in each other's embrace, breathing together. Slowly, she lifted her head. "You're right," she said. "It didn't happen. I stopped him."

Kayden grinned at her. "You stopped him with his own sword," he said. "That's utterly amazing."

His mouth found hers, and want rushed through her. They were alive. They were together. Suddenly, she wanted nothing more than to feel him against her.

When the kiss broke, she dragged him down into another one, her hand tangled in his hair. He groaned and pulled her to him, his arms wrapping tight around her and his hips rolling once against hers, making them both gasp. They broke apart for air.

"If you keep kissing me like that, we won't make it to a bed," Kayden warned in a low voice, trying to gain control of his breathing.

"Maybe I don't want to make it to a bed," she answered, giving him a saucy grin, her cheeks flushed and her hips shifting forward to press against his.

His eyes darkened, and his breath caught. His hands curled a little tighter around her hips. Mya took advantage of his stunned silence and slid her hand deeper into his long, dark hair, dragging his mouth down to hers once more. The second their lips touched, he startled back to life again, his hands sliding down over her ass and lifting her up so she could wrap her legs around his waist. He rocked slowly into her as he pulled her shirt loose from her belt and slid his hands up under it and over her breasts, keeping her pinned to the wall with his circling hips. Mya moaned and arched into the touch.

Kayden cupped her breasts in work-roughened hands and groaned deep in his throat, as though just the weight of them in his palms was enough to bring him pleasure. He roughly tugged the bottom of her shirt up further, huffing when it wouldn't do what he wanted and pulling open buttons, exposing her breasts to the cool air of the room, her nipples already hard and aching. He lowered his head from her mouth and brushed his lips against her collarbone, then lower, planting wet, open-mouthed kisses everywhere. He pulled each of her nipples into his warm mouth, teasing them with his tongue, gently nipping and sucking at them. Mya's back arched and she whimpered, wanting more. Needing his touch.

Kayden abandoned her nipples, then, and roughly grabbed her hands, pinning them above her head against the wall. Mya gasped in surprise and want, pleasure shivering along her spine. There was something about being manhandled, about the way his strong hands could place her exactly where he wanted her, that made her ache with want for him. He held both of her wrists there with one hand as he returned to his licking, kissing, and biting, slow this time, and teasing. Her arms strained against his tight hold, trying to work free and touch him: clutch his hair, squeeze his biceps. Anything. He was driving her utterly mad. But his grip held, and she could only writhe uselessly, her breath stuttering out of her in staccato bursts.

"Kayden..." she ground out. "Hell's fury. Please."

She twisted her wrists sharply, and perhaps his grip had loosened, because she managed to slip a hand out of his grasp. It dropped down to slide through his hair, fingers curling tight enough to pull when his teeth closed gently on her nipple. Kayden, to her disappointment, didn't allow it to go on. He gently unwrapped her legs from his waist and set her on the ground, making sure she had her feet before his supporting hands left her hips. Stealing a kiss from her lips, he followed it with another to her jaw, her throat. He pulled the unbuttoned shirt off and made his way lower, leaving a trail of hot, open-mouthed kisses down her stomach to the waistline of her skirt.

As he went, he sank slowly to his knees and ran his hands down her hips, along her thighs, molding the fabric of the skirt to her body. When he reached the hem, still damp from walking in the hills, he began slowly pushing it back up, thumbs stroking up the insides of her legs with a rough slide that made new heat wake in her core. He reached up, then, suddenly, and unfastened the belt, letting the skirt and arisaid fall. Mya stood still, legs shaking as he began to plant gentle kisses against her inner thighs, nudging one of her knees to step sideways so that she spread her legs. Standing before him, naked and spread open, she felt almost on display. It might have made her nervous, but when he looked up there was nothing but desire in his dark eyes. Nothing but admiration. She felt, under that gaze, like an incomparable beauty. Like a goddess.

Mya was breathing fast and shallow. His eyes on her and the giddy relief of having escaped Lachlan's plans for her were intoxicating. She felt almost dizzy with want.

His hands moved up, curving over her buttocks. Her breath caught in her throat. His nose nudged against her, his lips brushing a barely there kiss over her center, and Mya's hips bucked before she could pull herself back. She looked down to find him looking straight into her eyes as he stroked a finger over her, then two. It was a teasing touch, hardly enough to be what she wanted. He leaned in, then, flattening his tongue and pressing it up against her clit. Her head dropped back against the wall and her fingers scrabbled uselessly at the rock. Another lick. At the contact, her knees buckled and he easily caught her, lifting her thighs up so they rested on his shoulders and she was suspended against the wall. And then he buried his face in her sex and gave her what she needed.

Mya abandoned all restraint, moaning and rocking into his mouth, gasping his name. Her hands found his hair and tangled in it. She felt the hum of Kayden moaning into her when she writhed, crying out with the pleasure of it, and he quickened his pace, alternating between teasing her entrance and flicking his tongue relentlessly over her clit. One of her hands found its way up to her breast, cupping it and tugging at her nipple the way that he would. Pleasure slid down her spine to her core as her orgasm built, drawing her tense and tight. The motion of her hips lost its smooth rhythm, and Kayden's fingers dug into her thighs, holding her in place as he dragged his tongue up the length of her, pressing down hard on her clit. It was all she needed. Mya went over the edge with a cry, pleasure bursting like stars under her skin and behind her eyelids.

She was grinning when she opened her eyes. The muscles in her legs twitched with aftershocks, and her chest heaved with her breath. An easy, satisfied smile curled its way across her face, and she looked down to find Kayden watching her, his eyes dark with want.

"Damn, Mya," he murmured. "You're so beautiful."

After all they had just done, those words, of all things, made her cheeks heat, pink flushing along the curve of the bone.

"Come here, Highlander," she said, giving his hair a little tug.

He gently set her down, making sure her feet found the floor, and stood up. His hands curled around her hips and held her. Their eyes met, and for a moment they didn't move, lost in each other's gaze, breathing in each other's nearness. Mya's laughter had ebbed away.

Kayden tipped his head down, then, and met her lips with his own. His hands slid over her jaw, down her neck. The kiss, though it was tame compared to others they had just shared, languid and gentle, made Mya's stomach flip and heart jolt. He touched her like she was something precious, the most beautiful thing he had ever seen. It made her feel like her chest was filling up with buzzing light. It made her feel like she was floating, as though if she weren't caught between Kayden's body and the wall she could have drifted away on the wind. She deepened the kiss, pressing closer, and felt the hard length of him through the fabric that separated them.

"Kayden," she murmured quietly into his mouth. He hummed in response. She ran her hands down his chest and stomach, tracing the lines of the muscles there contentedly, skimming her fingers gently over the contours of his body. He sighed into the space between them and she breathed it in, sharing his breath. As his hips began to move, rocking gently into hers, she slid her hands down further still to the belt that held up the trousers he wore for riding. He gasped and she took the opportunity to take his exposed bottom lip in between her teeth, nipping gently, then soothing the slight sting with a flick of her tongue. Her fingers opened the belt and shoved the pants down his legs.

"Mya," he gasped. "You can wait a moment if you—"

She cut him off with a hand wrapped around his length, stroking him slowly. The words fell apart in his mouth.

"No," she said, giving him a wicked smile. "I want you. Now. I need to feel you inside me."

"You don't have to ask twice." He smirked at her, his hands curling again around her thighs to lift her up against the wall. Mya gasped. He held her as though she weighed nothing.

She slipped her hand down in between them to wrap her fingers around him, teasing him, stroking the sensitive tip. Kayden shuddered and returned the favor, rubbing his fingers over the lips of her sex where she was wet and wanting. The heel of his palm teased her clit as he slipped a finger inside her, and then a second one, testing her readiness.

The sensation of his fingers inside her, stroking against the places he knew made her helpless with pleasure, pulled a wanton moan from her, and Mya felt Kayden's hips jump against hers. He pulled back, fingers slipping from her, and she sighed at the loss before she felt him shift, pressing against her.

"Yes," she breathed. "Now, Kayden."

He lined himself up and pressed his forehead against hers, his eyes rolling back as he rocked up, burying himself inside her. He stayed there for a moment, eyes closed like he was trying to keep himself under control, like if he moved he might spill there and then. It made her burn with heat. Watching that, seeing Kayden trembling against her, so aroused by her nearness that he almost could not hold himself back, it was enough to make any woman wild with desire. She wiggled her hips impatiently, desperate for the friction. He groaned and finally began to move.

They were rocking together, Mya rolling her hips down to meet every thrust, noises spilling from them both. He caught her lips with his again, drinking down the moans that escaped her lips. They chased the pleasure, reaching for the edge together.

"Mya," he growled. "I can't...not much longer..."

He would have touched her, then, if they had shared a bed, making certain she found her pleasure with his. But he had no hands free, and so Mya reached down between their bodies and stroked her fingers over her clit, rubbing it in tight, small circles. Kayden looked down at her hand and made a sound she had never heard before, a groan wrenched from somewhere deep inside him, like he had never seen anything so arousing. She moaned again against his mouth as she neared the edge, everything in her pulling tight once more. She could feel Kayden close, ready to follow her over. Another thrust, another stroke of her fingers. She fell.

Her back arched and her hips undulated against his, her fingers abandoning her clit as she rode out her orgasm on the friction of his hips. He kissed her, hard and a little clumsy, and followed her over the edge with a low growl of her name. The world washed itself white with pleasure.

Mya felt Kayden's head droop against her shoulder and she pressed her lips against his neck. She felt an amazed laugh bubbling up inside her again, her body shaking and a smile on her face. But even as the laugh spilled out, her eyes welled with tears, and suddenly they were falling, tracing the curves of her smile. She tasted them, salty and burning on her tongue. A sob choked out of her throat.

Kayden lifted his head, concern written across his face. One hand lifted, and his thumb brushed the tears carefully from her cheeks.

"Mya?" His voice was soft. "Are you well? Have I hurt you?"

She shook her head. No, he hadn't hurt her. The words caught behind her teeth. She swallowed a sob, and tried again.

"No. Heaven's no. You didn't hurt me. I—" Her voice faltered. "It's just..."

"What is it, beloved?" His fingers tucked her hair behind her ear. "It's just...what?"

"Just the emotion from the day," she managed. "So much happened. I'm just so grateful to be here with you. So happy." Another sob escaped. "I—" She started crying in earnest.

Gently, as though she might fall to pieces under his touch, Kayden withdrew himself from her and gathered her into his arms, carrying her over to the fur in front of the fire and laying her down on its softness. He wrapped himself around her from behind. Mya reached for the blanket, pulling it up over them both, and rolled so that she faced him, burying her face against his shoulder. His hand stroked her hair.

Gradually, the crying slowed, and then stopped. Mya lifted her head, and tried to smile. It was a little watery, but she managed. "Thank you, lover," she said. "I'm sorry I dissolved into tears, just then. It wasn't a comment on your sexual prowess, I assure you."

Kayden laughed, and she felt it rumble through his chest under her hand. "I didn't think it was. I only wished to make sure that you weren't hurt."

"No." Mya took a deep breath, letting it out again slowly, and shook her head. "I'm fine. Better than fine. I'm so ecstatically happy I really don't know where to start."

"Start with this, then," Kayden said. "You are mine. And I've something for you, lass."

He slipped out from under the blanket for a moment, only to return with his sporran.

"Mya," he said, pulling a slim gold band from the pouch. "Will you wear this for me?"

"Do you even need to ask?" she answered.

He took her hand in his own, warm and calloused, and Mya watched him slide the ring down her finger, her heart fluttering in her chest. When he raised his head, she flung herself into his lap, her arms around his neck, and kissed him with a fervor that had his hands curling tight around her waist even as he laughed against her mouth. Mya kissed him silent.

They fell apart, breathless, and she sank back to the fur, looking up at him in the firelight. Outside, the wind was picking up, howling into a winter storm, but there in front of the fire it was warm. The door shut out the night. It was only the two of them, wrapped up in each other. Wrapped up in love.

It was a perfect moment. Mya smiled. The best, she was sure, still lay ahead.

She fell asleep, wrapped in her Highlander's arms, and dreamed of running under a blue and cloudless sky, his warm presence at her side.

Epilogue

Winter passed, and spring unfurled its banner over the Highlands. Kayden took Mya hunting.

He had gone on teaching her the sword as the winter stretched out long, had watched as she gained skill with the bow and began her own hunts. When she brought down her first rabbit, they held a private celebration, and afterward fell into bed together, falling into exhausted, blissful sleep only when the night had turned toward morning.

She had gone with him more often into the bustling little town of Inverness. Had spent more time with the other members of the clan, particularly the women. Not all of them had been as quick to accept her as Seonaid and Caoimhe, but they had come to it eventually, despite her indiscretions. In truth, she could no longer imagine life without the others. Without Kayden. The Highlands, even beyond their own little stretch of land, had begun to feel like home.

If there was a family out there somewhere looking for her, Mya had not heard from them. She did not think, anymore, that she needed to. With Kayden, she had all the family she needed, and all the love she required. They had their little house on the hill; that was enough. If her memories never returned, she would be content without them. She had, after all, so many new memories to make.

Memories like the one of walking beside him, her bow on her back, through the heather. The sun picked out sparks of bronze in his dark hair, and set her own aflame with red-gold light. And he was laughing.

Mya loved his laugh, deep and uninhibited. It rumbled through his chest and out into the clear spring air, filling her ears with the sound of his happiness. She smiled.

Overhead, the sky was blue and delicate as an eggshell, empty of clouds. The beech trees were unfurling their pale green leaves. Beneath their shade, bluebells rolled out underfoot, carpeting the forest floor in violet and sapphire. The scent of them, sweet and cool, filled the air. Mya stepped carefully, not wanting to crush the delicate flowers underfoot.

"There," Kayden whispered suddenly.

He had grown quiet in recent moments, his focus on the hunt. Now, he leaned forward, directing her attention to a flicker of movement in the trees. She saw it, and nodded.

"You go around. To the left. I'll go to the right. Don't go all the way behind him, though; the wind is coming from the north, and if you get upwind you'll spook him."

Mya had noted the direction of the wind even as Kayden had, but she only nodded, content to follow his direction in this. He was the experienced hunter. Leaning in to steal a quick, chaste kiss, she then turned and made her way through the trees, moving slowly and keeping low.

In the months since she had bagged her first rabbit, Kayden had taken her on other hunts, but she had never hunted a deer with him before. She had always been a little wary of that, remembering the night they had met and the stag he had almost brought down. But she would have to learn how to hunt bigger game, if they wanted to survive the winters. Their family would grow, one day, and with more than just the two of them, they would need more than a few rabbits.

It wasn't something they had spoken much about. Children. But Mya knew that Kayden wanted them. She had seen the longing way he looked at the little ones in Inverness. Once or twice, he had stopped to play with some of the older ones, tossing a ball back and forth, their laughter igniting his own. He would be a good father. A protector and a provider. He would love his children.

Mya turned to look ahead, her eyes seeking the stag they had glimpsed through the beech trunks. Her heart skipped a beat. It was the same stag who had stood over her the night she woke in the clearing.

Kayden, she was sure, would tell her she was being ridiculous, that all stags looked alike. But it was not that. Mya slid her bow into its place on her back, and stepped out of the trees into the glade.

The stag, grazing under the spreading branches of an oak at the edge of the tree line, lifted his head. Mya startled, almost losing her footing. He was white. The stag was the same. He did not flee from the sight of her, only stood as he had that night months ago, watching.

Slowly, so slowly, Mya approached him. She hardly noticed that Kayden was not yet in his place, though he should have been. Her entire attention was fixed on the creature before her.

He snorted, huffing a breath through his nose, and watched her come nearer. She was almost within arm's length, and her heart pounded. Her hand almost trembled. The stag watched her with wide eyes. His nostrils flared, and he too trembled, but he did not run. Barely daring to breathe, Mya reached out and laid a hand on his shoulder.

He hair was not coarse, as she might have expected. The hair under her hand was short and surprisingly soft, sleek and slippery beneath her fingers as she stroked her palm over the curve of his back. He watched her with his head lifted high, still as a statue beneath the touch. Mya breathed in, and out again. Her thoughts flickered.

For a moment, the barest fraction of an instant, she thought she saw something else. Some*where* else. The mountain rock rose before her, and at her side—

The image shimmered, and was gone. She couldn't see the one who'd walked beside her.

A room, greater on its own than the house she shared with Kayden, lit with golden light. A hand, held out to her. She followed it, up an arm clothed in white. But the picture was gone again. In its place, there was only the forest and bluebells, and Kayden standing at the edge of the clearing, staring. For a moment, Mya was disoriented by the change, and the world spun dizzily. What had those been, those pictures? Were they memories? And why had she recalled them there, standing in the forest beside the stag?

There was, of course, no one to answer. If they had been memories, she didn't know what called them up. Did not know what connected them. They had meant nothing to her.

Mya dropped her hand from the deer's flank. She stepped forward, already opening her mouth to speak, to explain to Kayden that it was the same stag, though he must know that he could not kill it.

He had an arrow to the string.

In frozen horror, Mya watched his arm draw back, his shoulders shift as he took his aim. The stag did not move.

"Go!" She snapped, rounding on it.

It watched her with dark eyes, and did not go.

The arrow twanged from the bow. She heard it cut through the air with a whistle. Saw Kayden's arm drop. A cry of denial burst from her lips. It did not, of course, stop the arrow. Her stag did not move. The world slowed, and she knew, in that instant, what she must do.

She flung herself forward, into the arrow's path. It hit. Pain shocked through her like lightning, burning along her spine, fire in her veins. The fall knocked the breath from her. She saw the stag run, then, finally. Slowly, she lifted a shaking hand to her shoulder. It came away wet with blood.

The last thing she heard as the world went dark was Kayden, screaming her name.

THE END
Victorian Bride

** Sneak peek included after this of book 2! **

Victorian Bride: Moment in Time #2

Remember enough of the past... You may be able to control the future.

She shouldn't be here... She doesn't even know how she got here.

There is always the dream. Mya can't recall all the details, but it wakes her up at night in a cold sweat with fear sending her heart racing.

Mya wakes in a bed she doesn't recognize, in a house she doesn't know. A woman tells her that they found her in their fields and have been taking care of her. As she gazes out the window, she sees a stag. A brilliant beast, white fur and strong, large antlers.

She also finds a scar on her shoulder that she doesn't remember getting.

A grown woman with no memory, no family, no money.

Kayden McGregor, a Scotsman who seems more a Highlander, owns an estate near where she is staying. When they meet, there is a fire between the two of them—one that is impossible to tell if it's furry or passion.

She resents him. He can't bare to look at her. Or stop himself from staring when Mya pretends not to notice. Trapped, and yet somehow destined to be together.

"You were made to be with me, as I was made to love you. No moment in time can take that away from us."

** Chapter Sampler of Book 2 included **

A Moment in Time Series

Highlander's Bride
Book 1
Victorian Bride
Book 2
Modern Day Bride
Book 3
A Royal Bride
Book 4
Forever the Bride
Book 5

Victorian Bride

Moment in Time: Book #2

By Lexy Timms

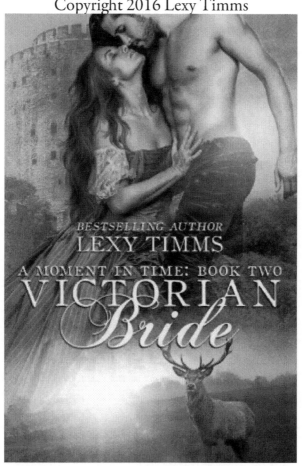

Prologue

Mya ran.

Behind her ribs she could feel the beat of her heart, steady and strong. Her legs pumped, carrying her, swift and easy. The sensation of air flowing over her skin and filling her lungs made her light. Beside her, she could feel another presence, matching her stride. They ran for the joy of it, just because they could, and it filled her up, overflowing in her chest. She bounded over a rock, and he jumped at her side.

Her footing faltered.

Mya stumbled. Something in her body shifted, and her feet became clumsy. Her legs would not obey her commands. The world looked strange around her, seen through eyes that were unfamiliar. She managed to catch herself before falling. It took a moment but she was able to start moving again.

Overhead, thunder crashed, unrolling itself across the clouds with a deep, displeased rumble. Lightning forked down, burning the skeletons of trees across the backs of her eyelids in silhouette. Her companion was gone. He hadn't stumbled. He'd run ahead, and in the darkness she had lost him. She ran on alone, because she had to. Fear drove her forward. There was no time, and she could not remember what she searched for.

Rain fell, sharp as needles. It pricked against her skin and chilled her through. To her left, she could hear the sound of surf falling against shoreline, violent and ragged as the wind that drove it. She shivered, and pushed her stumbling legs forward. Wet hair tumbled into her eyes and clung to her cheeks, obstructing her vision. She reached up to push it back.

Thunder boomed, and the earth split. The ground went out from under her feet.

Mya fell.

There was nothing for her grasping hands to catch. Only emptiness beneath her, and pain. Stabbing. Tearing. Pain that ripped through her chest and left her gasping in shock, struggling to breathe. Worse than anything she'd ever experienced. Enough pain to tear a heart. It burned along her veins.

A scream forced its way up from the depths of her, but no sound escaped, all the air gone from her lungs, her throat tight.

The pain dragged her up toward the light.

She woke.

Chapter 1

Mya came slowly up from the depths of unconsciousness.

Her first awareness was of quiet. Her ears rang with echoes of thunder she didn't remember. She let her senses roam outward, trying to determine her position without opening her eyes. There was something soft beneath her. A bed, maybe. The warmth of a heavy blanket covered her.

She took a deep breath, smelling clean linen, and the faint scent of cooking drifting into the room from somewhere else. For a moment, she simply lay still, basking in the peace of it. That didn't last long.

There was something whispering at the back of her mind. A worry that she couldn't quite put a name to. When she tried to reach for it, the warning slid further from her reach. The last vestiges of a dream, maybe, lingering at the edges of her thoughts before the daylight melted it away completely. It was not enough to aid her, in any case. Mya shook off the concern and opened her eyes to discover her surroundings.

The room wasn't what she had expected. Though what, exactly, she had thought it would be, she couldn't have explained. Smaller, maybe. Some part of her had thought it would be... Not this. She couldn't pinpoint more than that.

It was spacious, papered in cream and sky blue, and paneled in wood that gleamed the color of honey in the light spilling through the windows. A chest of drawers in the same wood sat against one wall, topped with a tall oval mirror. Next to the bed was a cabinet with a washbasin and pitcher sitting atop it. A pair of pastel pink chairs faced each other in front of the high arched windows, a little table between them. Through the glass, Mya could see a sloping yard set here and there with trees, and behind it purple hills rising up toward a blue and cloudless sky.

Mya didn't recognize it.

How had she arrived there? She tried to think back, to trace memories that might have led to the bed she was lying in, but there was nothing. Just blankness. Emptiness. It was as though all the time before that moment when she first returned to awareness had never existed at all.

She knew her name, and the names of the things around her, but she could not remember where she'd learned them. Or when. It was a disconcerting realization.

"Oh. My."

The voice from the door startled her, and Mya levered herself upright on one elbow, turning to see who spoke. Or, at least, she attempted to. The motion sent a jolt of pain through her shoulder that had her collapsing back to the mattress with a gasp, panting for breath.

"You ought not to move, dear," the voice that had spoken before said, low and worried, just as its owner bustled into Mya's view.

She was tall, clad in a gown patterned with sprays of pale green leaves and belted at her waist. As she reached Mya, she laid a hand on her forehead, tutting at whatever she discovered there.

"You are meant to be resting," she said as she turned to the basin sitting beside the bed and wrung water from the cloth sitting in it. "Young Lord McGregor found you in our back field, badly injured. It was quite uncertain for a time whether you would wake at all. Lottie was quite firm in her belief that you would, but even Doctor MacAslan had his doubts in the first days of your stay with us."

She was, Mya thought, rather pretty, perhaps a few years older than Mya herself, her pale hair touched with red. She laid the damp cloth over Mya's forehead, and stroked her hair gently back from her face so it would not catch.

"I need to take a look at your shoulder," she went on while Mya was still trying to process everything she had just learned. "If it will not trouble you for me to do so?"

Mutely, still not sure what to say, Mya shook her head. The woman folded back the blanket that covered her, revealing the nightgown she wore, which was partially unbuttoned to allow access to her shoulder.

"It has not begun to bleed again, I think," the woman said, when she had tugged the nightgown gently out of the way to check the bandage. "The doctor did wish me to tell you, though, if you woke while he was gone, to take care in using that arm. You have healing yet to do."

It occurred to her, abruptly, that the woman had spoken of days.

"How long have I been here?" she asked, the voice leaving her throat rough with disuse. She timidly tried to clear it.

"Three days," the woman answered. "We thought it best to keep you with us while you were unconscious, as we had no way of knowing who your family might be, and you were comfortably set up here."

Mya wasn't sure how to say that she had no way of knowing who her family might be either. The woman was looking at her expectantly, as though she awaited some sort of answer to the unspoken question.

"I..." Mya took a breath and let it out again. "I don't remember."

"You do not remember what, dear?"

"The accident. How I was injured. Or... my family." She bit her lip, glancing away from the serious blue eyes studying her. "I don't remember anything before waking up here."

There was a long moment of silence.

Mya was sure if she looked up she'd find the woman staring back at her. She had already watched over her for three days. They surely wouldn't be interested in keeping her around much longer when she couldn't pay rent or offer any useful skills. She wondered if there was protocol for that sort of thing. Would the lady, the doctor and whoever else, tell her where she might find lodging if she couldn't afford it? When she couldn't remember who she was or where she was from? Did she even have something to pay for her care?

"Nothing?" the woman asked finally.

Mya shook her head. "Not a thing," she admitted. "I tried. Everything is just blank. This empty space where memories should be."

"We will speak with the doctor about it." The woman reached out and turned the cloth on Mya's forehead over so the cool side rested against her skin. "And you need not worry about being thrown out, if you fear that. Lottie and I would not put someone out onto the streets with nowhere to go and no memory of her kin."

"You've given enough of your time already," Mya said. "I shouldn't take up more of it."

"Nonsense." When she finally looked up, the woman smiled at her. "We wouldn't hear of you wandering about Inverness with no memory and no money to your name. All that, and the clothes you were wearing when you were found are rightly ruined. You've nothing suitable to wear in public, so you shall just have to stay."

Mya opened her mouth to speak, and shut it again when she was stopped before she could start.

"You will not even think of arguing. I've made up my mind, and there's nothing to be done for it. You will remain here with us until we can find someone who knows where you are meant to be, or else until you have the means to strike out on your own. I will not hear otherwise."

The words were sharp, but Mya could see the smile hiding beneath them, and secretly she was grateful. If she wasn't allowed to argue, she would simply have to stay, and the knowledge that she wouldn't be turned out into the streets of an unfamiliar city was more of a relief than she cared to admit.

"Thank you," she said. "You are so kind—I don' t know how to repay you for such generosity."

Her benefactor lifted one shoulder in a shrug and let it fall again. "You need not, dear. We do what we believe is right, and what is right is aiding a stranger in need."

She stood, then, and picked up a cup from the cabinet top, which she offered to Mya, helping her sit up against the pillows so she could hold the cup in her good hand and drink.

"Now then," the woman said when she had finished drinking and given the cup back. "I imagine that you must be hungry."

Mya hadn't been; she'd hardly had time to think of her stomach with everything else that was going on, but once the words were spoken she realized that she was, in fact, quite hungry. If she had been in bed unconscious for three days, it had been at least that long since she had eaten, and the hollow ache in her stomach made itself painfully apparent.

"Yes," she said, voice a little smoother after the glass of water. "I could stand to eat."

"Lottie should just be sitting down to breakfast. We shall go and join her."

She slipped an arm under Mya's good shoulder again, helping her sit up. Mya swung her feet around to settle against the sleek wood of the floor, and slowly stood upright, using her good arm to catch herself against the mattress when her knees nearly buckled beneath her.

"Slowly," the woman said. "Doctor MacAslan said that you would need to go carefully when you first got out of bed. You've been unconscious for quite some time."

Slowly. Mya stood a little more carefully, the supporting arm still strong around her waist, and found herself steady on her feet.

"I'm not wearing anything suitable for breakfast," she said, looking between her nightgown and the clothing the woman in front of her wore, but her hostess simply shook her head.

"That is hardly of import when you have been so ill. We will find some clothing for you this afternoon, if need be, though in truth I think you will have to rest again. I believe you are close enough to Lottie's size to borrow a few of her things, if necessary, while we have something made up for you."

"I do not have money to—"

The woman waved away the rest of the words. "Lottie and I are blessed with more than enough to get by. If you wish to repay us when you have found work, or your family, we will discuss it, but until then do not even think of the money. As I said, we do what is right."

She slipped her arm through Mya's then, guiding her out into the hall. Mya blinked back the prickling sting of grateful tears, turning toward the windows that lined the passageway.

They looked out on the same neatly trimmed green lawn as the window in the bedroom where she'd woken. At the top of its slope, a stag stood calmly grazing, his hide ivory white in the sun. As though he sensed her eyes on him, he slowly lifted his head, turning his gaze to her. Mya's footsteps faltered, nearly a stumble before the woman beside her caught her weight.

"Are you well?" she asked, worry obvious in her voice.

Mya dragged her gaze from the stag to find her hostess regarding her with concern.

"Fine. Thank you," she answered.

When she turned to look back out the windows, the stag was gone.

Chapter 2

Her guide led Mya not to a room in the house, but out through a set of doors to a veranda on the side of the house opposite the lawn. Its paving stones were warm beneath her bare feet. A breeze, just cool enough to be pleasant, brushed against her cheek, smelling of green things and wildflowers and breakfast. Mya's stomach growled. Beyond the porch, the lawn gave way to a wooded slope rolling down into patchwork fields bordered with hedges. White dots of sheep moved peacefully over them.

Back on the porch, at a cast-iron table much burdened with food, a dark-haired young woman was sitting with a book in one hand, sipping a cup of tea. She rose at the sound of them stepping outside and turned, a smile lighting her face when she saw Mya and her hostess standing there.

She was, Mya couldn't help but notice, almost astonishingly beautiful, with the kind of looks that would have men falling over themselves to court her.

"Eleanora," she said warmly, setting the book she had been reading down and crossing the veranda to take the other woman's free hand in hers. "Good morning." Her gaze moved to Mya. "And to you as well. It is so lovely to see you awake. Please, do come sit and eat with me."

Mya found herself being guided over to the table before she even had time to answer, and placed gently down in a well-cushioned seat.

"Help yourself to anything you like," Eleanora said.

The breakfast spread was, Mya thought, a little overwhelming. There was fruit laid out on china plates, and yogurt in little bowls. Eggs. Buttered toast. Sausages and mushrooms. She hesitated a moment before reaching a little uncertainly for the kettle to pour herself a cup of tea.

"No need to be shy," the dark-haired woman, whom Mya assumed to be the Lottie earlier referenced by Eleanora, said. "Everything here is for sharing."

"Thank you," Mya said, wishing she had some more adequate way of expressing gratitude. "Very much." She poured herself the cup, and after some consideration served herself fruit and toast with some of the mushrooms.

"You ought to try the smoked fish as well," Eleanora suggested, indicating one of the plates. "It is quite good."

Mya added a little of the dish to her collection of food. If she hadn't eaten in a few days, would her stomach handle it? She decided to take her time, even though everything smelled beyond delicious.

"It occurs to me," Lottie said, "that we have not yet introduced ourselves. I'm terribly sorry for our dreadful lapse in manners." She smiled across the table at Mya. "I'm Ottilie, though most everyone calls me Lottie, and this is Eleanora."

She knew her name, like she knew she needed to breath to keep her heart beating. It seemed weird to know that, and only that. "Mya." She frowned. "I'm not sure why I know my name, as at the moment, I don't seem to know anything else." She smiled apologetically. "I cannot tell you how grateful I am for your aid."

Lottie shook her head. "It is hardly trouble. I've more money than I know what to do with." She said the words as though they were some sort of delightful secret. "In truth, I would rather it go toward helping those in need than to frivolities in the shops. I do not need any more gowns."

Eleanora laughed. "You would require a second—or third—closet, I think, if you acquired many more."

There was, Mya noted, no ring on either of their fingers, and she wondered how long they had been sharing the home they were letting her stay in, and where the money that Lottie seemed to think so little of had come from. She didn't ask. Though she could not remember any etiquette lessons she might have learned any more than she could recall the rest of her past, she had enough common sense not to stick her nose into someone else's financial business without an invitation.

"I have a dreadful addiction to nice clothing," Lottie said between dainty bites of egg and fish. "It is undoubtedly a sin of some sort or another."

"Avarice," Eleanora suggested.

Lottie turned to look at her, mock-displeasure on her face. "Are you accusing me of such, then?"

"I would not dream of accusing you, dearest."

Mya smiled down at her plate. They sounded for all the world like an old married couple, though how she knew what an old married couple sounded like, she wasn't entirely sure. The knowledge without source was rather frustrating. For an instant, she thought she could remember sharing such teasing, laughter and... But the memory was gone again almost before it had appeared, and Mya could not recall what she had been thinking of. She sighed and turned her attention back to Lottie and Eleanora, who were engaged in a spirited debate over just how many gowns qualified as too many.

"Mya will be on my side," Lottie said finally.

"I think," Eleanora chuckled, "That you are rather mistaken in that."

Lottie gave her a narrow-eyed look, and turned a sweet smile on Mya. "Tell me, dear, what is your opinion on the matter? How many gowns are too many?"

"I don't think I really have the experience to comment," Mya said, taking a sip of tea.

That earned light laughter from both her hosts.

"Clever," Eleanora said, with a conspiratorial smile for Mya. "A very eloquent answer."

Mya hid a smile in her teacup.

"Doctor MacAslan will be here later in the afternoon to check on you," Lottie said, the laughter faded from her voice and her dark eyes fixed on Mya. "I'm certain he will be quite pleased to see you awake. In the meantime, I thought perhaps we might take a stroll through the gardens, if you would be interested in such a thing? Or if you are tired you are welcome to return to your room, or rest on the couch in my studio, if you wish for someone to talk to."

It was a lovely summer day, the first fluffy clouds just beginning to drift across the blue vault of the sky. "A walk in the gardens sounds wonderful, actually."

Lottie's smile lit up her face. "A garden walk it is, then. Will you be joining us, Eleanora?"

"Unfortunately, I have work to attend to, but perhaps another morning." Eleanora set aside her napkin and rose from her chair, nodding a farewell to each of them in turn before she disappeared back into the house.

"She's a much harder worker than I am," Lottie said, in the tone of one confiding a secret. "Though of course we hardly need the money."

"Does she enjoy it, then?" Mya asked, setting her fork and knife across her plate the way she had seen Eleanora do. Interesting that the two women's focus was money. Why was that?

"Oh. Quite. Writing has always been rather a passion of hers." Lottie too laid her utensils on her plate, though more carelessly than Mya had, and stood. "Shall we?"

Mya got carefully to her feet, leaning a little on the table with her good hand before she straightened up. "Lead on, then."

As Eleanora had, Lottie slipped her arm through Mya's, and they walked together around the corner of the veranda and down a set of wide stone steps into the backyard.

"There is a greenhouse on the other side of the building," Lottie said. "If you would like to visit that later."

She paused, glancing down at Mya's bare feet, clearly visible beneath the hem of her nightgown.

"I forgot to ask you if you would like shoes," she said. "I'm not certain I have any of a size that would fit you, but we could take a look, if you wish to wear them. There may at least be house slippers."

Mya shook her head. She felt more comfortable barefoot. The grass was soft and cool under her feet in the shade of the tree that overhung the porch, and she wanted to feel the earth beneath her. Not the uncomfortable soles of someone else's shoes.

Lottie smiled. "I'm not wearing any either," she admitted. "I rather hate the things, if I am honest. And there is hardly anyone to care here at the manor. The servants undoubtedly gossip about it, but it will be just one more eccentricity Lottie Alan has picked up. The general populace love to pretend as though they are scandalized by such things."

"Do you think they aren't?" Mya asked.

They were moving out of the shade and into the sunlight, and she turned her face up toward it, basking in the warmth on her skin.

"I think they wish they had the courage to do it themselves. Which sounds arrogant, I suppose, but it is not as though it is an act of valor. Especially here, where I am allowed to do as I please, for the most part, so long as word of the worst offenses against society does not get out."

There was a quirk to her mouth that said the explanation was at least a little exaggerated, though Mya wondered how much of it was a joke, and how much of the joke was truth.

"It's your own property."

"Yes," Lottie agreed. "And since James died and left it to me, I've found that I do not care so much for what others think."

James. Mya didn't ask who he was, despite the way the question was burning on the tip of her tongue.

"I can see you are dying to ask." Lottie laughed. "James is my late husband. We were married quite young, and he didn't live to see our second wedding anniversary." Her expression softened to something almost sad. "He was a good man, despite being English, and left me more than was required of him. Most are not so lucky as I was. He was so sweet. So handsome. So... James."

"Do you think you will remarry?" Mya asked. She wasn't sure if the question was impolite. It just seemed that Lottie was too young to be alone. She had Eleanora, but it wasn't the same.

Lottie gave the question only a moment's thought before she shook her head, the curls of her chignon dancing against the nape of her neck. "No," she said. "It is hardly in a man's favor to wed me now, when I have the right to keep them from meddling with James' property. If they cannot steal my wealth off me, they have much less reason to woo me." She smiled. "And, in truth, I am happy as I am. Eleanora and I get along well here. We are both free to pursue our interests as we please, spend our money as we please, and generally live as we choose. It is not a bad life to live."

"I didn't realize it was so..." Mya wasn't sure what the word she sought was.

"Restrictive?" Lottie suggested as they stepped onto a path of smooth paving stones that wound through a carpet of bright bluebells.

The delicate scent of the flowers filled the air around them, and Mya, breathing it in, felt as though she had walked in such a place before. But she could not recall where, or when. Ahead, a latticework gazebo grew pink climbing roses. Lottie led her to a bench beneath one of the arches and they sat there together, breathing in the heady perfume of the blossoms, deeper and richer than the barely there scent of the bluebells.

"I suppose that is one way to describe it," Lottie said. "Though it does depend somewhat on the man. James was never fond of controlling me. Perhaps he knew how useless it was to try." There, again, was the flash of her smile, bright and amused.

"Did you love him?" Mya asked. She wanted that. The love that could move mountains. That could make time stand still. It was silly to think of that right now. She didn't know who she was or if she already had someone. She might even have a loving husband at a home, waiting anxiously for her. She might have... She sighed. She hoped Lottie had that kind of love with James.

Lottie was silent for longer than Mya would have expected, and she almost regretted asking the question.

"I'm sorry," she started to say. "I—"

"No," Lottie interrupted. "Do not concern yourself. It's not a bad question, only one that is not simple to answer." She looked down at her hands, folded together in her lap. "James and I didn't know each other well before our marriage. We courted, of course, but it was more a business match than a love match. We did, in time, grow fond of each other, and I suppose what we had could be called love, but it was not the romantic ardor I think you meant when you asked."

"I think I was in love," Mya said.

It was a thought that had been building throughout their conversation, making itself impossible to ignore. She did not know quite where it came from, but it was there all the same. Blurting it out to a woman who was still almost a stranger didn't entirely seem like the solution, but Mya couldn't help feeling that the woman sitting beside her would understand.

Lottie turned to look at her, brows raised in question. "What makes you say so?"

It was Mya's turn to be silent, wrestling with her own inability to describe the certainty settled somewhere deep in her chest. Like the phantom ache of another heart beating next to her own. There was meant to be someone beside her.

"I feel it," she said finally. "It's not a satisfactory explanation, I know, but I don't know how to describe it any further."

"You need not." Lottie reached up and plucked a rose from the vine winding its way along the wrought-iron leg of the gazebo. She turned the bloom over in her hands, stroking the soft petals with the tips of her fingers. "Some things simply are. We know them, and we cannot describe them, because the truth of them is deeper than the flimsy construct of words. Perhaps Eleanora could make a better attempt of it, but some things, I think, are not meant to be spoken. It is why I use a paintbrush and not a pen."

Mya thought of the white stag, turning his head to meet her gaze with his great, dark eyes, and the way her chest had filled with something bright and nameless at the sight of it. The stag. She couldn't remember things, but she remembered the handsome beast?

Without memory through which to view the world, too many of the things rattling around inside her had no words to describe them. No context in which to place them.

Perhaps, she thought, Lottie was right. Maybe some things were better left unsaid. Maybe even with her memories, she wouldn't know how to put words to the feelings that welled up in her. She breathed in the peace of the garden, and side by side they sat in companionable silence, neither of them saying anything at all.

Chapter 3

"We can come sit with you when the doctor arrives," Lottie offered as they made their way back up the path to the house. "If you would prefer it. He's a very kind man, and you have nothing to fear from him, but I know how intimidating such encounters can be. You've been... well, out each time he's come."

"I would like that, honestly," Mya admitted.

"One or both of us shall rescue you, then," Lottie promised. "If nothing else, medical checkups are not terribly exciting, and we would not wish you to suffer. Eleanora would be quite put out with me for failing as a hostess." She didn't quite manage to keep a straight face as she said it, a smile playing at the corners of her mouth and her dark eyes glittering with suppressed laughter.

Mya, despite the slight nervousness incited by the mention of the doctor's visit and concern for what it might reveal about her health, found herself giggling. "I believe agreeing to put me up indefinitely for free makes you both incomparable hostesses, purely by virtue of that action."

"Well, for heaven's sake, do not tell Ella that. If she thinks she has to impress you, we'll get to go to more parties."

"Are you telling me that you're using me as an excuse to go shock high society?"

Lottie gave her a wide-eyed innocent look that Mya didn't believe for a minute. "I cannot believe you would accuse me of such a thing."

Mya shook her head, laughing, and then winced at the pain in her shoulder. "I've known you for all of four hours, and I already know better than to trust that expression on your face."

Laughing, Lottie led her up the steps onto the porch. "Ella always falls for it, you know."

"I don't believe Ella does fall for it," Mya retorted. "I think she just indulges you and your whims."

Lottie attempted a wounded expression that dissolved almost instantly into hard laughter. "You," she said, panting to catch her breath, "are entirely too clever for my own good. Do you not know it is rude to call your hostess out on her little self-delusions?"

"I thought we were just discussing your fondness for bending the rules of proper behavior."

The dark-haired woman threw her free hand in the air. "I give up. You have defeated me utterly," she said, chuckling once more.

A disappointingly easy venture, Mya almost said. The words hovered on the tip of her tongue, but she did not speak them. They were, after all, still nearly strangers, and she was a guest in Lottie's home. She had no wish to cross a line that would offend. Instead, she merely smiled. Lottie gave her a look that said she knew what Mya was thinking, or at least that she was thinking something of the sort, but didn't press her to speak the words aloud.

"Unfortunately, as much as I would enjoy remaining here with you and continuing this conversation, I have a letter I must write before the day is out. Do you wish to return to your room, or would you prefer to remain outside?"

"I would like to stay here, I think," Mya decided. "And enjoy the weather."

"An excellent choice." Lottie made certain Mya was steady on her feet before stepping back. "I will send the maid to fetch you when the doctor arrives, and we'll make certain you have company for the visit."

"Thank you. Again. For everything," Mya said, taking a seat on one of the padded benches that sat along the back of the porch. "I'll be here."

Lottie nodded in understanding and went inside, pausing at the door to give Mya a little wave before she hurried off.

At least, Mya thought as she turned her eyes to the landscape below the house, staying here would not be dull.

When the doctor arrived, Mya was very nearly dozing. The maid who came to collect her had to say her name twice to get her attention, and looked a little amused when Mya startled up from the seat, blinking away the lingering sleepy lassitude.

"Doctor MacAslan here to see you, ma'am," she said when Mya had turned to look at her, her startled heart still beating a little too fast in her chest.

"Thank you," Mya said, touching her shoulder gingerly. The maid turned and Mya took a step after her. "Could you show me where I'm meant to meet him, please?"

"Yes, ma'am. If you'll just follow me."

Relieved that she wouldn't be expected to find her way through the still unfamiliar house on her own, Mya followed the maid inside and down the maze of halls to the room where she had woken. Thankfully the maid's guidance probably saved her several wrong turns.

Both Lottie and Eleanora were there already, talking with a gray-haired man in a suit. His doctor's bag sat on top of the cupboard beside the bed with the washbasin. When Mya entered, all three of them turned to look at her. Eleanora, she noted, was wearing a pink rose in her hair, tucked just behind her ear.

"Miss Mya, it is, I presume?" the doctor asked. It wasn't really a question. He knew exactly who she was, considering that he had been treating her for the past three days, but she supposed he hadn't actually known her name.

"Yes... Sir." Mya tacked on the respectful address a little too late to make them believe she had actually planned to use it, but the doctor only smiled. He had the kind of face that was easy to trust, open and honest, with lines at the corners of his eyes that suggested he spent much of his time smiling. Some of the nerves that had returned at the maid's summons settled themselves.

"It is good to see you up and about." Doctor MacAslan directed her as he spoke, beckoning her forward to sit on the edge of the bed while he retrieved a stethoscope from his bag. "It was a bit touch and go for a few days."

He pressed the tube of the stethoscope to her chest and had her breathe, then repeated the procedure at her back. "Your heart seems well enough," he said, leaning in next to examine her eyes. "Are you having any unexplained aches or pains? Any physical trouble?"

"My shoulder hurts," Mya said. "But I think you are aware of that already."

The doctor smiled. "Quite aware. We will take a look at that in a moment."

True to his word, he had her lie back against the pillows and folded the nightgown back to bare her shoulder. Carefully, he loosened the bandage that covered the wound.

Looking down, Mya could see that it had almost healed. Or, at least, it looked that way to her, though to her knowledge she had no medical training. But the wound was entirely closed, only slightly red at its edges. The raised scab that marked it was not entirely pleasant to look at, but she took from Doctor MacAslan's pleased muttering that it was a good sign.

He pressed his fingertips down against the flesh around the mark, and asked her at various times if it hurt. Mya shook her head. It felt a little tender, but there was no sharp pain. When the doctor straightened up, he had a smile on his face.

"You are coming along quite well," he said, packing the tools he had used back into his bag as he spoke. "You ought to still be careful of how you use that arm—vigorous exertion could cause pain or even reopen parts of the wound—but I believe that in time you shall get the full use of the limb back. And in a fortnight or so, the pain should be gone entirely."

"Can she travel?" Lottie asked.

The doctor turned to look at her. "I cannot see why she should not. So long as she does not lift anything too heavy. But a trip into town will hardly be dangerous for her."

"Thank you, Doctor," Mya said, glancing at her caretakers and wondering what they were planning. She'd just woken, and wasn't sure how much energy she'd have, even though she did feel quite rested. It was all strange.

"Don't thank me yet, Miss Mya," he said and winked. "I'm not finished with my examination."

"Oh."

He patted her hand. "Don't be anxious, my dear. I'm here to help."

She gave him a hesitant smile.

He sat in the chair at the desk and pulled out a leather notebook. He pulled out a pen and using the ink on the desk, filled it and wrote a few notes down. "The ladies mentioned that you remember your name is Mya, yes?"

"Yes."

"Do you remember anything else?"

Mya squinted, trying to press the recesses of her mind for some kind of knowledge, but she couldn't pull a memory or fragment from it. "Mya... Boyle," she said suddenly. "Boyle. Mya Boyle."

"Hmmm..." The doctor wrote something down in his notes. "You know your name?"

She nodded.

"Family?"

"I... I don't think so."

Lottie cleared her throat. "She mentioned she felt that she'd been in love before."

"Married?" the doctor asked.

Mya shook her head slowly. "I don't know... I don't think so."

"Father? Mother? Siblings?"

Mya chewed her lip as she tried to remember. Tried to see if there was a feeling inside of her that would tell her she had a mother, or a father. Even a brother or a sister. "I don't know."

"What about where you are from?"

She shrugged, biting her lip to stop the tears that threatened to fill her eyes.

"Your accent is different than this area. It's hard to tell where you are from. Maybe English? Or somewhere in Scotland near the border?" Doctor MacAslan wrote some more things down. "Boyle isn't a unique enough name to give you a territory. It could be Scottish, or even English. It could be a married name which wouldn't help tell us where you are from. We'll have to keep an open mind if there is news that someone is looking for you." He shook his head as he spoke to himself. He straightened suddenly and stood. "Have you had any pain in your head?"

"Like a headache?" She touched her forehead. "There's been a dull ache, but nothing sharp if that is what you are asking."

He nodded and moved close to her. "May I?" he asked and motioned to her head.

"Yes."

Doctor MacAslan pulled the loose bun from her hair and her auburn strands tumbled down, as if happy to be free. He felt along her scalp, checking with gentle, but expert, fingers. "No bumps or bruising. I don't see a blow to the head to indicate there may have been an accident." He stepped back. "You're a lovely girl. I can't see you disappearing unnoticed." He glanced down at her shoulder. "Unless it's for the better. Do you know who did this to you?" He pointed to the bad cut on her shoulder.

Mya shivered. Not from cold but from the realization of what the doctor was thinking. He believed someone had hurt her on purpose. Could that be why she couldn't remember? Maybe he thought she was running away. What if she was? "I don't know what happened." A tear slipped out of the corner of her eye and raced down her cheek.

Eleanora stood and handed her an embroidered handkerchief. She patted Mya's hand. "It's okay, dear. You don't need to figure anything out now. Or ever." She glanced at the doctor as if sending him a warning.

He nodded in understanding. "It may come back to you over time. Maybe in parts, maybe all at once." He shrugged. "Maybe never. Whatever is meant to be..." He turned and closed his notebook and gathered up his things. "I'd like to see you tomorrow again, Miss Bo—Miss Mya."

"No problem." Lottie stood. "We only want Mya to be safe. To be okay."

"Yes. I understand your concern."

Mya watched the three of them, sure there was part of a conversation going on that she was missing. "I'm not married. I'm sure of it," she said suddenly.

They all turned to look at her.

"Of course, dear." Lottie smiled kindly.

The doctor cleared his throat. "I shall drop by one morning soon, then," he said. "It seems you are doing fine. If anything arises, just sent for me. And make certain that there are no complications. No overdoing it." He turned to look at Mya. "You are a very lucky young lady. Such a wound could have easily done more damage than it did."

"I'm glad the damage wasn't much, then," Mya said, thankful the questions were over. "And I appreciate your help with it."

"As I said, it is no trouble at all. It's my job, after all, to look after the people of this town." He gathered up his bag, and tipped his hat to all of them. "Good day, ladies."

"Good day," they echoed.

"Well," Lottie said when he had gone, "that went quite well." She grinned at Mya. "Now that you know you won't drop dead if we let you leave the grounds, would you like to take a day trip with us tomorrow? We are headed to Inverness to do some shopping, and would rather not leave you here alone unless you have a preference for it."

"And if we are to get you some clothes that are not hand-me-downs," Eleanora added, "you will need to be fitted for them."

"That as well. So, what do you say?"

"If you do not mind taking me along," Mya answered. She hated that she had to have them pay for clothes for her. She would find a way to repay them. "I would love to visit the town with you."

Lottie clapped her hands together. "Excellent. We shall make a day of it, then. Shopping, lunch, and perhaps a walk down by the river before we return home in the evening, if you are not too tired."

Mya smiled. "Just you try and keep up."

The coach ride to Inverness from the estate was not a terribly long one, though the roads left a little to be desired. Mya, in a dress of Lottie's and a hat borrowed from Eleanora, leaned back against the seat as well as she could with the hat in the way and tried to ignore the jostling, despite the twinges of pain every bump sent through her shoulder.

When they arrived at the market, the coachman let them off, and Lottie stepped up to Mya's side, slipping an arm through hers as she had for the walk in the garden.

"Let's start here," she said, "and then later visit other parts of the city. The coachman will circle back around so that we can send our purchases with him periodically. Better that than lugging them all over Inverness."

"Just how many things do you intend on purchasing?" Eleanora asked from Lottie's other side, both eyebrows lifted.

Lottie shrugged. "Whatever catches my eye. The dry goods and such are already taken care of, but one never knows what exciting things one might find."

Shopping with Lottie, Mya discovered as they made their leisurely way through the covered market, was exactly what she might have expected. While the other woman had started out at her side, offering the support of an arm or a shoulder, she was quickly distracted, darting off to examine one thing or another almost constantly. Eleanora stepped in to take her place, a fond smile on her face even as she shook her head at Lottie's antics.

"Is she always like that?" Mya asked as they paused at yet another stall, Lottie talking animatedly to the shopkeeper as she turned a statuette over in her hands.

"Or worse," Eleanora said. "I think half of it is for show."

Mya turned away to hide a smile. It seemed she had been right the day before, when she teased Lottie about Eleanora's indulging her. She was fooling precisely no one.

"Though she is genuinely quite excitable, for lack of a better word," the blonde woman added as she and Mya followed Lottie to the next stall. "She takes a great deal more joy in life than most. It is a quality of hers that I rather wish I was better at emulating, however unfashionable it may be."

"That is—" Mya began, just as someone's shoulder knocked roughly against her own, making her stumble against Eleanora. "Excuse me!" she cried sharply, grabbing her injured arm.

The man who had nearly run her over stopped, turning slowly to look at her.

Mya's heart skipped a beat. He was gorgeous. His dark eyes swept over her, and Mya felt a sweet little shudder run down her spine.

"Your apology is accepted," he said.

It took Mya a moment to process the words. Her thoughts were caught on the way his voice sounded, deep and just a little rough, the kind of voice that would make any woman a little weak in the knees. At least, that was, until she caught up with what he had actually said.

"*My* apology?" Her eyebrows arched upward. "You're the one who ran into me."

"Mya," Eleanora whispered, voice so quiet that Mya doubted the man in front of them had even heard the quiet warning in the word.

He looked amused. "Is that so, lass?"

"I don't see how it could be interpreted otherwise."

For a moment, he simply stared at her, silent. A grin broke out across his face. "You are quite an usual specimen of femininity. Has anyone ever told you so?"

"And you are condescending and arrogant, but I suppose many have told you that."

"Mya!" Eleanora gasped beside her.

"Just what kind of scandalizing language are you using on poor Lord McGregor?" Lottie asked, appearing at Mya's elbow. "You've turned Ella completely red."

The man in question didn't seem at all perturbed by Mya. He was, in fact, laughing. Mya's jaw clenched. He was absolutely, insufferably annoying. The name, though, sounded familiar, and she wondered for a fraction of a second if she had known him before, only to remember that the name was one Eleanora had used the day before. Lord McGregor, the man who had found her in the back field. Mya felt her cheeks heat. The man who had likely saved her life. And here she was berating him on a public street. Not that he didn't deserve it.

"I am glad to see your encounter with that arrow doesn't appear to have dulled your spirits any, my lady," Lord McGregor said, bowing politely before straightening quickly.

Mya glanced down and then opened her mouth to answer him, but he was already gone, disappearing into the crowd. She snorted. Of course he had made thoroughly sure he had the last word. It was just the kind of thing a man like that would do.

"I cannot believe you spoke to Lord McGregor that way," Eleanora said, sounding as though she was not sure whether she wanted to be admonishing or impressed.

"Because he rescued me?" Mya asked. "Or because he has a title in front of his name?"

Lottie laughed.

"Both," Eleanora said. "Either."

"I spoke to him that way because he's a condescending ass," Mya pointed out to gasps from both of the other women. "And he completely deserved it. Running into me and then pretending as though I was the person who was in the wrong when he knew full well that it was his fault."

"Maybe he did not know," Lottie suggested. "Men can be rather oblivious."

"I think it's rather hard to be unaware of nearly stepping on a person."

"You would be surprised," Eleanora said, obviously speaking from experience in the matter.

"Either way." Mya shook her head. "I don't like him."

"The man saved your life, and you dislike him because he bumped into you at market." Unlike Eleanora, Lottie didn't sound conflicted. She sounded delighted by the whole thing, as though Mya had done something particularly thrilling.

When she put it that way, it did sound a little ridiculous, but she wasn't going to take the words back. "Yes."

"Living with you is going to be utterly fascinating." Lottie laughed, taking Mya's free arm. "I cannot wait."

They continued together through the market.

Chapter 4

The back field, Mya discovered, was a stretch of land at the foot of the hills that sloped up beyond the house. It was not landscaped the way the rest of the grounds were, only crossed by the tracks deer had worn through the vegetation. Lord McGregor, she was told, often walked there. Though it was Lottie's property, his land adjoined their own, and she did not mind him wandering through.

On a morning three days after their trip to Inverness, and her first encounter with the lord, Mya decided to take a walk there herself. Eleanora and Lottie were each in their studios, working on projects that she had no part in. Both had invited her to sit with them if she liked, but Mya found she was restless after the days of rain that had kept them all inside.

It was curiosity that led her back beyond the garden. Perhaps a rather morbid curiosity, actually. She wanted to see where she had been found before she had woken up in Lottie and Ella's guest room.

Finding the place, however, proved to be nearly impossible. There were no distinctive landmarks in the field beyond the occasional rock sticking up from the grass, and no one had told her any specifics. Some part of her had half expected to find a sign of some sort. Blood, maybe. Or grass trampled in odd patterns. But there was nothing. She had given up and was turning to make her way back to the house when a figure came over the rise ahead of her.

It had to be Lord McGregor, she realized almost instantly. Who else would be walking through Lottie and Eleanor's back field? Or someone as tall and roguishly handsome—even from far away. Mya briefly considered pretending as though she hadn't seen him and going on her way, but he had appeared so close to her that she was fairly certain he wouldn't be fooled. Before she could make a decision either way, he'd raised an arm and called a hello. Mya wondered if he thought she was one of the ladies of the house. It was highly doubtful that he had any interest in apologizing for his behavior at the market. Sighing, she waved back at him.

"Good morning, Miss Mya," he said as soon as he was close enough that he didn't have to shout.

"Lord McGregor," Mya said, only just verging on polite.

"I think, perhaps, we began wrong," he said.

"I wonder why that is," Mya retorted.

He laughed, a short, sharp bark of a laugh. "You are not like any woman I have ever met."

"And yet, you're exactly like every man I have ever met."

That wasn't strictly true. Mya had met a grand total of two men since waking up with no memory, and one of those men was Doctor MacAslan, who had been nothing but gentlemanly. But the sentiment felt real. Mya was sure she had known other men in her previous life, and the chances that at least a few of them had annoyed her as much as Lord McGregor did were high enough to gamble on.

The reply prompted another chuckle, and the sound of it settled low in Mya's belly, warming her from the inside out. Mya ignored the feeling.

"Laughing at me isn't going to convince me otherwise," she pointed out.

His eyebrows lifted. "If you are going to continue to look for things to be displeased with, I'm sure that you will find them, but might I suggest you stop and consider actually hearing what I am saying instead of immediately jumping at my throat?"

The reprimand stung. Mya lifted her chin, arms crossed over her chest, and stared him down. "I've heard what you are saying," she said.

"Yet you continue to behave in such a fashion. I thought I was doing you a favor, giving you an excuse, but I see now that you have none."

"Think what you like."

If he was going to lecture her, she was hardly going to remain and allow him to go on. She spun on her heel and started toward the house.

"Mya!"

She paused. Turned. He was standing closer than she had expected, near enough that she almost imagined she could feel the heat of his body against her own. Her throat felt suddenly tight. Her heart beat faster in her chest. "What?" she asked, forcing the word to come out flat.

"Are you truly going to walk away without so much as a word? I did save your life, you know."

Mya's fingers curled against her palms. "And just what does that have to do with this? Do you feel as though I owe you something for saving me?" she demanded.

"Of course not."

He sounded offended enough that Mya believed him. Still, she wondered what he'd meant by it. "Then why bring it up at all?"

"It is something a normal person might consider a good quality in another," he said, tone dry.

There was something about his voice, just then, the angle of the light on his face... Then it was gone. Mya shook her head. If they had known each other before her accident, he would have mentioned, surely. Unless there was something to be gained by keeping her in the dark. Maybe it wasn't luck that he had found her in the field.

But Mya dismissed the thought as quickly as it had come. Whatever she thought of him, he didn't seem like the sort of man who would be responsible for harming a woman.

"You can take a step back, now," she said.

One corner of his mouth curled upward. "Is that so?"

"It is so."

"And yet," he said, "here I am."

So close, he smelled faintly like ink and old paper, and beneath that of something warm and living. That too seemed strangely familiar, and Mya wondered if she was doomed to always be having flashes of familiarity that never resolved themselves into genuine memory, like a picture not properly developed. She found herself swaying forward, drawn toward him as though he exerted some physical pull.

His head tipped down. For the barest second, they almost touched, breath mingling warm between them.

Mya took a quick step back. Lord McGregor reached out, then stopped. His hand fell back to his side before it had even touched her. They stood for a moment, stock still, staring at each other, and then Mya turned and hurried back toward the house, feeling his eyes on her until the trees cut her off from his view.

END OF SAMPLER
Grab your Copy of Book 2 today!

CELTIC VIKING - SAMPLE

The Heart of the Battle Series
Book 1 – first 3 chapters –
By
Lexy Timms
Copyright 2015 by Lexy Timms

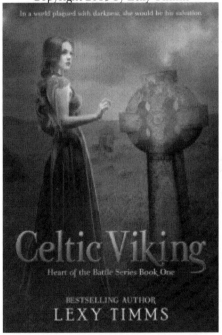

In a world plagued with darkness, she would be his salvation.

No one gave Erik a choice as to whether he would fight or not. Duty to the crown belonged to him, his father's legacy remaining beyond the grave.

Taken by the beauty of the countryside surrounding her, Linzi would do anything to protect her father's land. Britain is under attack and Scotland is next. At a time she should be focused on suitors, the men of her country have gone to war and she's left to stand alone.

Love will become available, but will passion at the touch of the enemy unravel her strong hold first?

** This is NOT Erotica. It's Romance and a love story.

* This is book 1 of a 3 book series *

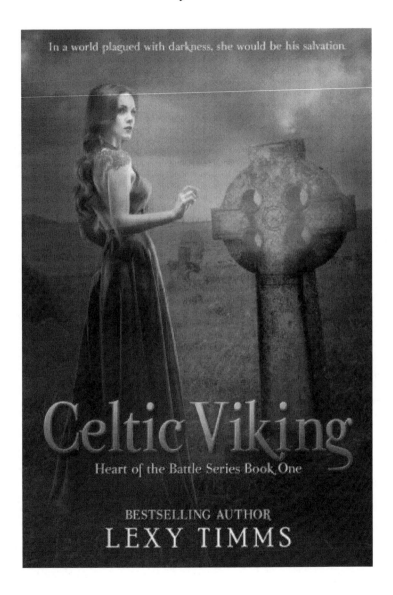

In a world plagued with darkness, she would be his salvation.

Celtic Viking

Heart of the Battle Series Book One

BESTSELLING AUTHOR
LEXY TIMMS

Celtic Viking Chapter 1

872 A.D.

Somewhere in North-East England

The fog hung in the air like a habit belonging to a monk, as if never meant to depart from the body. It was impossible to see more than twenty feet in front, or behind, or anywhere, as a matter of fact. The English could be standing in the middle of the field advancing and neither party would know until they bumped into the Viking army. They'd been awake since dawn, but no one knew what time it was now because the grey clouds would give no hint of where the sun might be. The Vikings were willing to battle and die for this country?

Erik squinted, trying to will his eyes to see through the thick, smoky-grey mist. He imagined the field before him, without the fog, the lush green of the grass and surrounding trees. The land stood perfect for agriculture, not battle. He tried to keep his thoughts in check. At twenty, he should be home in Denmark, maybe farming but definitely married, with a slew of sons and some daughters. Instead, he stood here, in the cold, wet mud of this forsaken country. All his training and education made him an excellent military commander. Except he really just wanted a simple life.

"The men are saying King Halfdan's going to speak with us. He and his guards are coming up the rear of the hill," Marcus spoke, bringing Erik back to the present.

"King Halfdan? Who's calling him that now, cousin?" Erik kept his face blank, though his insides were boiling.

Marcus stood beside him, grinning. "I think 'tis safe to assume the rumor was started by the *king* himself. He plans to lead this Great Heathen Army to battle."

Erik glanced the small distance he could see in front of him and glared. His body stood erect and it took an effort to unclench his jaw. "We are not the Great Heathen Army. It's the Great Danish Army." He bit the inside of his cheek, tasting blood. "Halfdan will not lead us today. He's a man of words," Erik couldn't hold back a snort, "and smart enough not to risk his life to appear heroic in this bloody fog. He'll do as he always does; talk with the commanders, ride amongst the men and then hide behind the dog's tail."

Marcus sucked in his breath. "As much as you don't like the man, I suggest keeping those opinions inside your head, or in the privy of your tent. I know how you feel, cousin, but there are many who disagree."

"The man's a tyrant. His goal is to pillage and conquer as much of England as he can. He has no respect for the people who have toiled to make this land livable. He would prefer to kill and burn them all." He felt Marcus' elbow sharp in his ribs, even through his chain mail. He'd seen the carnage Halfdan had created throughout Europe. Fighting for him was not something he would have chosen.

"Enough! If your father heard you speak –"

"I'm sure he's turning in his grave. I know who my father was and what he wanted of me. I'm here, am I not? I'm still doing his duty, years after his death."

"At least try to enjoy it." Marcus meant well and Erik was fond of his younger cousin. Marcus had risen through the ranks, both on his own accord but also through Erik's guidance.

Erik also knew only he himself had the power to speak his mind, and none of the other commanders would challenge him. He may be one of the youngest leaders of the Vikings, but he'd been fighting and organizing battles alongside his father longer than he could remember. He had earned their respect.

A murmur began through the men. Erik heard the quiet talk before those ones in his line of vision started to form two lines, bending down to one knee. Marcus dropped down, his right hand making a fist and covering his heart. Erik reached to settle his brown Arabian mare, rubbing her nose. He would bow to no leader who called himself a king. Their king was in Denmark, safe in his castle.

Halfdan rode in on a large, white horse. Erik didn't understand the white horse. It stood out in battle, like a target. Maybe it would be best if the man stayed at the rear of today's skirmish. As much as Halfdan loved the kill and fight, he would be marking himself for certain death.

"Erik," Halfdan spoke, his voice raspy and deep.

"Yes... Sire," he added grudgingly. He met Halfdan's unwavering gaze with no fear. Halfdan's blue eyes were full of ice and hatred, even as he spoke among his own men. The two were the same height, but Erik was lean, muscular and all legs. Halfdan was broader shouldered, still fit but age had begun to creep up on him. He hid his slight belly behind the full-length, fur cape.

"Are the men ready to fight?" It sounded like he needed to clear his throat though the man never coughed.

"They are, but visibility's very limited. The fog seems to stay connected to the ground, refusing to dissipate."

Halfdan waved his hand as if swatting a fly. "It will sharpen the men's senses. They'll have to be thorough; any English man partially alive could kill them."

"Yes."

Halfdan glared at Erik and gave him a once over. "You're not afraid to die?"

"No."

"You're fearless. Maybe stupid, but the soldiers follow you and that's good enough for me. Lead the men today, and when the victory is done give me the credit. You'll be rewarded as per your station. Make an example to the rest of the people in this god-forsaken country."

Erik rubbed his mare's neck. The horse snorted and side stepped. Erik forced himself to relax and scratched the horse behind the ears, bringing her back toward him. He said nothing to Halfdan.

"The men may loot the nearby town afterwards. They can help themselves to any valuables, food or cattle." Halfdan turned to go but swung the horse back around. He stared at Erik, a dark smile playing on his lips. "They're welcome to anything, but warn them not to touch the women. Kill them. No touching or gratifying from our men. I'll put a sword to any of the men who do. We will not weaken our Viking blood with this tainted, dirty race. No breeding, or death by my hand."

Erik swallowed, his throat now dry in the moist air. Halfdan's radical beliefs would be impossible to instill in the soldiers. Erik agreed with not touching the women but for entirely different reasons. They were not part of this war for land.

In order to prepare for the fight for the British island, the Vikings needed men, a lot of men. They took prisoners willing to fight and die for their freedom. Some of the men were decent but most fought for themselves, not their king and country.

On top of this, the men had been travelling for weeks with more time spent in preparing for battle. They hadn't seen, let alone been with, a woman in months, and for Halfdan to give them freedom to loot but not touch. Erik would have a bigger battle there than on this field.

"Is it understood?" Halfdan's raspy voice showed his impatience from Erik's lack of response.

"It'll be done, Sire," Marcus spoke, still kneeling on the ground by Erik. "I'll be sure and let the men know, and hold them to their word." He tapped his sword.

"Good. Get this battle done before sundown. I'll watch this one from the hill. This one's easy. Our next battle is critical, and I plan to be fresh to lead the men myself." Halfdan clicked his horse forward. "Erik, I expect a full report after." He turned and rode away, the fog swallowing him up.

Erik stood beside his mare, brushing dried dirt off her coat. He felt Marcus rise beside him and spoke, not bothering to look in his direction. "Do not tell the men they are free to loot but not to touch the women till after the fight. Some of our soldiers are short-witted and it will be enough to distract them from their duty. Let the combat finish and then tell them about their next charge."

"As you wish."

Marcus' curt reply had Erik turn his head in the direction of his second-in-command. Their mothers were sisters, but they looked nothing alike. Marcus had dark, curly hair and brown eyes. Erik's blonde, almost white, hair stood out on the battlefield like Halfdan's new horse.

Erik earned respect and loyalty. He knew his men would never forsake him. Marcus was different. He could command a group of men simply by the threat in his voice. When they played as lads, Erik often believed that Marcus could burn someone alive, simply by speaking.

"Don't be hostile with me, Marcus. I'm still above you."

"Fine, Sire. Might I suggest that you learn to reply to your king then, instead of leaving it to me?" Marcus stalked away toward his horse to prepare.

"He's not my king," muttered Erik. Lifting his chain mail shirt so it lay properly in place, he checked his clothing and gear. He'd sharpened his sword upon rising this morning. His axe had been sharpened the night before and he'd also attached his small, hand-size knife to the belt. It had been the last gift from his father, engraved on the handle by his mother.

He pulled it from his belt and held the handle, gazing at the knotted pattern and the name on the worn wood. He had been named after his father, Erik Jorgen. He could see the care his mother had taken to carve the pattern. He hoped to pass it on one day to a son. Turning it over, he noticed the red and brown stained into the wood. He meticulously cleaned it after each battle, but years of blood and gore had permanently stained the one side and found its way nestled into the carvings. It brought him back to the focus at hand.

The scouts had reported very little the days leading up the battle. They could find little information on the English army, almost like they were invisible. It made these grounds very deadly, for both sides. Erik would have preferred to wait, but Halfdan refused to stall any longer. He wanted to move toward Northumbria and capture the central waterfront shipping town.

Erik glanced around at the other commanders under him. The fog had begun to lift a bit, still thick, but he could now see fifty feet in front of him. It must be getting close to mid-morning. They needed to prepare to advance or all would be wasted another day.

A commander walked by, older than Erik by ten years but still under him.

"Johan, are the men ready to march?"

"Aye, Sire." He stood erect and faced Erik. "When would you begin?"

"Now. There is no need to wait or the day will be lost. Have the archers in front to hold the ranks. Hopefully, the heat from their fire will remove some of the damn fog. We'll advance on foot, and leave the horses until they're needed. Sound the warning. We march in half an hour." Let the bloodbath begin.

Celtic Viking Chapter 2

872 A.D.

In the Southern Tip of Scotland

Linzi stepped out of the house, dashing away from the shouts of her father and brother. She didn't need to hear the argument that never ceased to bore them. If her mother had still been alive, she would have swatted both men on the back of their heads and sent them to their chores. Plenty of work on the small farm always needed to be done. Kenton, her brother, felt the need to join the English army to stop the vicious Vikings, but her father bickered back that he was needed on the land.

Once past the stone wall surrounding the house, she slipped her shoes on and headed west, toward the sunset. Less than a mile walk brought her to the small hill on the edge of their land. Lifting her skirt, she trudged up the hill and sat down on one of the flat stones near the small burial plot. Her mother, grandparents and a baby brother who'd died at birth were buried here. She sat facing west, her back to the graves but near her mother's resting place.

Inhaling and slowly exhaling several long breaths, she let her shoulders drop as she hugged her knees. She watched the pink sky with the amber ball make its way into the horizon.

"Those men will always be boys, Mother." She often spoke to her while she sat here. "They both refuse to listen to me, or each other. Kenton shouts about the need for blood-shedding to save our country and drive off the Vikings. Those horrible beasts kill for pleasure. I see his point in fighting for what is rightfully ours, but I don't want him to join you here on the hill. Let the others fight. When the wolf comes knocking on our door, then Kenton can push his cause."

Having said the words aloud, she no longer felt the anxiety tightening inside of her. She wished she could say the words to her brother. He was two years her elder, nineteen years old, and full of vigor. He needed to find himself a wife to focus his energy. Three girls in town are vying for his attention and Linzi wished he would just choose one and settle down.

Sighing, she stretched her arms out behind her, leaning to let her fingers curl around the soft, green grass. She closed her eyes to enjoy the last bit of warmth the sun had to offer before it disappeared. She needed to head back to the house and finish making supper. Her boys, as she called her father and brother, had been working hard in the fields. Spring had come early this year and with the soil soft from the rain, it had the boys hungry by dinner time. That was probably the reason behind their argument, they needed to eat.

Standing up, she brushed off the grass on her skirt and blew a kiss toward her mother. Making the sign of the cross, she straightened her shoulders and headed down the hill. She thought about what she'd need to say if the argument still lingered. She hoped they'd be finished but knew that was not likely. They were as stubborn as each other.

The house stood silent as she rounded the old stone wall. She smiled to herself as she remembered as a child asking her father how old the wall was. He'd simply replied, old as the hills, old as the hills. It always made her smile when she remembered the look on his face. He'd been so serious, with a slight frown and creased brow. Her mother had shouted from the door that his face would freeze if he kept the look. He had laughed and bounded up the walk to swing her around in his arms. He now had laugh lines around his mouth and forehead to disprove her theory.

Blinking to clear her thoughts, she glanced around the yard and noticed her father out by the horses. He appeared to be giving them a brush down and checking their hooves. Cocking her head slightly, she thought she heard him whistling. He never held a grudge or stayed angry. He fought with intensity, but he could walk away and leave the matter until it needed to be dealt with again. Unlike her brother, who couldn't seem to let things go.

The savory scent of meat cooking brought her attention back to the house. It also brought a rumble to her stomach. She hurried inside and slipped her shoes off by the door. Kenton sat at the table cutting the carrots and peeling a few loose leafs off the sprouts. He tossed them into a black pot every few moments.

"I've had enough of Brussels sprouts. I can't wait to have some peas, or even spinach. The east field is almost ready for seeds. Hopefully by tomorrow afternoon we can start planting." He glanced up and smiled.

"Are you cutting my vegetables as a peace treaty?" Linzi couldn't resist asking.

He shrugged as he tossed the last of the carrots into the pot, splashing some of the water out. "My argument is not with you. I just wish he," Kenton nodded toward the barn, "would allow me to go."

"Father's right. You know he doesn't disagree with your feelings that this land belongs to us. However, rushing out blindly now would only be foolish. The farm needs to be looked after and I need to be fed." Her stomach rumbled again as if to add a voice. She took the pot and turned to put it on the hearth to boil.

"You do need to eat. You're tall and too thin. Even that long red hair of yours looks dull. You're never going to catch the eye of a man if you don't look after yourself."

Linzi swung around, feeling her eyes grow wide. "I think you need to worry about your mate-finding before you start criticizing–" She stopped when she saw the smile on her brother's face and the laughter in his eyes. Seeing an uncut carrot on the counter, she grabbed it and drilled it in his direction. It hit him square in the chest.

"Ow! I take it back." He rubbed his chest, by his heart. "That's going to leave a bruise."

"Good," she laughed.

"Who taught you to have such good aim?" He pushed away from the table and stood. He picked the carrot up and started chewing on it.

"My big brother. I may be thin, but there's muscle hidden under this woman's clothing. Lean and mean." She checked the potatoes and noticed they were done. Grabbing prongs, she set them away from the fire. "Dinner's almost ready. Go wash up and tell Da' that he needs to come in as well." She saw Kenton's mouth tighten into a thin line. "Be nice," she warned, shaking the prongs at him.

He raised his hands in mock surrender, the anger leaving his face. He slipped out the back door.

Linzi heard the water from the pump splash into a bucket. She looked out the window and saw her brother's back facing the house. She slipped into her bedroom and pulled the small chest out of the cupboard in the wash stand. Sitting on the edge of her straw bed, she reached in to take out a sterling, ornate vanity mirror. Her father had bought it for her mother a million Christmas' ago. The silver in the mirror had faded in a few spots, but the beveled glass still showed her reflection. She stared at her brown eyes, the small spray of freckles across her petite nose. She had always liked her lips, similar to her mother's. The full pink never needed rouge or paint on them.

Small benefit, but they made the rest of her face appear pale. The cloudy winter months didn't help to add any color. Hopefully, the next few weeks of planting would help put some color and hide her freckles. She pulled her dark, red hair and angled the mirror to see how dull it really looked. Her brother was right. Maybe later this evening she'd cut a few inches off and give her hair a wash tomorrow after planting. No need to do it tonight as the dirt in the fields would find its way to her face and scalp even with a scarf tied around it.

She did want to look beautiful. She dreamed of catching the eye of a gentleman one day, and hopefully, not too far in the future. She wanted a husband and children. She just didn't know how to find someone she could love like her father had. The boys her age that she knew still seemed young. A few of her brother's friends were nice, but none dared speak much with her, for fear of riling Kenton's infamous temper. Maybe this summer things might change and she'd get a chance to meet someone special.

Low, angry voices and stomping feet coming from the kitchen brought her attention back to the present. She slipped the mirror back into the wooden carved chest and pulled her hair back to tie it into a bun. She ran the few steps down the hall and into the kitchen.

The angry voices turned to weather conversation when she entered. Kenton moved to the window and looked into the early night sky. Linzi rolled her eyes at both of them and went to set plates onto the table. She pushed her brother out of the way as she pulled the meat from the hearth. The mouthwatering smell coming from the beef had the two men sitting quietly at the table in seconds. Tossing potatoes and vegetables onto each plate, she then grabbed the pitcher of ale and set it on the table.

She swatted her brother's hand as she sat down. "We need to bless the food before you make a pig of yourself." She pulled her chair in and said a short prayer of thanks.

They ate in content silence. The hard work from the day and cool evening air seemed to create an enormous appetite in each of them. All the food disappeared into bellies. As Linzi began to clear the table, her father poured each of them a glass of ale. He leaned back in his chair.

"Your friend Darren rode by on horse when I was out in the barn before." Her father looked at Kenton as he spoke.

"What did he want?" Kenton took a long drink from his mug.

"He was heading into town but stopped by to mention that he'd heard that war was breaking out in the south. It seems a large fleet of Vikings is determined to make a stand again."

Linzi's heart fluttered and she spun around to watch her brother. Kenton set his ale down but did not look angry.

"Those beasts are going to massacre the towns down there. Our army is building in the Midlands. They aren't ready to do battle, nor will they be able to reach the south in time." Kenton shook his head, his chestnut brown hair falling forward to cover his eyes.

"Darren said something similar. Looks like their leader, I think his name is Halfman, is hungry for bloodshed."

"Halfman? Ironic that the Vikings would choose a commander by that name."

"Darren said that the man already calls himself the King of England."

"Bah." Linzi couldn't keep her disgust inside. "King of England? Britain has no father. Not from Rome or France or anywhere and this Viking thinks he can step on our land and become our king? Shite!"

Kenton picked up his ale, but Linzi could see him grinning behind his mug. She was tempted to throw hers in his face. That would wipe the silly smirk off. She had every right to voice her opinion in this house. She opened her mouth to let him know her thoughts.

"Hold your tongue, Linzi," her father warned. He too had the corners of his mouth twitching upwards. "You're right to think that way, but you're also a lady, and there is no excuse for vulgar language."

"Sorry, Da'."

"Let's just pray the army in the Midlands stops them. Northumbria is a stronghold that the Vikings will want. That is no surprise. The ports and the farmlands are rich for trade and export. I can just imagine what'll happen if they sack the city." Her father picked up his ale and gulped the remaining down.

Linzi and Kenton both sat silent. Images of horror ran through her thoughts and she felt her brother might just be relieved that he hadn't joined the army – yet.

Celtic Viking Chapter 3

"Hold the line!" Erik hollered to the commanders under him. They shouted the phrase down the rows to their men. Erik heard his words turn into a murmur as it reached the front lines. He stood amidst the bloodbath and carnage. The men did not need to hold the line for their safety, they were annihilating the English. He wanted the men to stay in rank to avoid more death and let the English retreat.

Marcus appeared at his side, still on horse. Erik looked up at his cousin as he sheathed the handle of his axe, but kept his sword in hand. Marcus and his horse were covered in brown and deep red blood. Some had dried from the early start of the battle, the fresh still dripping off his boot and sword. Like Erik, Marcus refused to wear a helmet. His hair lay matted against his skull, his locks fighting against the sweat to curl unruly again. A dried cut and bruise were forming near his right eye.

"There's no need to hold rank. The English are fleeing as fast as the fog that disappeared," Marcus called down.

Erik gave a single nod, sweeping the field with a quick glance. "I know. I don't want my men killing for pleasure. We've taken the land and river. It's the main water supply for the nearby towns. Our, Halfdan's goal, has been attained."

"Let the men get the kill out of their system. They're enjoying themselves."

Erik grabbed the horse reins from Marcus. He knew the horse would be startled from the venom in his voice more than the screams of horror rising from the field. "This is NOT your battle. Hold your tongue, or I'll cut it out for you and place it in your hand."

Marcus opened his mouth but swiftly closed it. Erik watched him run his tongue over his teeth as he wavered on the alarmed horse. Erik spoke quietly to the animal until its ears no longer flicked back and its hooves stopped dancing.

"I'll tell the men to hold their ground." Marcus pulled the reins from Erik's grasp and hurried off.

Scowling, Erik watched him ride off and glanced at the soldiers around him. None looked directly at him, but they were no longer killing. *Just looting off the dead – theirs and ours.*

Finally sheathing his sword but keeping his hand on its hilt, he walked back through his men. He wanted his horse, who still rested at camp, and needed to report to Halfdan. The tents would now need to be moved forward. He needed to find infantry men and select soldiers to stay back to help while others went off to the towns within the radius they had just attained.

He stepped over several dead Englishmen and said a small prayer for each. These men were not soldiers, but farmers and villagers. These men were unprepared to do battle. They attacked with pitchforks, short swords and other weak weapons. Their archers had been boys, too young to fight, let alone die. He sighed, half of him not wanting to be there and the other half reminding him of his duty and his father's legacy.

The battle – or fight – it seemed more of a fitting word, had been finished in three hours. Oddly, even after the late start, the sun stood in the sky, slowly making its way toward the west. Shortly after the archers stepped forward, the fog had cleared so quickly the enemy had no time to react. The dissipated fog showed the small count of English against their vast army.

It had felt satirical when the sun poked through and cleared the skies of grey. Some of the men had said it was an omen, a sign that this battle was blessed. Erik had kept his opinion quiet, thinking that it was a sign for the Vikings to open their eyes.

No longer walking through bloody mud, his boots made little noise as they stepped across the trampled grass. He reached camp and sent a few men with instructions toward the front lines. He then called the page boy to gather his horse. No one else would approach him unless necessary. They never did after battle. He debated about entering his tent to wash his hands but decided against, knowing Halfdan would turn the action into a snide comment of some sort.

Mounting his mare when the page returned, he kicked her into a full gallop in the direction of Halfdan's tents. The sooner he spoke with him, the sooner he could gather his troops and let them know Halfdan's order regarding the women. He needed to get back to the front lines before many of them left. He didn't want to have to travel into the towns to give personal warning.

Halfdan stood outside his tents, talking to an elder that had once been Erik's father's advisor. The older man gave him a warm smile and clasped both hands on Erik's shoulders once he'd dismounted.

"Well done, Jorgen's son! You look like your father returning, and 'tis a welcoming sight." The elder's voice came out scratchy but still strong.

"Thank you, my lord." Erik rested his hands on the man's forearms but said no more. The look of disdain on Halfdan's face prevented him from addressing the man by his name or showing the affection he would have preferred to give. He straightened and turned to Halfdan, making a conscious effort to erase all emotion from his face. "The battle was quick and satisfactory. The English were not prepared to fight men of our caliber."

"Yes, I've already heard the reports. Do you have anything else to add?" Halfdan's voice grated with irritation.

"No. You asked me to personally let you know the result." He would have added a few other thoughts but knew better.

"You will address me as Sire," Halfdan reminded him.

Again, Erik bit a sharp remark back, knowing full well he had authority of Halfdan. It might not be military, however it represented more than that. "I'd like to return to the men to inform them of your orders."

"Orders?" the elder asked, still standing beside Erik.

Halfdan spoke before Erik could open his mouth to respond. "I will not have our men fornicating with the women of this country. Our Viking blood will not be watered down by this inferior race." His chest seemed to expand as he stared at the elder.

"I will have my leave then... if it's alright." Erik turned, not waiting for Halfdan's response or the elder's reaction to Halfdan's words. He swung onto his horse and headed back the way he had come.

It took less time than he wanted to reach the front lines. The battle finished, men cleaned their swords and weapons as the setting sun turned the sky a shade of pink. A few small fires burned in front of the field. Those in charge of clearing the dead worked out in the field behind the men. The English could gather theirs tomorrow in the daylight.

Erik spotted Marcus with another commander, Johan, near a fire, burning the blood off their swords. Their heads came up as Erik approached on horse. Letting his feet hit the soft earth, he reminded the men of the order. He tied his mare up near their horses and headed toward the next fire to speak to his men.

The reactions were as he had expected. The first group grumbled but knew better than to argue with him. The second lot included an enormous, burly Viking wearing a necklace of human ears. Erik spoke Halfdan's order, his hand resting comfortably on his axe.

"Like hell," the rogue yelled. "I've earned my right to a few tarts followed by a slag and a slapper or two." The idiot had actually jumped up and now stood inches away from Erik, challenging him.

Erik stood his ground, ignoring the stench coming from the rotting ears, or possibly from the man himself. "You will not touch a woman or child. That is the order."

The giant laughed, hot breath splashing down on Erik's face. "I have the right to the spoils of war. 'Tis my right."

"Find yourself a pale of ale. Halfdan's word were clear: Our Viking blood will not be watered down. You sire a child here and Halfdan himself will send an army after you."

The man took a step back and looked at the others in the circle, a cruel smirk on his face. "Fine, I'll find a woman and kill her when I'm finished. I'll even keep you happy, Master Jorgen, and kill her quickly with my knife. No teasing or torture." Spittle came from his mouth as he pronounced his t's, some landing on Erik's face.

Before the man had time to let his laugh erupt from his lips, Erik had his axe in one hand, the man's groin in his other. Gasps came from the circle but the giant said nothing, nor did he move a hair.

"Is it better I castrate you now? Prevent the wrong head from leading your thoughts?" Erik's voice split sharper than his axe. He'd not hesitate to remove the giant's manhood. If it would protect the innocent, he had no qualms about his actions.

The giant's Adam's apple bobbed up and down, however he said nothing.

"Answer me, soldier." Erik squeezed the man's bits tighter for emphasis.

"P-p-p-please d-d-don't." His voice now barely louder than a whisper.

"Not so fearless now, when your life mates are in my hands, are you? As I said, keep your bits in your pants." He gave a hard squeeze once more, putting the man out of action for probably the next week. He looked around at the men gathered around them. "This goes for all of you. Don't disappoint me."

Most of the men nodded or murmured in agreement. Erik knew the veterans would follow without question and they'd keep an eye on the new ones. He had no need to threaten them with spies watching and reporting back to him. His men would follow orders and most of Halfdan's would too. The crying giant now lying on the ground was example enough tonight.

He stepped over the man and toward the fire, warming his hands in the dancing flame. "Good job today, men. You fought like Vikings. Be proud of the land you've taken for our King in Denmark. Enjoy the spoils of the towns surrounding."

He glanced once more at the giant still lying on the ground and went back to the man. He leaned down and whispered in the man's ear, "Don't ever stand against me again. Next time I'll kill you before the words have finished rolling off your tongue." He stepped over the petrified man. Without looking back, he gathered his horse, and he headed to his tent to wash up.

~ END OF SAMPLE ~

Celtic Viking

Download for FREE!

More by Lexy Timms:

Book One is FREE!

**Sometimes the heart needs a different kind of saving...
find out if Charity Thompson will find a way of saving forever
in this hospital setting Best-Selling Romance by Lexy Timms**

Charity Thompson wants to save the world, one hospital at a
time. Instead of finishing med school to become a doctor, she
chooses a different path and raises money for hospitals – new
wings, equipment, whatever they need. Except there is one
hospital she would be happy to never set foot in again—her
fathers. So of course he hires her to create a gala for his sixty-fifth
birthday. Charity can't say no. Now she is working in the one
place she doesn't want to be. Except she's attracted to Dr. Elijah
Bennet, the handsome playboy chief.

Will she ever prove to her father that's she's more than a med
school dropout? Or will her attraction to Elijah keep her from
repairing the one thing she desperately wants to fix?

** This is NOT Erotica. It's Romance and a love story. **

* This is Part 1 of an Eight book Romance Series. It does end
on a cliff-hanger*

Managing the Bosses Series
The Boss
Book 1 IS FREE!

Jamie Connors has given up on finding a man. Despite being smart, pretty, and just slightly overweight, she's a magnet for the kind of guys that don't stay around.

Her sister's wedding is at the foreground of the family's attention. Jamie would be find with it if her sister wasn't pressuring her to lose weight so she'll fit in the maid of honor dress, her mother would get off her case and her ex-boyfriend wasn't about to become her brother-in-law.

Determined to step out on her own, she accepts a PA position from billionaire Alex Reid. The job includes an apartment on his property and gets her out of living in her parent's basement.

Jamie has to balance her life and somehow figure out how to manage her billionaire boss, without falling in love with him.

Hades' Spawn MC Series
One You Can't Forget
Book 1 is FREE

Emily Rose Dougherty is a good Catholic girl from mythical Walkerville, CT. She had somehow managed to get herself into a heap trouble with the law, all because an ex-boyfriend has decided to make things difficult.

Luke "Spade" Wade owns a Motorcycle repair shop and is the Road Captian for Hades' Spawn MC. He's shocked when he reads in the paper that his old high school flame has been arrested. She's always been the one he couldn't forget.

Will destiny let them find each other again? Or what happens in the past, best left for the history books?

The Recruiting Trip

Aspiring college athlete Aileen Nessa is finding the recruiting process beyond daunting. Being ranked #10 in the world for the 100m hurdles at the age of eighteen is not a fluke, even though she believes that one race, where everything clinked magically together, might be. American universities don't seem to think so. Letters are pouring in from all over the country.

As she faces the challenge of differentiating between a college's genuine commitment to her or just empty promises from talent-seeking coaches, Aileen heads to the University of Gatica, a Division One school, on a recruiting trip. Her best friend dares who to go just to see the cute guys on the school's brochure.

The university's athletic program boasts one of the top hurdlers in the country. Tyler Jensen is the school's NCAA champion in the hurdles and Jim Thorpe recipient for top defensive back in football. His incredible blue-green eyes, confident smile and rock hard six pack abs mess with Aileen's concentration.

His offer to take her under his wing, should she choose to come to Gatica, is a temping proposition that has her wondering if she might be with an angel or making a deal with the devil himself.

Seeking Justice
Book 1 – is FREE

Rachel Evans has the life most people could only dream of: the promise of an amazing job, good looks, and a life of luxury. The problem is, she hates it. She tries desperately to avoid getting sucked into the family business and hides her wealth and name from her friends. She's seen her brother trapped in that life, and doesn't want it. When her father dies in a plane crash, she reluctantly steps in to become the vice president of her family's company, Syco Pharmaceuticals.

Detective Adrien Deluca and his partner have been called in to look at the crash. While Adrien immediately suspects not everything about the case is what it seems, he has trouble convincing his partner. However, soon into the investigation, they uncover a web of deceit which proves the crash was no accident, and evidence points toward a shadowy group of people. Now the detective needs find the proof.

To what lengths will Deluca go to get it?

Fortune Riders MC Series
NOW AVAILABLE!

Undercover Series - Book 1, PERFECT FOR ME, is FREE!

The city of Pittsburgh keeps its streets safe, partly thanks to Lt. Grady Rivers. The police officer is fiercely intelligent who specializes in undercover operations. It is this set of skills that are sought by New York's finest. Grady is thrown from his hometown onto the New York City underworld in order to stop one of the largest drug rings in the northeast. The NYPD task him with uncovering the identity of the organization's mysterious leader, Dean. It will take all of his cunning to stop this deadly drug lord.

Danger lurks around every corner and comes in many shapes. While undercover, he meets a beauty named Lara. An equally intelligent woman and twice as fearless, she works for a local drug dealer who has ties to the organization. Their sorted pasts have these two become close, and soon they develop feelings for one another. But this is not a "Romeo and Juliet" love story, as the star-crossed lovers fight to survive the deadly streets. Grady treads the thin line between the love he feels for her, and his duties as an officer.

Will he get in too deep?

Heart of the Battle Series
Celtic Viking

In a world plagued with darkness, she would be his salvation.
No one gave Erik a choice as to whether he would fight or not.
Duty to the crown belonged to him, his father's legacy remaining beyond the grave.
Taken by the beauty of the countryside surrounding her,
Linzi would do anything to protect her father's land. Britain is under attack and Scotland is next. At a time she should be focused on suitors, the men of her country have gone to war and she's left to stand alone.
Love will become available, but will passion at the touch of the enemy unravel her strong hold first?
Fall in love with this Historical Celtic Viking Romance.
* There are 3 books in this series. Book 1 will end on a cliff hanger.

Knox Township, August 1863.

Little Love Affair, Book 1 in the Southern Romance series, by bestselling author Lexy Timms

Sentiments are running high following the battle of Gettysburg, and although the draft has not yet come to Knox, "Bloody Knox" will claim lives the next year as citizens attempt to avoid the Union draft. Clara's brother Solomon is missing, and Clara has been left to manage the family's farm, caring for her mother and her younger sister, Cecelia.

Meanwhile, wounded at the battle of Monterey Pass but still able to escape Union forces, Jasper and his friend Horace are lost and starving. Jasper wants to find his way back to the Confederacy, but feels honor-bound to bring Horace back to his family, though the man seems reluctant.

Now Available:

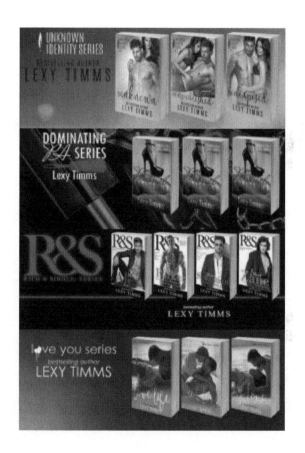

Coming Soon:

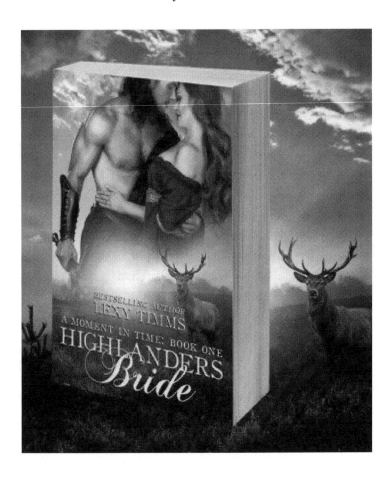

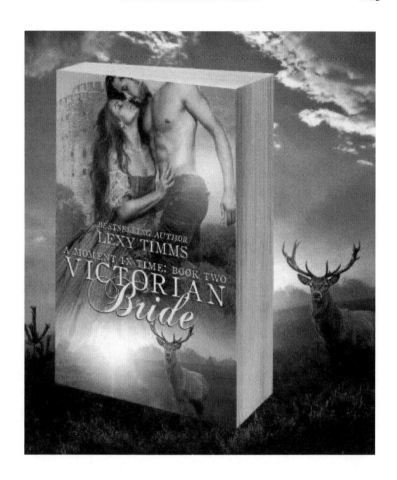

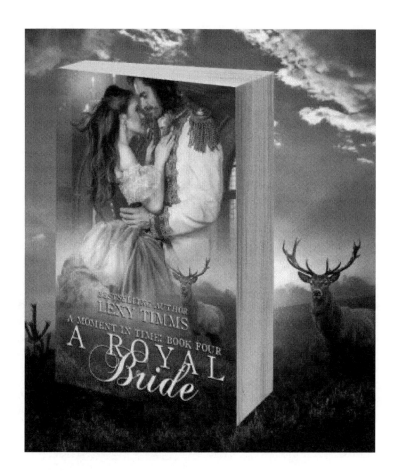

Don't miss out!

Click the button below and you can sign up to receive emails whenever Lexy Timms publishes a new book. There's no charge and no obligation.

Did you love *Highlander's Bride*? Then you should read *Managing the Bosses Box Set #1-3* by Lexy Timms!

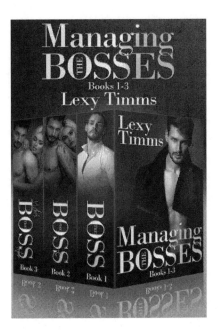

Grab Managing the Bosses Box Set Books #1-3!

Book 1 The Boss

From Best Selling Author, Lexy Timms, comes a billionaire romance that'll make you swoon and fall in love all over again.

Jamie Connors has given up on finding a man. Despite being smart, pretty, and just slightly overweight, she's a magnet for the kind   of   guys   that   don't   stay   around.

Her sister's wedding is at the foreground of the family's attention. Jamie would be fine with it if her sister wasn't pressuring her to lose weight so she'll fit in the maid of honor dress, her mother would get off her case and her ex-boyfriend wasn't about to become her brother-in-law.

Determined to step out on her own, she accepts a PA position from billionaire Alex Reid. The job includes an apartment on his property and gets her out of living in her parent's basement.

Jamie has to balance her life and somehow figure out how to manage her billionaire boss, without falling in love with him.

Book 2 The Boss Too

Jamie Connors has decided a job is more important than a boyfriend. She's landed an awesome position working as billionaire Alex Reid's personal PA. It is not meant to be a job with benefits and yet she finds herself in Alex' bed. Despite being smart, pretty, and slightly overweight, she doesn't believe she's attractive enough for a man like Alex.

Trying to manage work and put as much time into her sister's wedding, Jamie finds herself trying to please everyone. Her sister's wedding is at the foreground of the family's attention. Jamie would be fine if her sister wasn't so bossy, if her mother would stop nagging and her awful ex-boyfriend wasn't about to become her brother-in-law.

Jamie has to learn to love herself again, speak up for herself and have the confidence to go after what she wants. She also needs to prove to Alex that she's perfect for her job and for his bed.

Book 3 Who's the Boss Now
How close can you get to the fire and not get burned?

Landing the dream job, working and dating her incredibly hot boss and at the same time gaining the confidence she never had,

Jamie doesn't think live could get any better.

She's helping to manage a multi-billion dollar company. Her family issues seemed to be resolved and even though she and Alex have to figure out the wrinkles, it looks like they'll be able to be professional at work and romantic after.

Except perfect isn't quite exactly how Jamie imagined it would be.

Managing the Bosses Series:
The Boss
The Boss Too
Who's the Boss Now
Gift for the Boss *Christmas Novella*
Love the Boss
I Do the Boss
Wife of the Boss
Employed by the Boss
Brother to the Boss
Senior Advisor to the Boss

This is a steamy romance, NOT erotica.

Also by Lexy Timms

Alpha Bad Boy Motorcycle Club Triology
Alpha Biker
Alpha Revenge
Alpha Outlaw

Conquering Warrior Series
Ruthless

Diamond in the Rough Anthology
Billionaire Rock
Billionaire Rock - part 2

Dominating PA Series
Her Personal Assistant - Part 1
Her Personal Assistant - Part 2
Her Personal Assistant - Part 3
Her Personal Assistant Box Set

Firehouse Romance Series
Caught in Flames
Burning With Desire
Craving the Heat
Firehouse Romance Complete Collection

Fortune Riders MC Series
Billionaire Biker
Billionaire Ransom
Billionaire Misery

Hades' Spawn Motorcycle Club

One You Can't Forget
One That Got Away
One That Came Back
One You Never Leave
Hades' Spawn MC Complete Series
One Christmas Night

Heart of Stone Series
The Protector
The Guardian
The Warrior

Heart of the Battle Series
Celtic Viking
Celtic Rune
Celtic Mann
Heart of the Battle Series Box Set

Justice Series
Seeking Justice
Finding Justice
Chasing Justice
Pursuing Justice
Justice - Complete Series

Love You Series
Love Life: Billionaire Dance School Hot Romance
Need Love
My Love

Managing the Bosses Series
The Boss
The Boss Too
Who's the Boss Now

Love the Boss
I Do the Boss
Wife to the Boss
Employed by the Boss
Brother to the Boss
Senior Advisor to the Boss
Forever the Boss
Gift for the Boss - Novella 3.5
Christmas With the Boss

Moment in Time
Highlander's Bride
Victorian Bride
Modern Day Bride
A Royal Bride
Forever the Bride

RIP Series
Track the Ripper

R&S Rich and Single Series
Alex Reid
Parker

Saving Forever
Saving Forever - Part 1
Saving Forever - Part 2
Saving Forever - Part 3
Saving Forever - Part 4
Saving Forever - Part 5
Saving Forever - Part 6
Saving Forever Boxset Books #1-3

Southern Romance Series

Little Love Affair
Siege of the Heart
Freedom Forever
Soldier's Fortune

Tattooist Series
Confession of a Tattooist
Surrender of a Tattooist
Heart of a Tattooist
Hopes & Dreams of a Tattooist

Tennessee Romance
Whisky Lullaby
Whisky Melody
Whisky Harmony

The Debt
The Debt: Part 1 - Damn Horse
The Debt: Complete Collection

The University of Gatica Series
The Recruiting Trip
Faster
Higher
Stronger
Dominate
No Rush

T.N.T. Series
Troubled Nate Thomas - Part 1
Troubled Nate Thomas - Part 2
Troubled Nate Thomas - Part 3

Undercover Series
Perfect For Me